Harley L. Sachs

MS# 115Sam/75,364 words
10/30/13

SAM IN LOVE

A Romance
by
Harley L. Sachs

ISBN (paper) 978-1-939381-37-8
ISBN (ebook) 978-1-939381-38-5

Harley L. Sachs

A Review of "Sam in Love" by Doc Macomber:

In Mr. Sachs's latest novel set in Post WWII Europe an American GI attempts to find love in all the wrong places. In this splendid coming of age tale, "Sam in Love," a twenty-one-year-old draftee stuck in a dead-end job on a United States Army base in Germany, Sam just waits out his time like a prison sentence before he can return home. Filled with self-doubt and worry about his seemingly failed relationships with women, the soldier sets out on a quest to find the "Right Girl." In this war-torn environment Mr. Sachs paints a somewhat Fitzgerald-like atmosphere, airless, bleak, and yet captivating – one that has the intrepid cast of amorous malcontents venturing out at every opportunity to find adventure. Whether barreling down icy European countrysides, middle of the night border crossings, hopping high-speed trains, finding romance in the backseat of cars, or drunken nights in dinghy clubs, it's a story worthy of its author and his former overseas work. Mr. Sachs's sentences flow with consistency and purity often only found on the top of a mountainous peak. Take a journey and discover the joys of youth and what happens when life can take an unexpected turn. You won't regret it...

Doc Macomber, author of the Jack Vu Mystery Series.

Books by Harley L. Sachs

Novels

Queer Company
Never Trust a Talking Horse
The Gold Chromosome
Murder by Mail (Scratch—out!)!
Ben Zakkai's Coffin
The Search for Jesse Bram
The Mystery Club Solves a Murder
The Mystery Club and the Dead Doctor
The Mystery Club and the Hidden Witness
The Mystery Club and the Serial Widow
Deliver Me from Evil
White Slave
Conspiracy!
Murder in the Keweenaw
The Lollipop Murder
Betrayal
Retribution
Burnt Out

Collections of short fiction

Ahoy! Quarterdeck! (Irma Quarterdeck Reports)
Anna-Lena's Troll and Other Stories
Threads of the Covenant: The Jews of Red Jacket
Misplaced Persons

Non-Fiction

Freelance Non-Fiction Articles
The 1957 Sachs Arctic Expedition
From Tent to Castle: Memoir of a Year-Long Honeymoon
IS
*Chilly-Chilly BANG! How We Freelanced Through Europe's
    Coldest Winter in a VW with a Kid*
Essays and Columns: 1992-2011
The Writing Life

Cartoons

Hunting the Mail Buoy and Other Hazards to Navigation

Harley L. Sachs

Author's Note

Sam in Love is a revision of a revision of my MA creative writing thesis, *The Golden Grape*, which I first wrote in 1956 while on the GI Bill at Indiana University after military service as a company clerk in Heidelberg, Germany. Later, while living in Stockholm, Sweden, I showed the thesis manuscript to Mrs. Lindblad, an editor at *Året Rund*, a women's magazine. She suggested I revise it, which I did in 1957 under the title *A Woman for Sam*. Mrs. Lindblad decided that Sam was based on my own life, and forever afterwards called me Sam.

Unfortunately, in those days, before Xerox and other copy machines, before computer word processors, the best I could do, hammering on my 1940 vintage Underwood portable typewriter, was an original typescript and two ever fainter carbon copies. No Swedish publisher would be interested in a romance about an American GI in Germany. Submitting the book via sea, the slowest snail mail, to a New York publisher or agent risked it being lost en route. For someone on the G.I. Bill, the expense of providing international postage coupons for the manuscript's return should it be rejected, as was inevitably the case, was prohibitive.

The result was that the revision was never published and languished along with other failed projects in my desk drawer. Now, after more than 50 years, I have taken it up again with the benefit of much more writing experience and practice and maturity as a person and as an author.

Sam in Love has its literary antecedents. Military life has been the inspiration for many authors, notably Eric M. Remarque who wrote *All's Quiet on the Western Front,* which was followed by *Three Comrades* and *The Way Back.* Michener got his start with *Tales of the South Pacific,* and Neil Simon with his Army book *Beloxi Blues.* Ernest Hemingway's war book, *The Sun Also Rises,* also fits the pattern. Then there's James Jones' *From Here to Eternity,* Curt Vonnegut's *Slaughterhouse Five,* and *Catch 22,* were all novels coming out of war, so I am in good company.

When my faculty advisor at the University of Stockholm, Professor Sletvig, read *A Woman for Sam,* he said it was like life in an airless room. Foreigners living abroad tend to stick together in cliques of expats. The Golden Grape hotel in Heidelberg was a billet for female employees of the U.S. Army in Europe (USAREUR). The British living abroad in E.M. Forster's *A Passage to India* at least had interaction with the locals, as George Orwell did as a colonialist in *Burmese Tales.* That interrelationship is the core of those books, but Sam and the women in my book have little or no interaction with the Germans. They do live in an airless place and Sam isn't sure what he's looking for.

Harley L. Sachs

For Ulla

Acknowledgments

With thanks to the late Professor William Wilson of Indiana University, Dr. Sletvig, my advisor at the University of Stockholm; and Mrs. Lindblad of *Året Rund* who advised me to revise the first version of the book.

Thanks to my wife Ulla, my most critical reader and editor, and to Doc Macomber and Mary Jane for their thoughtful input. Thanks to Cynthia Sachs-Bustos for her valuable copy edit.

With homage to Smiley, Sonja, Ray, Ingrid, Åse, Gunilla, Barbro, Patricia, Sally, Beth and others whose names I have forgotten, but who all contributed to my understanding of the meaning of love.

Table of Contents

Chapter One

The First Weekend—The Kreutzek

He liked her at once. Months later he tried to understand just why he liked her from that first moment, explained to himself that she had been the first girl he had really looked at in a long time, but that wasn't enough. He would say that she was slim, just as he was slim, and they had that in common, but slim wasn't enough, either. They had both come to ski... yes. They were both Americans in Germany... yes. They were both in one way or another connected with the occupation Army. Yes. But those were all superficial surface details that could never explain what drew him to her.

Sam, looking pale and unnaturally weak, had just emerged from Marty's aging Volkswagen, the Green Beetle, and was unfastening the skis from the rack at the back of the car when the brown, Army bus ground up the hill from Garmisch and stopped. There were only two passengers, a plump girl who got off first, and Fran. Of course, he didn't know her name then. He only noticed—at once—that there was a simultaneous hesitation and eagerness in her manner and that, when she caught sight of the Kreutzeck's looming peak above them, the sight didn't register with the here and now, but with something far away, deeply hidden in herself.

Marty's reaction was one that Sam had come to accept as typical and couldn't help admiring for its almost primitive frankness. "Sam—women. That's for us, eh Buddy Boy?"

Sam only nodded and went on studying Fran as she followed a half step behind the other girl toward the cable car station. He wasn't sure whether she had noticed him, but she looked back over her shoulder with a far away expression on her face and a smile that might have been at him or at nothing in particular.

"The fat one looks like a woman of the world," Marty said.

"She does?" Sam wasn't sure what a woman of the world was. He noticed only that her tight black ski pants made her look plumper than she really was, and that she swung her American suitcase as it if were no weight at all.

"Sure." Marty sucked on the tiny pipe that he affected but almost never lit. He looked out from under his heavy black brows with an expression he used when he was trying to look older. "Tell you what. You need a woman of the world more than I do, so I'll make the sacrifice. You take the fat one."

"Thanks, old buddy."

Marty shouldered his skis. "I'd flip a coin for choice if you insist, but my hands are full. Besides, you might win."

Sam smiled, took a deep breath, and was suddenly shaken with a fit of coughing. It was a deep cough from down in his lungs and when he wiped his mouth on the sleeve of his parka his already pale face was grey. "It's all right. I'm out of condition anyway."

"That's what I mean, Buddy Boy. A woman of the world. Just the thing to recuperate with."

They followed the girls into the cable car station and got in the cab. It swung precariously like a small boat about to go under, and then bumped against the cradle in a reassuring way. Sam kept looking at Fran, but glanced away now and then so she wouldn't think he was staring. The cable car started up, swung briefly, and in a moment they were passing the tops of pine trees.

Pines, snow, and ski clothes, Sam thought. A fresh chill in the air that cleared his nostrils and made the breath run deep. There had been another day like this—the last time he had skied in the States. It was Christmas, before he left for overseas, and he had been with a girl, Betty. Her name still unsettled him. He had taken her to the north and to bed. It was all very romantic, except that he had felt guilty afterwards and miserable. They'd gotten into an argument at breakfast and she had cried. He had sat there, helpless, picking at his scrambled eggs and wondering why she was crying.

The truth was he was not an experienced lover, was not adept at seduction, and was prone to premature ejaculation that made him feel stupid and inadequate.

"Excuse me, can you help me with this light meter?" It was Fran, only then he was thinking of her as the slim girl, handing him a light meter before he could collect himself. "I just bought it and I don't know how it works."

"Sure," Sam said. He took the meter and stole a glance at Marty who was glowering from under those heavy eyebrows. "This way. Just press the button and read it here. You get a number and then you have a choice of aperture and shutter speed, depending on what film you have. What's your ASA?"

Fran blushed. "I don't know what ASA is."

"It's the film speed. Yours is probably 100 unless you're using color film."

"You know a lot about cameras," she said with admiration. "I should have practiced with it on the train but I forgot."

Before Sam was discharged from the hospital he spent his accumulated pay on a twin lens reflex camera at the hospital store. He would have preferred a Leica or Pentax, but couldn't afford that and didn't like the small 35mm negatives, so settled on a clone of a Rolleiflex that took 10x10 cm negatives, easier to work with in the service club darkroom. His camera was heavy as a brick around his neck, but took excellent pictures.

Sam handed back the meter. When she took it their fingers brushed together. Sam felt a sudden flush of excitement as he looked up from the meter to her face. Her eyes didn't seem unfocussed now. They looked right at him, or through him, not with a cold, calculating penetration but with an expansive, enveloping warmth. She gave him a quick, embarrassed smile. "I just got this camera and it's a lot more complicated than my Baby Brownie. With it you just pointed and clicked." She turned away to set her camera's speed and aperture and take a picture.

Marty clutched Sam's arm and drew him to the other side of the cable car. "What do you mean, making out with my girl?" he said with a harsh whisper that Sam was afraid could be overheard. "I told you to take the fat one."

It was no place to argue. Sam changed the subject. "Look at that ski trail down there. You think you could make it?" Down below tiny figures were expertly maneuvering between the trees.

In another moment the car suddenly slowed and stopped, suspended in its cradle at the top of the mountain.

The two girls had no skis to unload and were gone when Sam and Marty entered the station waiting room. There was a crowd of people buying souvenirs and waiting for the next cable car—GI's in uniform, dependents, assorted parts of the occupation Army community. But they looked out of place, dominating the confiscated cream of German vacationland. The atmosphere made Sam uncomfortable. He had seen graffiti in some places that said "Ami go home," and he knew they were not welcome in Germany. Welcome or not, he reminded himself that Garmisch was one of the places he would not have missed if he were an ordinary tourist and there had never been a war.

But if there had not been a war in Korea and he had not been drafted, he would never have been sent to Germany in the first place.

"Hurry up, Sam. The girls are probably at the hotel by now."

Still, Sam felt more like a tourist than a soldier. Being drafted, serial numbered, uniformed, and trained didn't make you a soldier. Soldiers were trained to fight and kill. Sam wasn't a fighter and he was certainly no killer.

Marty gripped the tiny pipe between his teeth and pushed through the crowd with his skis on one shoulder and his overnight bag in the other hand. "This time remember, the slim one's mine, understand?" Marty pushed his way through as if he were fighting for a seat on a bus back in Newark. Not carrying his skis vertically, he almost knocked someone out.

"Hey!"

"Sorry."

Marty forged ahead on the steps up to the hotel. He announced that he wanted to see the girls sign the register so he could learn their names, handed over his luggage, and left Sam to puff up the stairs in the high altitude air and get caught in the revolving doors on his way into the hotel. He had bundled the poles with the skis, which were white, surplus from the Mountain Division Italian campaign of World War II, and he almost dropped the whole mess when the revolving door caught the tips.

The girls turned to look at him, tangled in the lobby with skis, poles, and his suitcase. The plump one chuckled good naturedly at his clumsiness and Fran smiled as though she felt sorry for him. They had both already checked in and were on their way to their room.

Sam asked Marty for his report. "What did you find out?"

"They're Department of the Army civilians stationed in Heidelberg. Names are Fran and Yetta. They're in room ten."

"Which is Fran and which is Yetta?"

Marty shrugged inside his tent-like Army overcoat. It was one part of the uniform, along with the GI-issued shoes that you could wear when not in uniform. "I got there too late for that."

Sam put his skis in the rack in the lobby. "Yetta sounds like a fat name. I bet the fat one is Yetta."

"Then that one's yours, Buddy Boy."

Sam asked the clerk, "How's the skiing?"

The clerk was German and had an inconsistent mid-western American accent. "The lift isn't working. It will be repaired in the morning. If you ski now you have to climb back up."

"Climb!" Sam was disappointed. He had been in the hospital with a lung disease and wasn't in condition for climbing.

The hotel had been commandeered by the occupation forces for exclusive R&R for military personnel, so the room price was cheap. They filled in the usual police forms with their GI ID cards and registered for a room for two. It was room eight, either next door or across the hall from the two girls. The room keys were attached to a couple of varnished pieces of wood that looked like bowling pins, large enough to not to be carried away by accident.

"Join me at the bar, Sam. You've been off your feet too long to knock yourself out." Marty turned to the desk clerk. "He's been in the hospital."

The clerk looked sympathetic.

At the mention of the hospital Sam self-consciously looked down at the floor and rubbed the bony ridge of his nose. He picked up his bag and started toward the exit.

Room #8 was small, possibly because, being built at the top of the mountain, there wasn't much space for large bedrooms and guests would spend their time either out skiing or in the bar or dining room. They had bunk beds, and Marty immediately commandeered the lower. They didn't wait to unpack.

Mention of the hospital had thrown Sam into a funk again. Marty knew him well enough to recognize the sign and slapped him on the back. "Sorry. old buddy, I didn't mean to make you feel bad again. Stick with me. I'll cheer you up."

It wasn't that easy to turn off the memory. The hospital—eight weeks, and for what? The Army doctors were willing to err on the side of caution. First they thought he might have TB, even though the new medicines had almost stamped out that scourge. The x-rays could show TB, or pneumonia, even cancer or some undefined tropical fungus, but Sam had never been in the Pacific. That sort of thing was what GI's picked up in the war in the Pacific campaign, but then he had been exposed to some of those veterans when they turned up at college on the G.I. Bill. Maybe what they had was catching. He didn't understand it, either, and the doctors would rather tell him nothing than reveal their own ignorance.

They made all kinds of tests while nurses and ward boys exercised full contagion precautions, treated him like a dangerous, infectious thing. They took no chances. They parked him in a remote isolation ward and, he feared, forgot him like they'd exhausted all possibilities and given up.

His condition was chronic, but not an emergency, too severe to let him return to duty, but not severe enough to discharge him from the Army with all the paperwork that went along with a medical discharge.

He had lain in bed for eight weeks staring at the green walls, a color that frightened him now every time he saw it. He'd been left to review his thoughts, his life, his plans if he had ever had any, everything mulled over and over until they lost all meaning. He'd been suspended in a womb of pale green.

The cough had never quite gone away. Breathing deeply still hurt. When they finally released him as being no danger to anyone else, they burned all the personal items he'd left behind.

But the damage to his spirit had been done. Weeks of lying in bed, staring at the walls, was like being a prisoner in solitary. He'd had no radio and no contact with the outside world. The sensory deprivation made it hard for him to come back to reality when he finally did get out.

He had emerged uncertain, having discovered that the world was a chaos of contradictions where he must, somehow, find something or someone he could believe it. Whenever he did get a discharge, he didn't want to join Logan Associates, his father's advertising firm in Chicago. He was no longer sure he wanted to finish college. He felt he had no purpose.

Fortunately, his roommate Marty had taken him under his wing, adopted him like a lost puppy. Marty might not have been the sharpest tack in the box, but he had good instincts and meant well, in his own way of thinking. "The way I see it," Marty was saying as they settled into their room, "is all you need is a good woman. Get somebody to shack up with and you'll find your troubles are all over."

"That's your cure-all, is it?" Sam opened his bag and searched for his ski goggles. "Get laid?"

Marty grinned. "If that doesn't cure you, at least you'll have your ashes hauled." He dropped his grimy Army overcoat over the back of the only chair. It slid off onto the floor and he didn't bother to pick it up.

Sam looked out the window. The view of the valley below was spectacular, but the late afternoon shadow of the mountain had turned the town into grey twilight with a few lights beginning to glow.

Marty took off his boots and dropped into the lower bunk. "I guess I'll sack out until dinner."

Sam had found his goggles and was adjusting them on his forehead.

"You aren't going to ski, are you?"

Sam nodded hopefully. "I've got to get back in shape. I've been dormant too long."

"Better be careful. At this time of day the temperature's dropping. There'll be ice. You don't want to break a leg out there. Save your energy for later. It may be a long evening."

"I'll be careful. I don't want to be put back in the hospital." Sam closed the door behind him and headed toward the lobby where he'd parked his skis in the rack with the others. He felt like some sort of Rip Van Winkle who'd waked up from a long sleep twenty years behind everybody.

The snow was crisp and dry. It was late afternoon and the sun had moved behind the peaks to the west to cast long shadows on the trails. Sam fastened his ski bindings and watched the skiers so he could judge the difficulty of the turns. When he straightened up he did it slowly, and when he kick-turned away from the steep edge of the hotel veranda it was with deliberation born of lack of practice. But when he started to ski he found his speed the same as all others' and, not ready for the first turn, he fell.

Falling was what he did best. He fell down a lot.

...

When Sam and Marty entered the dining room the only people left at the top of the mountain were those staying at the hotel. The last cable car to the valley left at 6:00, and after that the only way down was to ski, a tricky business in the dark. Only serious skiers were guests at the hotel. The touring Americans in uniform had stayed in town where they could get drunk at the Casa Carioca night club created for the military.

Casa Carioca was hardly a south German name in the cuckoo clock part of Germany. No doubt it had been cooked up by someone without much sensitivity to the local culture. No wonder the locals hated the Amis.

Fran and Yetta were settled among the guests and Marty, without hesitation, lead Sam to an adjoining table. Sam had thought he might bump into them on the slope but hadn't seen them. Perhaps they had taken another trail. "How was the skiing?"

The plump girl turned in her chair to look at him. "We didn't get to ski, They were all rented out at the ski hut."

"Should have been like us," Marty said. "We checked some out at Special Services in Munich. Connections." He smiled around the stem of the tiny pipe in his teeth.

"This man's got all kinds of connections," Sam added proudly.

"Thank you, constituent."

After they sat down, Sam whispered, "Why didn't you ask if we could join them? I thought you were an operator."

"And end up paying for their dinner? Have more faith in me than that, Buddy Boy."

"Oh, of course." Sam looked around. There was something about the dining room that made him feel uncomfortable. He suddenly realized why. The menu was in English. There was ice water on the table. The coffee mugs were G.I. issue, porcelain made in Germany, but the same as the ones at the hospital. Near the end of his eight

20

weeks he had been allowed out of isolation and visited the dining room.

"I'll have the T-bone steak," Marty said to the waiter. "With French fries and lots of catsup."

"I'd like to feel like I was in Germany for a change," Sam grumbled. "You'd think the Army would die of culture shock if they ever got away from the American atmosphere."

"So what'll you have, Sam?"

"The whole thing irritates me. It's the same in the snack bar and the PX, a fake, all contrived. Do we have to drag our culture around with us?"

The waiter looked uncomfortable.

Marty was impatient. "Allow me on behalf of SAC, Southern Area Command, to apologize for the American atmosphere, Private Logan. How about placing your order? I'm hungry."

Showing off his high school and college German, Sam said stubbornly, *"Ein rumpsteak mit pommes frites."* A steak by any other name was still a steak.

The waiter smirked and wrote down the order. "Do you wish catsup on the potatoes, sir?"

Sam looked at him blankly. Suddenly he started coughing, turned his head and held a linen napkin over his mouth.

"Bring him catsup, too," Marty said. "And a beer. I think he needs a beer."

When the waiter disappeared again Marty leaned toward Sam with a worried expression plucking his shaggy brows. "You all right? How's the cough?"

"The cough's all right. Mox nix." It was the Army version of the German *es macht nichts*, meaning O.K.

"I think I understand your point, Sam." Marty wiped the stem of his pipe and put it in his shirt pocket. "But I frankly like the American atmosphere. It keeps me from getting homesick."

"All the time? The PX, snack bars…it's all the same. We even have commissaries so the dependents can shop without making contact with the Germans. I think it's a rotten shame."

"Where else could they buy peanut butter? I think it's a good deal. Things are cheaper in the commissary."

"There's got to be some alternative to peanut butter. While we're in Germany we could at least gain something by the experience. Look at those people living in Little America. They stay here three years and when they leave they can't speak a word of German and haven't benefited from contact with the German culture."

"Culture? You mean like having some old dame come in to mop the floor while you're in the john taking a leak?"

"You don't get what I mean."

"Relax, Sam. I'll ask the girls what they think." Marty rose. When he was sure the girls had noticed him he withdrew an imaginary pencil and notebook from his sport coat pocket and dropped his voice to a lower register. "I beg your pardon. I'm from the Gallop Poll. Can you tell me whether you buy your items at the commissary to avoid contact with the Germans, or take advantage of the cheaper prices, or to keep from being homesick?"

Fran and Yetta looked at each other. The plump one spoke. "We get everything at the cutest German shop around the corner from our hotel. It's much more convenient."

"Aha!" Marty made an imaginary check mark. "Then you speak German."

The thin girl smiled. "No. The man at the delicatessen speaks wonderful English."

"I see." Another imaginary check mark. "But allow me to introduce someone who claims to speak German, in case you ever need an interpreter." Marty turned with a flourish. "This is Sam Logan."

Sam rose with a slight bow. "And this is Marty Vidal." They never mentioned rank. For two clerks, one a PFC and the other a corporal, there was not much prestige in the Army hierarchy.

"I'm Fran," the thin girl said.

"And I'm Yetta."

"So I was right," Sam said. Yetta had been a fat name. Must be karma at work.

"About what?" Yetta asked.

"Nothing," Sam said. "I'm usually right about nothing."

"Nothing at all?" Fran asked. She looked at him with her faraway, unfocussed eyes as if she were, if not blind, at least too nearsighted to see clearly.

"Not if the First Sergeant has anything to say about it," Marty added.

Sam saw that a three piece band was forming up at a little stage at the far end of the dining room—an accordion, drum set, and a guitar. The three musicians were wearing white shirts and lederhosen held up with brightly colored suspenders. They wore hats with decorations. What would they play, polkas?

Sam asked, "Would you like to join me for dancing after dinner?" In spite of Marty's claim on her, Sam directed the invitation to Fran.

Fran stared briefly at her hands, folded in her lap, then looked up and smiled. "Depends on what they play. I'm not good at polkas."

"Whatever." Sam smiled. He returned to his table and sat down. He poured himself a glass of dark beer from the bottle but was staring at Fran and spilled some beer on the table cloth.

Marty was surprised. "Good God, Buddy Boy, you asked her for a dance. You cutting me out?"

"I guess I did."

"You never did anything like that before, not so quickly. There's been some changes made in that hospital."

"I don't think so. Wasn't anything to change, nothing important, anyway."

Marty squirted catsup on his steak. "I don't get you."

"I don't know if I can explain it. I just feel sort of empty and new."

"You looked plenty discouraged when you got back from the hospital."

"It was pretty horrible."

Marty chewed vigorously on a large mouthful but managed to say, "You'd think a guy would crack up being so long in there."

Sam tried to concentrate on his steak. "I almost did."

...

Ordinarily two strong German beers would have made Sam feel drunk, but instead of feeling dizzy he felt like he'd lost his dimensions, his boundaries, like a bleeding water color mingling with his surroundings. For some reason he seemed as alert as ever even if out of focus. While dancing with Fran on the tiny floor near the bar he was aware of every clink of glassware, every voice, every whispered conversation that made up the general murmur that the jumpy oom-pa-pa three piece band seem to rise above. In spite of Fran's protests, it was a polka.

He was also aware of Fran, slim, uncoordinated in her movements, stumbling now and then as if she were aware that her slimness made her legs seem longer than average. She was not accustomed to drinking beer. Out of deference to Sam's budget—PFCs didn't earn much—she had drunk beer, unlike Yetta who had called Marty's bluff and ordered a double scotch.

To their great relief as dance partners, the band changed the pace and did a Teutonic arrangement of Hoagy Carmichael's "Stardust." Unlike the polka, what was later to be called touch dancing was an embrace. Sam felt the texture of Fran's sweater, soft and sensual. He was conscious of her waist, her small bosom and her long thighs against him. There was no bulge of excess flesh at the waistband of her ski pants and she wore no girdle. She was dancing close, her hair brushing his lips,

25

her hips bumping against his groin, a movement that was an invitation.

Sam said. "It's wool and cashmere, isn't it?"

"What is?"

"Your sweater. Wool and cashmere?"

She laughed. "You're the first man who ever analyzed the composition of my clothes."

"I'm always analyzing something. Maybe it's a failing. Makes me too introspective."

"It is wool and cashmere. How did you know? You told me you were a supply clerk at some signal unit in Munich. You don't knit, do you?"

Sam laughed. "I grew up reading *The Women's Wear Daily*. My father's in the advertising business in Chicago. Handles mostly textiles and women's wear accounts. Gets a lot of samples."

"I see. Does your mother work with him?"

"She did when she was alive, I guess. She died when I was little. I hardly remember her. After school Dad wanted me to hang out at his office. He said he wanted to teach me the business, but I think he just wanted me to stay out of trouble."

They danced a couple more numbers before Fran said something about herself. "My father died a few years ago. He was a wonderful man. We all tried to get him to retire, but he insisted on one more season in the lumber business. He wasn't quick on his feet any more. There was an accident on the green line."

"The green line?"

"The part of the mill where the lumber is rough cut. If a blade kicks back it can fire wood like a missile. If you don't get out of the way, well…"

26

Fran brightened. "They closed down the mill the day of the funeral. Everybody in North Creek was there." She paused. "It was bound to close anyway. The Forest Service and Bureau of Land Management basically shut down the forest. It's been a ghost town ever since."

Sam wondered if when he died anybody would shut down anything for his funeral. Probably not. Nobody knew him. He had done nothing for any community, had few friends. He couldn't even boast of any enemies. He'd just never got started at anything.

"Are you going in your father's business when you get out of the Army?"

"I thought I might. Now I don't know what I'll do."

"I suppose you have time yet."

Sam turned his head to face her. The dance number had ended. Fran's remark made her sound older, superior, more mature. He knew she must be older than he was, but until now it hadn't made any difference. Now she'd put him on the defensive because he had no idea what he wanted to do with the rest of his life. The point was he didn't have time.

Time was like running water. You couldn't catch it or stop it. In the hospital he had thought maybe he didn't have any time left at all. One of the orderlies had mentioned Valley Forge hospital and joked that some of George Washington's troops were still there. It was a warehouse for the chronically ill. Once you were sent there you might never get out. So Sam felt he didn't know how much time he did have left. His nagging cough still persisted. That made everything urgent, uncertain.

"What do you plan to do?" Sam asked, anxious to turn the question back to her.

She winced, not her face, or the muscles around her small mouth. They remained calm, but her back stiffened under Sam's hand. After a time she answered, "I used to think I'd get married, have a family of woodsmen. Three boys and a girl. She'd be the youngest." She caught herself fading into a daydream, shook it off. "But now I don't know. Maybe I won't ever get married."

"Is that why you came overseas?"

"There was more to it than that…" She drew away.

"Sorry," Sam apologized. "I shouldn't have asked."

"It's… it's not really so important." She drew closer to him, suddenly realized, "How long have we been dancing without music?" She looked around, embarrassed.

"I don't know." They moved back to where Marty and Yetta were trying to drink each other under the table. Sam was reluctant to let Fran go, and his hand lingered at her waist. Too long. She noticed it, looked up at him as she sat down and briefly squeezed his hand.

Sam sat down, feeling guilty, as if he had received something he didn't deserve.

"You owe me a buck," Marty announced thickly. "Two beers and some other stuff. One buck."

"He's a great guy for money, isn't he Sam?" Yetta said. "What's he do with it all?"

"Please, you're speaking of the subject I love. You know, when my folks and I travel in Europe we do it right: no luggage."

Fran gave Marty a quizzical look, then back at Sam, smiled, sipped her beer tentatively, as if it might make her as drunk as Marty was getting.

Marty continued. "Just one suitcase," he boasted, "full of money." He laughed. So did Yetta, but it wasn't clear that she was laughing at Marty being a jerk or if she thought his joke was amusing. Perhaps she though his bragging about money had some basis and he might prove to be a big spender. They had gotten along fine ever since she took the chair he had planned for Fran.

The fact was, Marty was only a corporal and never saved anything. Owning an old Volkswagen was a status symbol that ate much of his monthly salary.

Sam asked, "Just what do you do in Heidelberg?"

Fran had been watching Marty who seemed occupied in filling, for the first time, the tiny pipe he often sucked on like some baby's pacifier. She turned to Sam. "I work in the comptroller's division of USAREUR headquarters."

That meant she was either a typist, file girl, secretary or maybe an accountant. Accountants were, well, dull, and Fran wasn't dull. Sam hoped she was a secretary. She didn't strike him as an accountant, and the lesser jobs didn't fit his impression of her. "Why come to Germany in the first place?"

"To see Europe." There seemed to be more than that, something she didn't tell. Aside from a desire to travel she might have needed a new horizon, was running away from a failed relationship, might even be divorced. Sam wished she trusted him enough to tell the rest of her story.

"What about you, Sam?"

"I was drafted, shipped over." He remembered the circumstances of his induction. In spite of poor grades he had hung onto his deferment until the actual fighting ended in Korea. Thousands of men had been killed or simply froze to death in the North. The truce was tentative.

If he served his two years in the Army, the G.I. Bill would pay for the rest of his college expenses. His rudimentary language skill got him to Germany instead of Korea. In spite of Cold War tensions along the East German border and the Soviet Army poised there, Germany was safer.

"I came over to have a ball," Yetta said, joining in. "And I'm having one, right Marty?" She raised her almost empty glass.

"You sure are, baby." Marty was trying to pack his pipe with the remains of someone's cigarette. He never actually carried tobacco. The pipe thing was an affectation.

"You try hard enough," Sam said, counting the empty glasses. Though run by Americans, the German hotel staff used the local method of marking the paper coasters to keep track of how many drinks were served.

Yetta took sudden, unexpected offense. "Don't you worry about little Yetta. When she wants to have a party, she has one, see?"

Sam raised his beer glass, toasted apologetically, "Alright, alright." He was still feeling clear headed and his sharp eyes twinkled in the smoky room. He wondered why she tried so hard to have fun, why Fran had really come to Europe, how other people ran their lives, how they thought, what they did. He didn't know how to run his own and needed some successful example to emulate.

Marty blew smoke in his face. "Look, Buddy Boy, I got it lit. Surprised?"

Sam coughed. "Easy with the smoke, Marty. I'm convinced."

Marty blew a second puff slightly out of the way, but Sam still got a whiff and coughed again. "Forgot about your lungs. Sorry old buddy."

Sam looked at Fran. "Like to go for a walk? The smoke is getting to me."

"Alright."

They rose, leaving Marty and Yetta. "We're going outside," Sam said. He put his arm around Fran's waist to steer her toward the exit. He wanted to hold her in his arms again.

The Kreuzeck at night was a disorderly pattern of snow, trees, and shadows in between. The moguls were tied together by ski trails that wove and interlocked among the drifts. Down below in the valley Garmisch pulsed with lights that glowed in the chimney smoke. No sounds came from the valley, but there was a hammering from the ski lift shack a few hundred yards below. Repairs were still going on.

Sam pulled up the hood of his ski jacket against the night cold and slipped on a glove. He couldn't find the other one, searched through his pockets.

"Lose something?"

"My other glove. I'm always forgetting them. It's probably back in the room."

"Got a pocket?"

"Oh, sure." Sam took her hand, held it, felt the cold nip his wrist, and put both their hands into his pocket. She was wearing wool gloves.

They walked to the edge of the mountain to where they could look down at the valley. Snow squeaked under their boots.

"Beautiful, isn't it?" Sam asked.

"Romantic."

"Like a desert island." Sam felt the isolation, the gap of darkness between them and the pulsing lights of the world below. Garmisch was vastly removed.

In spite of the presence of the girl, Sam felt a loneliness clawing at him, a feeling that he might never bridge the gap. In the silence he sensed the rush of blood in his veins and the beating of his heart. Each beat a moment, each beat a moment gone; something irrevocably over, past, dead. He felt his life slipping away into the darkness, in the shadow of the mountain a presence of death, in his lungs the lurking cough he could never be sure was harmless. The doctor had said that every cough could damage the little sacs in the lungs that transferred oxygen to the blood. He shuddered and looked away.

"Cold?" Fran asked.

He became aware once more of her hand clutched inside his jacket pocket. "A little."

She studied his features in the half light. His nose was a little larger than average, broken once when he foolishly went out for high school football. Still, his square jaw had a soft appearance and his ears, had the light been right, would have shone pink from the cold.

"It's too bad Charlie and Jim can't be here," Fran said. "They'd love the skiing."

"Who are Charlie and Jim?"

"My brothers. They used to ski all the time at North Creek. It's a little lumber town with a lot of tourists in the winter. Charlie and Jim were in the ski patrol. Jim wanted to be a ski instructor, maybe buy part of a mountain and put up a tow, but he didn't have the money and when he got out of the Army he got a head start on a family. Mary—that's his wife. She's from North Creek, too—had twins, so Jim had to go to work in the mill just to make ends meet. But they're beautiful children, a boy and a girl. You should hear them call me Auntie Fran. It's funny."

She paused. "Then the mill closed."

Sam didn't ask what a young family did to survive when the town's only employer went bust. He looked at Fran beside him at the edge of the mountain. Her shoulders were hunched against the cold. Inside his pocket, her fingers clutched his as if she were using him as a focal point, an anchor this side of her memory.

"Your brothers are older than you."

"Yes. I've a sister, too, younger."

"She go to school?"

"No. She's married." The lines around her mouth were grim and the strange light reflected from the snow made her face look pale and lifeless.

"I suppose you get homesick for your family."

She shrugged. "Sometimes. I try not to think about it."

"You think coming to Europe might have been a mistake?"

She didn't answer.

Sam felt it was time to change the subject. "I'm an only child. There's just my father and me. Dad's got an agency on Michigan Avenue. He's going to move into the Prudential Building when it's finished. In advertising you need an address with prestige." He trailed off. She hadn't been listening.

Sam stopped talking and stood uncomfortably beside her. A thin layer of clouds had crept over from the south to turn the sky a milky grey and blot out the stars. It was starting to snow.

"Auntie Fran." She drew her hand from his pocket and turned to face him. "Do I look like somebody's aunt?"

"I don't see what's wrong with being an aunt," Sam said. "I'd like to be an uncle. Why not?" She might think being an aunt was awkward because she wasn't married. Maybe it was the stereotype of that maiden aunt thing.

Fran smiled. The hood of her parka was up and she tucked her hair under it. "It is silly of me, I guess." She took his hand again and put it back in his pocket.

"Let's go back inside. It's starting to snow." He suppressed a shiver.

They walked silently back up to the hotel. The guests had almost all gone to bed and the bar was closing. Lights glowed in the empty hallways and the carpets silently received their footsteps and flecks of snow from their jackets.

"I'm afraid I've been rather poor company," Fran said as she stopped at her door.

"Not at all. I enjoyed it very much."

"That's probably not true. Thanks anyway. I'm a terrible bore sometimes." She put the cumbersome key in the lock. Apparently Yetta wasn't back yet.

"Can I see you at breakfast? Maybe do some skiing with you tomorrow?"

"We'll see. Breakfast is fine. Yetta and I are going to try the downhill course tomorrow. Think you can make it?"

"I'm afraid not. I'm out of shape." Sam cursed the hospital and his weakness. Eight weeks mainly in bed had caused his muscles to atrophy.

"She and I are skiers from way back." Fran paused, her hand on the door.

Sam was sorry that tomorrow he would have to leave the real skiing to the girls and instead struggle through more of the basics with Marty pin wheeling along behind him. Fran was close. He bent and kissed her on the cheek. When he did, she pressed her face against his mouth.

"Thanks for the beer, Sam," She said quickly. "Good night." She closed the door behind her, leaving him in the hall.

His own key had not been at the desk, and Sam wondered for a strained moment if Marty and Yetta were both in their room. He hesitated, knocked softly. There was no answer but the door was unlatched. It swung open at his touch.

Neither Marty nor Yetta were there. Sam wondered briefly where they were, dismissed the thought as none of his business, and went to bed. He was suddenly exhausted, wondered if it was the thin air at that altitude. He fell asleep almost immediately.

. . .

Sam was still groggy the next morning when he stumbled into the dining room for breakfast. The few falls he had taken on the ski slope the afternoon before had given him some bruises to remember them by.

Outside the light was brilliant on the new snow. It hardly seemed possible that this was the same dining room he had been in the evening before, when the night outside the hotel revealed only the dark outlines of mountains and a landscape filled with mysterious, hidden places. Now everything was sparkling with light and people sat having breakfast, excited at the possibility of getting outdoors as soon as possible.

A few children with freshly scrubbed faces ran between the tables, laughing and alarming the

German waiters. Sam was still groggy. The thought of food was a shock to the system. If he hadn't made a date with Fran he might have slept in, but that would be a waste of his weekend pass. If all he wanted to do was sleep in he could have stayed in the barracks.

He thought he was early, but Fran and Yetta were already having breakfast. He joined them.

"Morning, Sam." Fran smiled brightly over the last of her orange juice. Except for the orange juice it was a German breakfast in spite of the fact that the hotel had been taken over by the occupying Army: rolls, coffee, butter, jam and slices of German salami and cheese.

"Hi!"

"Morning." Yetta's voice was flat and her hair disheveled. "Where's Marty?"

"Still in bed."

"That's where I should be," Yetta said and quickly added, "in my own bed." She cleared her throat, frowned at her glass as if she wished it were whiskey.

Sam ordered breakfast without looking at the waiter. He studied Fran instead. He had wanted to know how she looked when she got up in the morning.

Yetta pushed aside her empty juice glass. "What's Munich like, Sam?" She picked at the waist of her heavy, black sweater. She seemed to have dressed in a hurry.

"Big town. Lots of shopping. Not many hotels. It's eighty-five percent rebuilt since the war, but there's still ruins around. I suppose you have ruins in Heidelberg, too."

Fran smiled. She had been studying him so closely he wondered if he'd shaved properly. "We have the castle. That's our only ruin. Heidelberg wasn't bombed. The allies saved it for post war headquarters. USAREUR. That's where I work."

"I mean, what's it like for DA civilians?" DA was the abbreviation for Department of the Army.

She simply cocked her head, nothing to report. "What about you, Sam?"

Sam's own private life was pretty mundane. He hadn't yet got into any sort of groove since his release from the hospital. "I'm the supply clerk, and Marty's the company clerk. We're roommates. Some of the guys hang out at the service club. I'm always saving money for the next excursion, then spend evenings in the darkroom making prints of the pictures I take on the weekend."

"I've been thinking of taking a job there," Yetta said. "Comptroller's division and the Finance branch are being reorganized in Heidelberg and I think I'll take advantage of the break and get out."

"Why?"

"I'm tired of Heidelberg."

Was she tired of Heidelberg, or was this some whim? Perhaps she liked Marty and was one of those people who rush off without thinking very clearly of the consequences. Sam wondered what had gone on the night before. Marty had been too sleepy to answer questions.

"What's wrong with Heidelberg?"

"Sam, I came to Germany to have a ball. I've been in Heidelberg for a year and it's been great, but I'm getting tired of the gang there. I feel like meeting some new faces. I don't like to stay too long in one place anyway. Makes me feel settled in."

Sam's attitude was the opposite. He preferred a sense of security. "Settled in sounds good to me. I guess you can't ever do that in the military. Maybe it's deliberate. If someone is stationed more than four years in a foreign country their loyalties might be influenced. So they keep moving."

"You like some stability," Fran commented. "So do I."

Sam turned sharply to see what she meant. She was dreamily staring out the window at the mountain scenery, but maybe not actually seeing anything.

"You're both wrong," Yetta insisted. "The most fun you have at a place is when it's all new and different. New faces..." She winked at Fran. "New men."

Sam winced. In mixed company he never spoke of what Marty referred to as "the hunt."

Yetta continued. "I've an old friend working in Munich who is fixing me up with a place down there."

Fran asked, "Which friend is that?"

"Sally Ann. You remember the Berlin trip? The tall blonde?"

"Yes." Fran's smile was far away. "We had only three days that time. Hardly time to see anything."

"It's pretty tough to see anything on just a weekend," Sam said.

"We used to work in the same office back in the States. Left for Europe together, but Sally Ann was sent to Munich. She's been there the whole time."

"And you went to Heidelberg."

"No, Sam. I went to Wiesbaden. I was there a year and now I've been in Heidelberg a year. That's enough for anybody."

"You say her name is Sally Ann?"

"You probably don't know her. Ever been to the *Goldene Traube*?"

Sam thought a moment. The *Goldene Traube*— the Golden Grape. Yes. A hotel confiscated for dependents or DAC's. "I think I've seen it. I don't spend much time in downtown Munich."

"What do you do, Sam?" It was Fran, back from her thoughts of Berlin.

"I'm gone every weekend."

"But I thought it was hard for an enlisted man to get a pass."

Sam didn't correct her and say he was a draftee, not enlisted. The proper term was non-com. "It is, but Marty's the company clerk, and since we're both cadre we have passes every weekend. We're always going someplace together."

Yetta grinned knowingly. "It's his car, isn't it?"

"Yes." The question slightly angered him. "The Green Beetle is his car, but he doesn't know any German, so I'm his sort of translator. But that's not why I stick with him. We're cadre. We're not supposed to mix with the rest of the guys in the detachment. If we did, they'd be asking for extra passes or equipment."

Fran stirred her coffee. "Then you are the elite of the company."

"We're just discouraged from association. Kind of miserable, in a way. The First Sergeant and the rest of the NCOs are all married. The officers are a bunch of dodos and that leaves just Marty and me." He almost added "alone," but that would sound like self-pity.

"No wonder you go away on weekends," Fran said.

"They got to have some fun, don't they? I like to see the boys have some time to themselves." Yetta winked. "More power to you, Sam."

She sounded like she was taking on the role of mother hen, which made Sam wonder how old she was. Older that him or Marty, he guessed. "Thanks."

Marty appeared in the dining room. He had his usual morning look, as if he'd forgotten to comb his eyebrows. His sleepy expression and sagging posture made his clothes look like rumpled pajamas.

Yetta saw him and waved. "Hi there, doll."

Like a sound in a rusty pipe a "good morning" rumbled up from Marty's throat. He ignored the menu, asked the waiter for some coffee, black.

"You look like hell, honey," Yetta said.

Something of her tone reminded Sam of home, something unpleasant.

"Yetta's thinking of moving to Munich," Fran said.

Marty seemed to be falling asleep at the table. His eyes were almost closed and he sagged in his chair. "That's nice."

"She's tired of Heidelberg," Sam added.

Marty showed no reaction. Yetta was getting peeved. "I'll be coming down for part of next weekend to see about a job."

"Will you be coming down, too, Fran?" Sam wanted to see her again.

"My colonel's giving another party. I have to be there."

"That's too bad." This would probably be the only weekend he could see her. He wished that for once he could meet someone and that the relationship wouldn't end with the weekend pass. Each weekend was another adventure, complete or incomplete in itself, but separate, a unit with no connection to the other weekends or to the wearisome routine of the supply room. It was like being trapped on Square One.

Fran understood his disappointment. "Maybe I'll get to Munich sometime, Sam. "I'll look you up."

"That'd be great. Give me your address and phone number in Heidelberg so I can do the same."

They exchanged addresses and Yetta rose. "Anyone for skiing?"

Marty stirred in his chair as if finally waking up. "Aren't you going to wait for me to finish my coffee?"

Yetta smoothed back her hair and started toward the stairs. As she passed him she patted

Marty on the shoulder. "The early worm gets the bird. See you on the slope, honey."

Sam rose. Now he remembered what she had reminded him of. "Honey." That's what the whores at Mother Green's had called their customers. He had gone there with the boys from the fraternity when he was a sophomore. Horrible.

"You coming, Sam?"

"Be right with you."

. . .

The sun was still behind the next mountain, but to the east Sam could see the brighter spots where the early light came between the distant peaks and lit their rocky edges. He looked down toward the valley to see how Garmisch looked after a fresh snowfall. A sea of grey clouds lay between the mountains, obscuring the valley, silent, unmoving, turning the neighboring peaks into islands. The only suggestion that something lay beneath that sea of cloud was the arc of cables that hung down into the mist from the Kreutzekbahn station.

On the far side of the valley Sam could make out the shifting wisps of cloud, partly transparent, moving like trapped smoke among the trees. Again he felt the isolation from the world that had chilled him the night before. But this morning the brilliance of the snow blinded him with a wild exhilaration. It didn't matter if his muscles were tired from yesterday or if the slope was too steep. He'd follow the girls on the downhill race trail even if he broke his neck. For an exhilarating moment he didn't care.

"Let's go kiddies," Yetta was shouting. She stood at the edge of a terrace waving a ski pole. Her yellow goggles were low on her stubby nose and her black ski outfit clashed with the fresh, powder snow.

Sam pushed his way toward her. "Won't we wait for Marty?"

Yetta's smile faded. "Hell with him." She waved her poles at Fran who was slipping her Arlberg straps around her ankles. If a ski came off it might fly down the mountain on its own like a spear, leaving her on only one ski. "Let's go, Fran. Have a ball!"

Fran straightened, started toward them. Yetta pushed off into the upper trail, did a quick turn to the left and was off, suddenly graceful, swinging her broad hips with perfect control. Sam was amazed.

"What are you waiting for, Sam?" Fran asked, and followed Yetta. He could see at once that she wasn't as good a skier, for her long legs seemed a hindrance, but she outclassed him. Definitely.

"Wait for me!" Sam did a sloppy snowplow turn as he reached the trail, wobbling at the knees and fighting for his balance. By the time he reached the second mogul Fran and Yetta were out of sight. He looked for them, missed a bump, and careened over the rise. Only his desperation and insistence on being able to follow the girls down the mountain got him under control without falling. He was too determined to be scared, but he fell three times before he reached the base of the upper slope. By the time he got there he was convinced he needed more practice and training to put back into his legs the strength he had left behind in the hospital.

Yetta and Fran waited for him at the top of the Olympic downhill race trail. "Coming along?" Yetta asked.

One look at the flags set out to mark the slalom race track convinced him. "I... I'd better not. Sorry. You've got me outclassed."

Fran looked at him a little sadly. "We'll be back, though."

"How about lunch?"

"I'd enjoy it."

"Two o'clock at the top of the ski lift?"

"Fine."

He reached out and took her gloved hand. Her smile was warm, the welcoming look he'd got on the cable car. Their ski poles dangled from their wrists, swung together, tangled, separated and then she was off, down the trail in a less graceful copy of Yetta's perfect form. Sam stood a long time looking down the steep trail after they were out of sight.

There was a crash behind him, a yell. Sam turned.

The sprawled figure untangled, reassembled itself and got to its feet. "Hi, Sam. How do you like my new way of stopping?"

"Effective."

Marty side-stepped down to Sam, looked over the edge. "Holy shit, they didn't go down there, did they?"

"Yeh."

Marty spat in the snow. He wiped the snow out of his goggles.

"What happened last night, Marty? What time did you get in?"

"Pretty late, I guess."

"Where were you? With Yetta, I suppose."

Marty smirked. "That's right, old buddy."

Sam waited for more, got none, was convinced that nothing had happened. If there had, Marty would have bragged about it. When Marty did score, he gave Sam a blow by blow description. "We're meeting them at 2:00 for lunch."

"OK." Marty turned. "How about teaching me that snowplow turn or whatever you call it? I can't figure it out."

. . .

The Kreutzek station was crowded with people waiting for the four o'clock cable car. Weekend passes were running out and there were suppers to wolf down before the train connections to Munich or farther north. Sam looked in vain for the girls. He hoped that they might show up at the last moment before he and Marty left for Munich.

"Stop moping, Sam. They wouldn't have met us for lunch anyway."

"She said she would. Fran doesn't look like the type who wouldn't keep her word."

Marty shoved his hands deep into the pockets of his Army overcoat. "Yeh, it's too bad. You know how it is, each weekend another couple of guys to buy 'em drinks. Have a ball. Maybe make out a little just for excitement. It doesn't mean anything. Not anything. She probably didn't even give you her real address."

Sam's disappointment was obvious.

"Come on, Sam. We better get in line or we'll miss the cable car."

Sam hefted his borrowed mountain division surplus skis and took a lingering look over the crowd, searching.

"There she is! Fran!"

The girls were just coming down from the hotel. Fran was carrying their overnight bags. Yetta looked pale. Fran noticed Sam, came forward, pushing her way past some GIs in uniform.

"Hi, Sam. I was looking forward to our lunch date."

"So was I." Sam coughed, the old lung thing again.

"We would have been there in time, but Yetta fell. It was misty and her goggles fogged. She ran into some Austrian."

"I hurt my back," Yetta said, obviously in pain. She started to sit on one of the suitcases, got half way down, winced, and slowly stood up again.

"Serious?" Sam asked.

Marty was indifferent.

"We spent the afternoon in the infirmary in Garmisch. Had to come back up to turn in the skis and get our things," Fran explained.

A bell rang and a German attendant opened the gate. People rushed to get into the car. "Grab your stuff, Marty, Fran. This thing only runs once an hour."

They got aboard and assembled in a corner where they were crushed by the crowd. Everyone was snapping pictures. Sam remembered that his camera was packed in his bag. "Do you take the train by way of Augsburg or Munich?" he asked.

"Munich," Fran said. "It's a rough ride. Train's always crowded on Sundays."

"You may not get a seat." Sam looked at Marty.

Marty took the hint. "You can ride with me to Munich if you want." He took the little pipe from the bottomless depths of his overcoat pocket and chewed on the stem. His bushy brows made him look like a dog poking his head out from the folds of a big khaki blanket.

Sam was surprised that Marty didn't ask the girls to share the gas. Perhaps he didn't have the nerve, or didn't want to look cheap. Maybe he wanted to do them a favor so they'd be indebted to him after. People did things for many reasons. Sometimes it was hard to figure out what was the most important.

The cable car descended into the cloud bank that had hidden the valley all day and had caused Yetta's accident.

The tops of the fir trees moved silently past the car. Had it not been filled with passengers the only sound would have been the humming of the cables and the clicking of the pulleys as the car passed the Kreutzeckbahn's supporting towers.

When they arrived at the lower station Sam looked back toward the mountain. Clouds obscured the top, and the valley got none of the brilliance the sun made on the snows above. Here everything was grey, subdued. It must have been an inversion, for the smoke from the chimneys of the houses hung in the air trapped in the valley between the mountains. Sam's pass was ending and all he had to look forward to was another week of trying to straighten out the mess of paperwork the supply sergeant had let accumulate while Sam had been in the hospital.

Marty pointed. "That's my car there, the Volkswagen with the U.S. Forces in Germany plates. I call it the Green Beetle."

Getting their accumulated luggage into the compartment under the hood took some ingenuity. Yetta had a hard overnight case, but Sam and Marty had soft, nylon bags that could be squeezed into the corners.

"Better sit in front, Yetta," Sam suggested. "No sense in trying to cram your sore back into the back seat."

Fran got in. "You think you can squeeze your long legs in here, Sam?"

"If you can, I can."

She blushed. "My legs aren't that long."

Sam followed her in, swiveling his hips. Once crammed into the small space they would hardly be able to move during the drive to Munich. Sam noticed that Yetta was eyeing him coolly, a grin flickering at the corners of her mouth.

"Say, boy. You sure you'll behave back there?"

Marty kicked the starter and put the VW in gear. He let the clutch out too quickly and the car lurched forward, kicking back cinders that had been strewn for traction on the few inches of fresh snow that had fallen. The car ground gingerly down the hill on the narrow road toward Garmisch. When they reached level ground Marty shifted up and they increased speed. The old Volkswagen careened along the road, skidding now and then.

"Take it easy, Marty," Sam cautioned.

"You know me, Buddy Boy. I like to drive fast." Marty was hunched over the steering wheel. His overcoat cuffs almost hid his hands.

After a few kilometers everyone grew confident in Marty's driving and relaxed. Sam turned to Fran and asked, "What time's your colonel's party next weekend?"

"Three o'clock. Why?"

"I mean, if you really wanted to, you could still come to Munich with Yetta when she looks for that job."

"I don't know."

"It wouldn't be hard to manage." Sam had made a hobby of studying the Deutsche Bundesbahn timetable. "You could come down Friday night and leave Sunday morning. Easy connections. I'd like to see you."

"I can't say just yet." She paused, her thoughts again in some distant place. "I'll have to see."

Sam suddenly seemed very occupied with the zipper of his ski jacket. He toyed with the leather thong he used as a pull tab and thought, *"She's going to wait for a better offer."*

"It's a long way to travel for a little over one day, Sam." She looked at him, studying his features.

One of the first things he did when he was released from the hospital was get a haircut. He was self-conscious about the lump on his nose where the old break was. What was she looking at? It was as if she were studying the shape of his jaw, like an artist who wanted to recreate his face in a sketch.

She asked, "Do you really want to see me?"

"I, sure. Yes, I do." He clumsily took her hand.

"Why?"

"Well, I… I could show you around Munich. I know something of the town. I don't usually make any plans until Friday so this way I'd have something to look forward all week." Something to plan for would be a departure from his ad hoc life.

Fran was thoughtful. "I know what you mean."

Did she? It was like a hesitant, preliminary dance, like two courting birds, the male displaying plumage and hoping to get the female's attention. Sam meant to kiss her on the cheek but she surprised him and turned and met his mouth with hers. Not breaking the kiss, he tried to turn in the back seat of the Volkswagen to put his arm around her. She gently broke away and sat still and pale, looking out the window with blank, faraway eyes. Houses decorated with Bavarian paintings swept past. The speeding car kicked up little sprays of snow behind them.

The taste of her kiss reminded Sam of other kisses, of Betty, their first night at Iron Mountain, the tiny cabin and the fireplace, the rug on the floor where they had lain a long time looking at the flames snapping and sparking at the birch logs.

They'd tussled on the floor, kissed, laughed, and by mutual, wordless agreement decided that the floor wasn't comfortable enough for sex and went to bed…

She asked, "Why don't you call me on Wednesday?"

"Fine." He fumbled in his pocket for his pencil. "What's your number at the office?" But he was still thinking about that other kiss, the brief goodbye at the Union Station in Chicago when he left for Camp Kilmer and the troop ship bound for Germany. Things hadn't worked out with Betty after all. That kiss was a sad goodbye that marked disillusionment and disappointment.

"Heidelberg Military 7530. That's the comptroller's office. Yetta's on the same phone." Sam nodded, wrote on the back of the receipt from the hotel, the only bit of paper handy.

"You already have the number of the Hotel Schrieder. Heidelberg 7-7003." She looked at Sam uncertainly, the look a man gives a woman when he wakes up with her in the morning and can't remember what happened the night before.

Sam put away the pencil and took her hand again. She gripped his fingers fiercely, not looking at him. "I don't make any guarantees. I may be busy Saturday, too. I…"

Sam kissed her again. She didn't respond immediately, then suddenly squirmed in her seat. Trapped in the back of the Volkswagen she could hardly break away. Sam was only aware of the taste of her lips and her skin. The roaring of the air-cooled engine behind them faded in his ears and

Harley L. Sachs

the Green Beetle ground on recklessly toward Munich, the *Hauptbahnhof*, and the Heidelberg Express...

Chapter Two

Detachment A, 50th Signal Battalion

There were three desks in the orderly room of Detachment A. At the front, inside the railing, was the First Sergeant's. Always orderly, it maintained the freshly-arranged look of a desk made ready for the night. The dish of paper clips was carefully arranged at the edge of the blotter, and the pencils were sharpened and placed points to the left in their tray. The IN-basket was full and the OUT-basket missing. The desk always looked neat because it was hardly ever used. There was no one at it now.

Behind the First Sergeant's swivel chair was a second desk. Here, under a pile of assorted papers, was a heavy duty manual typewriter and Sam, standing at the gate, could see a corner of the First Sergeant's OUT-basket showing under a stack of pass requests. This was the company clerk's desk, but Marty wasn't there, either.

Sam started to push open the swinging door to go inside the railing but he stopped. The captain's German Shepherd puppy was standing guard in the middle of the floor. It watched Sam with its six-month-old eyes and growled. Sam waited at the gate. "Sergeant Bird," he asked, "where's Vidal?"

At the third desk a skinny SFC put down a training manual and took a cigar from his mouth before speaking. "Gone to get the mail. What're you standing at the rail for, Logan? Still afraid of that dog?"

"No, sergeant. I just don't like him."

"You aren't used to him yet."

The puppy growled again. Sam growled back. The dog suddenly leaped up, barking wildly, and jumped at the gate. It couldn't clear the top and dashed around the office, barking. Sam stood back and chuckled. He barked.

"Goddamn it, Logan. Whataya got to excite that dog for?" SFC Bird rose behind his desk. Manual in hand, he approached the dog. "Quiet, General. Quiet now."

The puppy grasped the training manual in his jaws and hid behind the desk with it. SFC Bird followed closely after. "Gimme that." After a moment of frustrated poking under the desk the sergeant gave up. "Alright Logan. Now he's eating it. I don't know why they draft you college kids. Got no sense at all."

"The orderly room's no place for a dog, sergeant."

"If the captain wants to keep his dog here, that's his business, not yours." The sergeant made another try for the manual. "I've had enough of this. Logan…!"

"Yes, sergeant." Sam wondered what he'd started this time.

"I'm going to the mess hall for coffee. You get that manual away from that dog and take care of the orderly room."

"Where is everybody?" In the Army it was important to know where everybody was.

"It's the lieutenant's afternoon off. Sergeant Adams is at the mess hall having coffee. The captain's bowling, but if anyone calls you'd better say he's at the quartermaster sales store."

"That's what we said yesterday."

"Well, say anything then. Say he's at the commissary."

"I'd better lock the supply room."

"I'll lock it. You stay in here and answer the phone and get that manual before the stupid dog chews it up. I'll need that for training tomorrow morning." SFC Bird let himself out through the gate. He paused briefly at the supply room to snap the padlock and continued down the basement hallway, a skinny man puffing cigar smoke. His uniform was so heavily starched it look like cardboard.

Sam let himself in behind the railing and looked cautiously around the office. The adjoining room, belonging to the CO and the Exec, was empty. General was still chewing noisily on the manual under the First Sergeant's desk. Sam placed himself at the door and took his fatigue cap, crushed and shapeless, from under his belt. "Here, General," he said, waving the hat. The growling under the MSGT Adam's desk stopped. The German Shepherd dropped the training manual, crept suspiciously forward. "Here, General. Here's a hat." Sam lured the dog into the Captain's office and closed the door on him. Then, stuffing the hat back under his belt, he sat down at the First Sergeant's desk. "Stupid dog."

Marty came into the room dragging a sackful of mail. "Hi, Sam. Where's Bird?" Marty wore wrinkly fatigues, said he couldn't stand starched ones because they chafed.

"Gone for coffee. Any mail for me?"

"Haven't sorted it yet, but there's another love letter for Bird. Slip it into his desk drawer."

Sam took the crisp, blue aerogram letter and went to SFC Bird's desk. On the way he picked up the chewed training manual. "You'd think that gal of his would give up. She knows he's married."

Marty leafed through the bundle of letters. "Bird doesn't care. Have you seen one of those guys who gave a damn about their wives? I don't see why they got married. All they do is chase the German broads. You want this bag of packages put in the mail room?"

"I'll take it later." Sam looked at the pile of pass requests on Marty's desk. "These the weekend passes?"

"Yeh."

"Don't forget to make out mine, will you?"

"Where do you want to go?"

"Gee, I don't know. I have to call Fran back."

"I thought you talked to her Tuesday." Marty sat down at his desk and rocked back in the swivel chair. His boots were unpolished and the bloused fatigue cuffs had slipped down.

"She didn't know then. Said to call Friday."

"Well, here's the phone."

Sam moved the phone to the First Sergeant's deck and lifted the receiver. "You want to see Yetta, don't you?"

"Sure. She's a nice gal. Lots of laughs." Marty rocked forward in his chair, stood up.

Sam dialed Headquarters Area Command. Somewhere, a series of switches and relays carried his connection through the Munich circuits. A lot of buzzing and clicking and a recorded voice said, Headquarters Area Command, dial your number." He dialed again. He hoped that this time Fran would give him a definite answer about the weekend. He had held off making any plans because of her. "Heidelberg Military, dial your number..." He dialed Fran's office number. Strange how he remembered it right away. He really wasn't very good at remembering things. Even in basic training he had a terrible time learning his serial number.

Marty walked aimlessly around the orderly room. He picked up the chewed manual from Bird's desk. "Hey, Sam, don't you get enough to eat in the mess hall?"

Someone picked up the phone at the other end. "Comptroller's Office, Miss Wagner."

"Fran?"

"Shame on you, Sam, eating Sergeant Bird's training manuals. He had trouble enough on his little mind...."

Sam covered the mouthpiece. "Quiet, Marty. I'm on the phone."

"Who's speaking, please?"

"Sam. Sam Logan. I'm calling from Munich."

She hadn't recognized his voice at first. Hers sounded far away and thin. The connection wasn't very good. Still, Sam thought immediately of the long ride from Garmisch in the back of Marty's Green Beetle the weekend before.

"Glad to hear your voice, Sam," she said. "I was just going to call you. I'll be coming down tomorrow morning early. Be glad to see you, but Yetta's taking me shopping in the afternoon. We'll have to make it just an evening date. Say, seven-thirty? After supper?"

Marty's voice came through Sam's other ear. "Sam, where's the dog?"

"That'll be fine. Where?" It would be great to see her again. Maybe they could be alone for a little while.

As if in answer, a whimpering and scratching came from the adjoining room.

"We'll be at the *Hotel zum Bahnhof.* Know where that is?"

"I think so. I'll find it anyway."

"Christ, Sam. General'll crap all over the captain's rug. Damn, you're stupid sometimes." Marty opened the door and let the puppy out. It sulked in a corner by the railing.

"Bring Marty along," Fran was saying. "Yetta might like to see him."

"I know I'll be glad to see you," Sam said. "Been looking forward to it." Sam was trying to think of something else to say, to indicate indirectly and subtly how he felt about her. A sudden tugging at his leg distracted him. "Hey!"

"Sam?"

The dog was taking its revenge out on Sam's fatigue pants. Gnawing and tugging, its young teeth were firmly engaged in the fabric.

"Get away… Fran, I can't talk to you now. I'm having trouble with the captain's dog. Get away, General, stop!"

"What's that? Did you say something about a general's dog?"

"I'll tell you when I see you tomorrow night. Seven thirty?"

"I think we have a bad connection, Sam. What did you say?"

Sam was getting desperate. A misunderstanding now would spoil everything. "It's all right. See you tomorrow at seven-thirty. Tell you all about it."

"All right." She sounded puzzled, her voice even farther away. He could imagine how her eyes looked when she spoke like that… wide, unfocussed… looking at some dream… but there was a ripping sound that distracted him.

"Damn it!" Sam kicked at the dog. "Not you, Fran." But she had hung up. He wasn't sure whether she had heard him swear or not. Sam put the phone back and tried to disengage the dog.

Marty sat, laughing, on SFC Bird's desk. "See what you get, Buddy Boy? Mistreating that innocent dog."

Sam struggled helplessly, was finally helped by Marty who came to the rescue. Taking the dog by the scruff of the neck, Marty pushed it into the captain's office and closed the door. "Stupid dog." He returned, still laughing. "How's the fatigues?"

"Just a little rip. I can sew it up."

"While you're at it, sew some patches on my shirt, will you?"

"You still wearing those Second Army patches? Sergeant Adams told you to fix them months ago when you made corporal."

Marty sat down at his deck and picked up a pass form. He inserted it into his typewriter. "You know how it is. I never have any time."

A figure in white had appeared at the railing. "Can one of you boys give me my pass?"

"Hi, Strycklan." Marty was pleased to have an excuse to stop typing. He leaned back in his chair, took the tiny pipe out of his pocket and jammed it between his teeth. "Done in the bakery already?"

The small man smiled shyly. His whole attitude, the way he stood in his white baker's jacket and fatigue pants, the white, cook's hat in his hands, spoke of humility. Good humor sparkled in the corners of his eyes. He had brought with him the fresh-baked smell of pastry and frosting. "I finished the cake for dinner, so I'm free now. Don't have another shift until Tuesday. Is my three day pass ready?"

Marty shuffled through the papers on his desk. "Hell. It's typed but the captain hasn't signed it yet."

"When will he be back?" A fumbling with the white hat. My shatzy's waiting for me. We're going to visit her folks for the weekend."

Sam looked up from the First Sergeant's desk. "He's at the bowling alley. Might not get back until four-thirty."

Disappointment and worry. "That's awful late."

"We can't call him, Strycklan. Might catch him in the middle of a frame."

"Can't one of you boys sign the pass?"

Marty shook his head and looked out from under his shaggy brows. The pipe clenched in his teeth, he said, "That's forgery. You wouldn't want me to get in trouble, would you?"

"No. I don't like any kind of trouble."

The phone rang. Sam answered it. "Detachment A, Private Logan, sir."

Sergeant Stryklan turned to go. "I'll take a chance on my permanent pass, then."

Sam waved him back. "Wait a second. It's the captain… Yes, sir. Everything's fine here, sir… The dog's right here."

"Arf, arf." Marty had mastered the puppy's bark the first day it had been brought to the orderly room for housebreaking.

A more distant barking came from behind the door to the captain's office.

Sam continued. "Sergeant Adams is at the mess hall, sir."

"He's gone home," Marty interrupted. The barking in the next room continued.

"…Yes, sir. Just a minute, sir. There's a man here for his three-day pass. Sergeant Stryklan, the baker… I know, sir, but he needs it right away. He's going to Stuttgart again." There was a silence at the other end of the phone. Sam paused, then handed the phone to Marty. "He wants to talk to you."

Marty put the pipe in his pocket, took the receiver. "Afternoon, sir. How's the bowling? … Yes, sir. The baker. Fine man."

Strycklan smiled hopefully.

"Is that an order, sir? Yes, sir. In that case I'll do it... No, there haven't been any calls for you. ... Sir? Don't forget to pick up General on the way home. Goodbye." Marty hung up the phone. "How do you like that?" He took out his pipe again. "He says I'm to sign your pass for you, Strycklan."

"Thanks a lot, boys. I sure appreciate it."

Marty took out an expensive pen that looked out of place in contrast to his grimy fatigues. With a practiced hand he signed the captain's name to the pass. "The First Sergeant does this all the time, but I wouldn't do it without a direct order from the Captain. You understand that, Strycklan?"

"Sure." The baker took the pass, blew on the ink. "Not a bad job."

"I've watched Sergeant Adams doing it. Remember, I had a direct order if there's ever any question."

"Thanks a lot." Stryklan returned behind the railing.

Marty got up, showed the chewed training manual. "Those cooks have our poor supply clerk starving. Look how thin he is. He's taken to eating SFC Bird's training manuals."

Stryklan smiled.

"Next time you make pies, do you think we could have one in the orderly room? Sam here is hungry all the time."

"I'm getting in some apples next week. Probably make apple pie on Friday. Just pick one up on your way through with the mail. But you got to promise to return the pan."

"We'll do that," Sam said, smiling.

"It's awful hard to get pie pans. Thanks a lot, boys." Strycklan put on the white hat as he passed through the orderly room door and disappeared around the corner.

Chapter Three

The Second Weekend—Mixed Signals

Party time. Sam and Marty took the stairs to the third floor of the *Hotel zum Bahnhof* where Yetta and Fran had booked a room. It was a seedy, travelers' hotel near the railway station, but cheap. Sam, still not in shape or over his persistent cough, was out of breath. His hand sweat on the neck of the wine bottle. "I'm sure glad she decided to come down."

"You told me that about six times today, Sam. I'm just happy we aren't taking them out to dinner."

"You're always thinking of money. I hope this four mark wine wasn't too much to invest in."

Marty was silent as they rounded the corner of the stairs.

Sam continued. "I can't understand your attitude. You're the one who was telling me I needed a woman to help me recuperate, and now that we've got a couple of nice girls on the string you're indifferent."

Marty shrugged. "I'm not so interested in nice girls, Sam."

"I thought you like Yetta."

"I do, but I'm not going to get all shook up about it. I don't like to get involved."

This time Sam was silent. Marty went on. "This is a hell of a way to waste a weekend. One evening in a crummy hotel. We could have driven someplace instead of hanging around Munich."

"Yeh, I know. I'd like to get as far away from that orderly room as possible. That stupid dog. I thought we'd never get the captain's rug clean again."

"That was your fault, Sam. You shouldn't have locked him in the office in the first place."

"You put him in the second time."

Marty stood, complacent and self-righteous, nibbling at the stem of his tiny pipe. His misshapen, khaki Army overcoat hung to his calves, almost hiding his baggy pants. Sam, bottle in hand, was wearing the Gestapo-like trench coat he had bought so the Germans wouldn't recognize him as a soldier. They stopped in front of the girls' room on the third floor and knocked.

"Hi Sam, Marty." Yetta had opened the door with a big, forced smile.

The room had once been elegant but now looked worn, the furnishing old fashioned, the chaise lounge in the corner threadbare.

"How's your back?" Sam handed Yetta his coat. He looked around the room, didn't see Fran.

"Much better." Yetta hung up the coat in the amoire. Clothes closets weren't standard in Germany. "Fran's in the bathroom. She'll be right back."

Marty, like a buyer instead of a visitor, inspected the room. He sat down on the bed, opened the window, shut it again, walked up and down, and finally sat on the chaise lounge in the corner. He sucked on the pipe, made a wry face and extracted a small package from his pocket. "Look what I bought today, kiddies. A special long cigarette holder." He pulled on the ends and the cigarette holder expanded about twelve inches. "My doctor told me to keep away from cigarettes."

"It's different," Yetta remarked. "I'll say that for it."

Sam turned away.

Their ration was a carton of cigarettes a week, which Marty then sold on the black market to cab drivers in the alley beside the main railway station. The pack of cigarettes he had with him were Camels from an outdated can of C rations left over from World War II. The cans always contained a pack of cigarettes, some waterproof matches, a packet of halizone tablets for purifying water, and a can opener. Marty opened the pack of stale cigarettes and with some difficulty got one out. He bent it getting it into the cigarette holder.

Sam looked at him, remembered the squabble in the orderly room about the captain's dirtied rug. "Don't tell me you're actually going to smoke that?"

Marty lolled on the couch. "Sam's just jealous. The doctor told him not to smoke." There was an awkward silence.

Sam put the bottle of wine on the bureau. "We brought some refreshments." He didn't want to think about the doctors and the hospital again. "Want to open this now?"

"Not just yet." Yetta sat down at the foot of the chaise lounge. Marty began to feel uncomfortable, got up indifferently and sat on the bed. "I'm not thirsty," Yetta said, giving Marty a cold look. Marty pretended to ignore her and calmly lit the cigarette.

Fran came out of the bathroom carrying a towel. "Sam! Are you early or am I late?" She hung the towel by the ornate, ancient wash stand.

Sam approached her, wondering if he would get a kiss hello. "How was the train?" It was a five hour run down from Heidelberg to Munich. He longed for news of a trip. Except for the stay in the hospital every weekend had been a train ride someplace, or the wheels of Marty's Green Beetle carrying him away from Munich and the Army.

Fran looked at Yetta, then edged away from Sam. "I see you brought some wine."

"It's from both of us," Marty added from the bed. He puffed a cloud of smoke that was supposed to be a smoke ring.

Sam sat on the bed. There was something unpleasant about this situation. He couldn't figure out if it was the peculiar mixture of being mad at Marty, being stuck in Munich, and looking forward so long to meeting Fran, three feelings that didn't mix well, or something else. Granted, Marty was being an ass with his phony cigarette lighter. His affectation with a tiny pipe was bad enough. What was he trying to prove?

At a loss, Sam went to the window. "Not much of a view from here." The buildings across Fuerstenstrasse were shabby and old, a pre-war contrast to current new construction. At this point Fuerstenstrasse was narrow and ended in a few meters in one direction and turned a few meters in the other. The view from the window was more like a glance into an ill-kept courtyard.

Yetta's expression was blank. "No, there isn't."

Sam thought, *What's going on?'* Yetta didn't seem her usual party girl self at all. Now she sat, stiff in a knit suit ill-chosen for her figure.

"But then, this part of Munich isn't much on scenery." Sam looked at Fran and Yetta. There was nothing gay and have-a-ball-ish about Yetta this weekend. Fran looked uncomfortable. Marty still lay on the bed assuming his attitude of studied indifference. He wasn't helping matters any.

No one said anything. Was this the big evening he had looked forward to? Sam had hoped, perhaps, some serious, personal conversation, a chance to get better acquainted, to find out what it was that drew him to Fran, made her so interesting, such an enigma. He had a feeling that if he found out about her he would better understand himself.

Fran picked up the bottle of wine and studied the label.

"I've got an opener." Sam produced the imitation Swiss Army pocket knife he always carried with him. "It opens into a twelve inch cigarette holder." It was a stupid joke. He laughed, realized he was the only one laughing, and coughed to hide his embarrassment.

After a short silence Fran looked at him, almost apologetically. "We only have two glasses."

Sam went to her and awkwardly took her hand. She briefly returned his grasp, glanced past him at Yetta, and pulled her hand away.

Sam took the wine bottle and screwed the opener into the cork. He bent and held the bottle between his knees. In the quiet room the noise of the cork seemed unbearably loud. "Marty and I can drink from the bottle."

Marty asked Yetta, "Did you get the job?"

"I start next Friday. I'll be moving down on Wednesday."

Marty studied the ashy end of his cigarette. "Going to stay at the *Goldene Traube?*" It was the billet for female employees of the U.S. Army in Munich.

Sam breathed easier. At least someone was talking.

"Yes. A friend of mine is helping me get a room there." Yetta fetched the two glasses from the wash stand.

"Yetta has a friend named Sally Ann," Sam explained. "Worked with her in the States and when they both came over here. You weren't around when we were talking about it." He poured some wine.

Marty seemed suddenly interested. "Sally Ann? What's her last name?"

"Ross. You know her?" Yetta asked.

Marty seemed confused. He came out of his thoughts like a school boy caught at something he shouldn't. "I, well, I met her once. And I've seen her around." He seemed to know more than he claimed.

Sam was curious. Perhaps this had something to do with those nights when he was in the service club darkroom and Marty went out.

Marty sat on the edge of the bed and puffed coolly on the cigarette. Were it not for the long holder he might have looked like an interrogator, for he kept a studied eye on Yetta and when he asked a question it sounded as though he were expecting her to give herself away. "Where did you work in the States?"

"In New York at an advertising agency on Madison Avenue."

"Yes?" He waited for her to continue, but she didn't.

"Ever hear of Logan Associates in Chicago?" Sam asked.

Yetta shook her head, sipped some wine.

Marty asked, "Where does Sally Ann work?"

"Armed Forces Network."

Marty nodded, satisfied.

"She sounds interesting," Sam said. "You'll have to introduce us some time."

Yetta had no answer and Fran looked at him suspiciously. Could she be jealous?

Sam buttoned his baggy, maroon sport jacket, the only one he had with him in Europe. He had worn it when he was a freshman in college but it was out of style now. He had brought it to Europe where he thought the solid color would fit in better than his alternative, a gaudy plaid. Of course, it was an American cut, nothing like the tailored jackets the Germans wore. His German trench coat might help his disguise, but the sport coat gave him away. He thought of school, of leaving, of the Army, of Fran. She had drunk from the wine bottle and was holding it out to him. But she seemed only polite, not interested, and he thought hell, what's the use? But he'd make one last try. "What are you doing next weekend?"

"I'm going to Feldberg in the Black Forest to ski."

"Oh?" Perhaps she'd want company.

"I'm going with some friends."

"Oh." Sam paused. "I'm glad you could come down this weekend."

Marty gave him a disgusted look, then turned his back irritably. "The trouble with Sam is he has too much imagination."

"I'm afraid you're right, Buddy Boy," Sam said sarcastically. "I'm always making something out of nothing."

"Marty makes something out of nothing," Yetta said. There was a canny look on her shrewd, plump face, as if she didn't expect anyone to understand what she said but wanted to say it anyway.

Sam stood, puzzled. He held the bottle in one hand, buttoned and unbuttoned the old sport jacket with the other. He coughed nervously and had the feeling that he must look like a surprised rabbit that hasn't made up his mind which way to run. Perhaps, he thought, the direction doesn't matter as long as it's running. He wondered whether they had gotten on too well, necking in the back seat of the Green Beetle the weekend before, and the girls wanted to nip things in the bud before anybody got ideas. Maybe there was something between Marty and Yetta that hadn't been explained and was causing this cold shoulder now.

Whatever the reason, it was no go. There was no point in prolonging a painful situation. Sam studied Fran. There was no faraway look in her eyes tonight, but when she noticed he was looking at her she turned away with what seemed like a guilty expression. Best to bail out before things got more awkward than they already were.

It dawned on him that the girls had made up their minds that any expectations he and Marty might have had were not going to materialize. Sam asked, "Why don't we take off tonight, Marty?"

Marty looked puzzled. "Take off? Where?"

"You remember. We were going to check out that big castle at Oberammergau. We could leave tonight. I hate sleeping in the barracks on weekends."

Marty no longer looked puzzled. "We could leave at 9:00 and still get there in time to get a room."

Yetta didn't seem surprised or disappointed. "Leaving tonight?"

"We'll have to go." Sam handed Fran the bottle. "You can finish this. It's on me."

"On us," Marty corrected. He tapped the cigarette holder against the bed to loosen the sections, collapsed it, and turned to Yetta. "When you come down I could help you move into the billet."

Fran handed Sam his trench coat. He put it on, conscious of Fran's plucking at the collar to get it neatly in place. He was thinking of a weekend wasted in the barracks. Maybe he should get a bottle and sleep late on Sunday like a regular Army guy with no imagination. A wasted pass. That's what he got for daydreaming too much.

When they left the girls' room Fran said goodbye to him rather sadly, apologetically, like the cold shoulder they'd got was not her idea. Later, he would remember her look, but at the moment he thought only of buying a bottle and getting drunk. It was a relief to get away from the tension in the room.

...

They walked to the car and had driven in silence for some minute before Marty finally spoke. "I told you all the time, roomy. Just a couple of DA's looking for a good time. Just one weekend. That's all we were allotted, and we got more than that. I hope you're satisfied."

Sam coughed. Again he felt the congestion in his lungs that had persuaded him to go to the doctors. It still persisted in spite of their diagnosis. Perhaps they were wrong. Perhaps he was still destined for a sanitarium and a life making useless souvenirs stamped with "Made by patients of Valley Forge Military Hospital." "Let's get a bottle. My throat needs something for medicinal purposes."

"I need more than that, Sam."

"Are you really going to help Yetta when she moves in on Wednesday?"

"Maybe I can drop her trunk in the river to get even."

Sam had a fleeting vision of a trunk floating, sinking in the swift current of the Isar. "I know a place where we can buy a bottle." It would be better to get drunk than to lie in bed staring at the

74

barracks ceiling the way he had in the hospital, that pale green inaccessible ceiling. He shuddered.

"Hell, Sam. Let's go to the Dolly Bar. There's always some action there."

"I suppose you want to pick up a broad."

"Why not, Sam? The weekend doesn't have to be a total loss." The stem of the pipe forced Marty's mouth into a cruel, sensuous grin. He had been driving aimlessly before. Now he swung the VW around a corner and headed back toward the *Hauptbahnhof*. As usual, it was brilliantly lit and boasted a stream of arriving or departing passengers. Sam was sorry not to be among them. He resolved to have a big evening in spite of Fran and Yetta. For a change he'd go along with anything Marty suggested.

The Dolly Bar was one of a group of dives near the railway station. It was a favorite hangout of those GI's who preferred to wear their uniforms, who had come to Europe for the big party and the girls.

And the girls were there. Almost every table was occupied by a girl sitting behind a Coca-Cola. Those sitting alone seemed to be waiting for someone.

Sam had looked into the place briefly one night when he had first arrived. It had not changed much from what he remembered. He didn't dare hang his coat near the door for fear it would be stolen. The juke box, an American import, was playing a screeching, stomping country western song and the voices in the room were raised accordingly so conversations could be heard above the racket.

"What do you think?" Marty asked, offering Sam his choice of tables.

"I think I want a drink." None of the girls looked very appetizing. If anything they looked tired and used.

Marty sat down at a table. Sam, feeling uneasy and vaguely rebellious, hung his coat over the back of a chair and sat down. The light wasn't good in the Dolly Bar, but it was good enough for him to see that the girl at the table wasn't a doll. She had a double chin and bleached blonde hair with dark roots. Her heavy makeup had been carelessly applied and didn't cover an unhealthy skin. She sat, bored, ignoring the coke in front of her, and assessing the room to see how her cronies were faring. When Marty joined her she was more alert. "Buy me a drink, GI?"

Marty didn't appear interested. "What do you want? Another coke?"

"I like cognac." A waiter was already on his way to the table. In most restaurants the wait staffs were women with black aprons that concealed the change purses under them. At the Dolly Bar the waiter was a tough looking man. The prescribed apron had once been white.

"I only buy beer," Marty said. "I'm broke."

"It ain't that long since payday, shatzie."

"I'm broke all the time."

The girl turned to Sam and got right to the point. "You got thirty marks?"

Thirty marks would buy more than a cognac. "I... no." He was surprised that he would say anything to her. He had never haggled with a prostitute. His only experience with one—besides that fiasco at Mother Green's—was when the fraternity had thrown a big party at a pledge's home in Gary, Indiana. Afterwards half the boys had come down with the clap. As he thought of that party now he wondered if tonight was going to end the same way.

The girl made a wry face. "Why the hell you come in here?" Taking her Coke with her, she got up and moved to another table. She sat down to talk to one of the unoccupied girls.

The waiter had arrived, saw that the girl had left, made a quick appraisal of Sam and Marty. Were they trouble?

"Two double cognacs," Marty said.

The waiter moved away without having said anything. Sam sat back, fighting down a feeling of sick anger that had unaccountably come over him. What a life for those women, sitting like second hand, shopworn merchandise in a seedy store, and having to haggle over the price of their own bodies.

At another table a GI with his OD jacket unbuttoned and his tie off was leaning forward in earnest but drunken discussion with a plump blonde who seemed better looking than the rest in the room.

Marty looked at the plump blonde, winked, frowned at the drunken soldier with her.

Sam settled back and waited for his cognac to come.

Marty asked, "How do you like the blonde"

"All right, I guess."

"I wonder how much she wants."

"Thirty marks, I suppose. Isn't that what the first one wanted?"

"That's what she asked, Sam. She'd take less."

The waiter arrived and put the cognacs down on the linoleum-topped table. Sam ignored him and suddenly realized that Marty had paid the bill. Usually a customer paid when he left a German restaurant, but here certain Americans had brought about a "pay when served" policy. It made Sam feel distrusted.

Sam reached for his wallet. "How much was that, Marty?"

"Forget it. You take the next round."

This was untypical. Sam wondered why.

The drunken GI left the blonde and headed for the men's room. Marty beckoned and the blonde rose to come over. "On with the hunt," Marty said from the corner of his mouth.

'*The hunt*'? Sam thought with disgust. *The hunt for what?*

The blonde sat down immediately. "Buy me a drink?"

"That's not what we're here for." Marty moved the tiny pipe to the other side of his mouth.

"Looking for business?"

Sam listened, a reluctant observer. He sipped his cognac. She seemed young, though it was hard to tell. Some months ago she might have been really attractive. A few pounds off the hips and a better bra would do her some good in the flesh market, but night life, dim lights, beer and whatever else were wearing away her looks. A few months more and she would be no different from the other burnt out whores. Sam frowned. At least here was one life cycle that wasn't hard to detect, examine, and toss away, the truth extracted. But the truth about disposable young girls wasn't the truth he looked for.

Abruptly the din of conversation in the Dolly Bar diminished. The juke box blared alone. Sam turned in his chair to see what was happening.

Two MPs in white helmets, arm bands, and polished leather boots had come in and were quietly looking over the crowd.

"Got your pass?" Marty asked.

Sam checked his wallet. "Sure."

The MP's continued their assessment, walking from table to table. Around the room there was a general checking of ties and buttoning of uniforms. One of the older women at a table crowded with soldiers turned and waved to the shorter, more nervous-looking MP "Hey, curly, buy me a drink?" She leered and the women at her table laughed. The soldiers with them tried to avoid the scrutiny of the MP's.

"Baby!" It was the drunken GI who had been with the blonde. He came staggering from the direction of the men's room. His tie hung from his pocket where it had been stuffed and his fly was unbuttoned. When he saw that she had moved to Sam and Marty's table he was suddenly angry. "Hey!"

The MP's moved in from opposite sides. They spoke in low voices.

"Hell, yes, I got a pass." The soldier pulled away and made for Marty. "Hey, buddy, get away from my gal."

The MP's intercepted and, watched by the approving looks of the waiter and bartender who had been relieved of the task, guided the protesting soldier from the bar. With their exit, conversations renewed as if never interrupted. Sam gulped the remainder of his cognac. He tried not to think of Marty and the blonde, wanted an exit strategy.

"Yes, we're looking for business," Marty continued.

"You can come home with me for thirty-five marks. Make it fifty and you can bring your friend."

"What do you think this is? Payday weekend? We're not flushed, you know. Been buying Christmas presents."

The blonde started to get up.

Christmas presents. It was too late now to send any home. Sam wondered if he should have sent one to Betty.

"Twenty marks," Marty said.

"You crazy? What you think I am, old whore like those others?"

Besides, Betty probably had forgotten him by now. Or hated him. It was too bad. How could he have been such a fool?

"Twenty-five?"

"Well…" She was weakening. "What about your friend?"

Betty had not been what he wanted. He had thought so, briefly. One night.

"He comes along, too," Marty said.

"Fifty marks."

He had been what Betty wanted, he thought, but it was all a horrible mistake.

"Forty."

She agreed.

Sam pushed thinking aside, reduced himself to his lowest common denominator.

"Deal." Marty looked at Sam. "OK with you, Sam?"

Sam shrugged. He hadn't been paying much attention. "Sure." Right now he couldn't care less. It was cheaper than going to Oberammergau, castle hunting, or taking a train somewhere for eight hours. Here was something quick and obliterating.

"Let's go," Marty said, rising. He turned to the girl. "We'll go in my car. I call it the Green Beetle..."

They passed in front of the *Bahnhof* again, passed the crowds, the shops and the stares of the German civilians who knew a whore when they saw one with a GI whether he was in uniform or disguised in civvies.

Marty bought a bottle of cognac without asking Sam to chip in. Sam didn't know how to handle a VW stick shift, so Marty had to drive through the dark streets past bomb-ruined buildings with staring, empty windows. Marty tried to steer with his knees so his hands were free to grope the blonde. She pushed his hands away and said in her coarse English. "Take it easy, shatzie. We got plenty of time."

Sam sat in the back seat, stupidly felt like the third wheel. He didn't want to be doing this.

The girl's one-room apartment was on the shuttered ground floor of a run-down building. She went into the bathroom to get ready while Sam and Marty had a quick drink in the alcove galley that served as a kitchen—a stained sink with a single cold water tap and a two burner gas hot plate.

Marty flipped a coin, covered it with his hand. "Call it, Sam. Heads or tails?"

"You go ahead, Marty. I'll wait."

"You want sloppy seconds?" Marty grinned, hung his Army overcoat on a hook inside the door. "Don't drink all the cognac, Buddy Boy."

The girl came out of the bathroom barefoot and wearing a faded pink bathrobe open enough to show that she had nothing on underneath it. She didn't have a separate bedroom, just an alcove that concealed a bed behind a curtain. She went in first. Marty followed her and drew the curtain.

While trying not to hear Marty's grunts and the girl's theatrical groans of "Oh, shatzie!" Sam took in the details of the room. On the bureau Sam glimpsed a little glass souvenir, one of those that looks like it's snowing when you shake it. The lamp on the bureau had no shade, just a bare bulb.

Now the girl was pretending to be in ecstasy. It was very disconcerting to Sam. He tried to distract himself by taking inventory of the apartment's scanty furnishings. The linoleum floor was a collection of unmatched pieces that had never seen wax. A single table with two chairs that didn't match. He sat on one of them, discovered it was wobbly. He was uncertain whether it was because the floor was uneven or the chair. He waited for them to finish.

Above the sink was a cupboard with the doors sagging open to reveal very little food and a couple of heavy cups Sam recognized as having been stolen from an Army mess hall. There was no TV, but sitting on a crate there was an old pre-war radio in a wooden case.

Gosh, they're taking a long time, Sam thought. He stood up, taking the bottle with him, and listened. He hadn't taken off his trench coat and stood, looking at his reflection in the cracked mirror mounted on the wall beside the bedroom door. He needed a shave again. His black eyebrows made his face look pale in spite of the five o'clock shadow. He wished he'd gotten a tan on the Kreutzek last weekend. High altitude sun could do that. He wished Fran had acted differently at the hotel. He guessed that was all over. It had never really been anything but wishful fantasy. He took a pull on the bottle. *Hell.*

Sam pulled at the bottle again. It was nearly a year since he had been with a girl. Last Christmas. Tonight was simpler. No worry about this girl being a virgin. No hesitation or anxiety this time. No having to talk and persuade. It had seemed strange to him how Betty hadn't needed much persuading. That had surprised him. Maybe she had decided for herself that now was the time. Crossed signals.

Sam pulled at the bottle again. He had to remember to leave some for Marty. Marty and his girls. A woman wasn't so hard to find after all, and they were all the same in the dark, weren't they? Pay 'em in D-marks or in free drinks and rides to the station. Pay 'em under the pillow or with security and a home. Transactions. It was business. If a girl married for money to better herself, wasn't that a form of prostitution, too?

Another sip from the bottle. But if buying sex wasn't honorable, what must selling it be like? The horror of there ever being a necessity to submit to sex for a price must be depressing if you had any self-respect.

Buttoning his fly, Marty came quietly out from behind the curtain. "Did you leave me any cognac, Buddy Boy?"

Sam didn't answer. He handed over the bottle and looked behind the curtain. In the back wall was a shuttered window that let in some light. He waited until his eyes got accustomed to the darkness.

She was sitting up, waiting. He could see that she was naked but the sight of her breasts left him cold.

He told himself, what was the difference? As long it was a transaction for a price, what was the difference? It was meaningless.

It was an old, brass bedstead, probably pre-war, scene of many encounters. Funny, he thought. He had hoped for a German bed this weekend. Now the barracks cot seemed more inviting.

What did it mean? Nothing. It was just meaningless sex. Sam sat on the bed, defeated, angry for being put in this situation. He stood up, cold, gathering his coat around him. He didn't want nothing. He tried to think of anything, anything but that girl and his twenty-Mark obligation. Not want nothing. The double negative amused him.

"*Was ist los, shatzie?*" the girl asked. The sound of her voice was a surprise. "Don't you like me any more?"

Sam stood up. "*Ich kann nicht. Leider.*" He didn't want any part of this. What he had said was ambiguous. It might mean he couldn't, that he thought it was an immoral act, or he wasn't capable, that is, impotent.

Marty looked up in surprise when Sam came back out of the alcove. "So soon? That was a quickie."

Sam shook his head, avoided Marty's contemptuous look. "Hell with it. I'm not interested."

The girl came out of the alcove. She was barefoot and wore the shabby quilt draped over her shoulders against the chill. "*Was ist los* with your friend?"

Marty took out the tiny pipe. "He doesn't like girls."

Sam choked back his anger. "Knock it off."

Marty took out his wallet, careful not to let the girl see the contents. He extracted two ten mark notes. "Looks like you got only one customer."

The blonde tried not to drop the quilt while she reached for the money. "*Scheise.* Twenty-five, GI"

Marty put his wallet away and picked up the almost empty bottle of cognac from the kitchen table. He took a final sip and gestured with the bottle. "Not from me. Sam, pay her the other five Marks just to show how ashamed you are."

Sam crumpled four five-mark bills and closed the girl's hand on them so Marty couldn't see. He whispered, *"Entshuldige,"* knowing Marty didn't understand that he was apologizing to the girl. "Come on, Marty. Let's get out of here."

Marty glowered under his heavy brows. "You're disappointing the lady, Sam."

The girl had counted the bills, looked at Sam with understanding and sympathy. Whatever his reason for not taking advantage of his opportunity, he was a gentleman, and she appreciated that.

Marty put the top back on the cognac bottle. There wasn't much left. He put it in the pocket of his GI overcoat. His voice was loud and sharp-edged. "Sorry blondie. Next time I'll bring a man."

"Blondie," Sam thought. She didn't even have a name. Outside on the narrow street Sam was stiff with anger. He turned to say something to Marty but a wave of nausea made him swallow quickly. Wordless, he followed Marty to the car.

Somewhere up above a shutter banged open. Someone emptied a slop bucket out the window. They jumped aside just in time to avoid the splash.

Chapter Four

Housewarming

Sam's room in the Detachment A barracks was great improvement over the wooden buildings he had lived in while stationed in the States. Those were little better than the buildings housing interred Japanese during World War II, clapboard sidings, unfinished inside, no insulation, raw plank floors and single pane windows and bunk beds. In Munich he was quartered in a four story brick building with thick walls, tile floors, and double windows. The attic floor, which he had visited once out of curiosity, was covered with four inches of dirt spread there during the war to prevent damage from incendiary bombs intended to penetrate the tile roof and set fire to the contents below.

The room that he and Marty shared was steam heated and kept reasonably dusted between inspections. Besides the two Army cots along one wall, the cadre's room was furnished with two large wall lockers and a table with a lounge chair. The chair, the wood painted a dark Army brown, was not on the company A inventory. A previous company clerk had "liberated" it from the day room of another unit and it still had "Property of Fox Company" stenciled on the back, a mark turned toward the wall during inspections but, as a nod to Army supply procedure, never painted over.

Sam was alone and sitting in the big chair in his undershorts, looking over the latest batch of pictures fresh from the darkroom, when the Wednesday night charge of quarters came bursting in.

"Logan!"

Any surprise in the Army had to be bad. "What's up?" He didn't like to be disturbed by company business after duty hours.

"Phone call for you in the orderly room." He didn't wait to explain but dashed back to his post as quickly as he came.

Using his unlaced combat boots for slippers, Sam thumped out into the hall and down the three flights of stairs in his underwear, wondering who could be calling him. Was it his father? There was a seven-hour time difference. He'd still be at the office. As Sam entered the orderly room he asked, "Who is it? The Captain? He's probably got some stupid job that can't wait until tomorrow."

"I think it's Vidal." The CQ went back to his copy of Stars and Stripes and pretended to be reading it.

Sam picked up the phone and stood at attention. "PFC Logan here, sir."

"Sam? This is Marty. What're you doing?"

"I just finished the pictures we took at the Kreutzek. You should see them…"

"I suppose you're moping about Fran again."

Sam hesitated. He had been looking wistfully at the picture Yetta had snapped of the two of them with his camera. "No. Not exactly."

"Forget about that gal, Sam. Come down to the *Goldene Traube*. We're having a big party at Yetta's room."

"Got her moved in all right?"

"I helped her with her trunk this afternoon. Now we're having a housewarming. Want to come over?"

"Sure." Sam scratched his stomach. "I'll have to get dressed." At school they'd occasionally have a come as you are party, inviting people to show up in what they were wearing when the phone rang.

"Naturally, Buddy Boy, if you're naked, get dressed. And bring the rest of that cognac we bought last Saturday."

"You nearly finished it off at that whore's place." He winced when he said it, for the CQ was listening.

Sam absent-mindedly dipped his fingers into the first sergeant's bowl of paper clips on the desk. Someone had clipped them into a long chain, a small prank that would cause a big explosion when the first sergeant discovered it.

"And one more thing," Marty's voice was hushed and confidential. "Sally Ann's here. You remember... Yetta's friend?"

"So?"

"She's the one I told you about. A couple of drinks and she'll drag you off to bed. Or aren't you interested in girls yet?"

There was no mistaking the dig about his having backed out of the deal with the blonde from the Dolly Bar. "Well, I... why don't you take her?"

"I'm with Yetta. Look, Buddy Boy, they're crying for men in this place. They'll even take you."

"Lay off, will you?" Sam glanced at his watch. "Do you think they can wait half an hour? I've got to get dressed."

"Take a cab. Don't be stingy like me."

"OK, Marty. *Wiedersehen.*" Sam put down the phone and stood up. He had been sitting on the first sergeant's desk. Between a thumb and forefinger he held up the long string of paper clips. "Hey, CQ."

"Yeh?" The charge of quarters looked up. He was a sergeant and a squad leader, but to Sam, being cadre, he was nothing more than Wednesday's charge of quarters.

"Did you do this?"

"Nope."

"The first sergeant will think so. Anyway, he'll say you're responsible. You'd better unhook these things before he blows his stack in the morning."

The C.Q. reluctantly got up, came forward from Marty's desk.

Sam paused at the gate. "And thanks for coming up about the phone call. Looks like we have a party on."

. . .

The *Goldene Traube* housed most of the female civilian employees of the Army in Munich. Unlike many of those buildings damaged in the war it was not a patched building. It was not large as German hotels go. In its old days the *Goldene Traube* might have been an inn. Like many of its kind, it had outgrown the original building and had annexed another, so the corridors were a maze and the stairways tucked away in odd corners. It had grown without a plan, gaining a piece with each generation, and was steeped in the traditions that hang about old buildings—an old hotel that had lost its original plush.

Though Sam followed the instructions he'd been given at the desk, he had difficulty finding Yetta's room. The hallways were confusing, and the rooms did not seem to be numbered consecutively. He felt like a rat in a laboratory maze, a rat searching for a reward hidden at the end of a blind alley. Intelligence and random movements finally led him to Yetta's door. He had to knock twice before getting an answer.

Yetta's voice had an explosive, overwhelming quality, what happens to people who have been drinking and whose hearing is impaired. "Greetings, Sam!" She handed him a glass of wine. "Welcome to the great housewarming."

Sam was glad to see she was in a good mood again, but he was never comfortable around people who had been drinking. You never knew what they would do once their inhibitions were down. "Hi," He produced the remainder of the small bottle of cognac. "I come bearing gifts."

He was immediately aware of the smoke in the room. It reminded him of his damaged lungs and he coughed self-consciously.

Yetta took the bottle and nudged the door shut. "Just in the right yuletide spirit." She shook the bottle. "You didn't have to drink most of it on your way here."

He hadn't drunk anything, but joked, "Had to get a head start." It was a lame excuse.

The room wasn't large and much of the space was taken up by an old-fashioned double bed. There weren't chairs for everyone, so, typical of American practice, guests had piled their coats on the bed. Marty, a glass of wine in his hand, was sitting on the floor talking to a blonde woman posed seductively on an old-fashioned chaise lounge. He looked up at Sam and gestured with the glass. "Sit down, Buddy Boy. Pull up a slab of rug and make yourself comfortable."

Careful not to spill his glass of wine, Sam sat down on the floor and checked out the room. At one end was the wash stand, typical of rooms that didn't have a private bath. A low bureau stood against one wall below a tall window that might provide a view of a central courtyard. At the other end of the room was a footlocker, the trunk Marty had spoken about. It was now doubling as a coffee table with a towel for a doily, and an ash tray already loaded with cigarette butts. Next to it was a bookcase topped by an elaborate German Grundig radio.

It wasn't a big space, but if all Yetta did was sleep there, who needed more? It wasn't an apartment. He wondered where she took her meals. Perhaps the *Goldene Traube* had a restaurant or a mess hall, since the residents were all government employees.

Marty interrupted Sam's perusal of the room. "Sam, I want you to meet Sally Ann."

Sally Ann managed a thin smile as though she were tired or simply tired of smiling. She was how old? Thirty-ish? More? What the French called a woman of a certain age, the age when she knew what she wanted and how to get it. "Hello." Her voice had a dry quality, what some people called a cigarette voice.

She refilled her glass from a bottle that stood open at the foot of the lounge. "Do you drink, Sam?"

"I've already got a glass." Hadn't she noticed?

"Well, drink it and let me get you a refill."

Sam wasn't in a hurry. He didn't have to get drunk to have a good time. "I don't drink very much. I'm afraid if I'm drunk women will take advantage of me."

She liked that. "I know men. The shyer they pretend to be the more you can expect from them. I bet you're a guzzler." She made him finish his glass, then filled it to the brim. When he took it she toasted him. "*Prosit!*"

Sam wondered if she knew more German than that. "Cheers." He sipped the wine. He wanted to stay alert. He didn't know Sally Ann and her verbal sparring wasn't telling him her real self or what she expected. He was on his guard.

Yetta was at the wash stand dividing up what remained of the cognac. "Where's your cigarette holder this week, Marty?"

"Can't use it. Sold all my cigarettes."

"I always smoke all of mine," Sally Ann said. "A carton a week doesn't go far with me. How much do you get for your cigarettes?"

"About ten marks a carton," Marty said. At four marks to the dollar, the weekly black market profit wasn't much, but if you only made a bit over a hundred bucks a month, the extra D-marks helped.

C rations had always included a pack of cigarettes and waterproof matches. The cigarette industry was pushing its product, but in post-war Germany American cigarettes were sometimes used for barter, so soldiers were permitted only a carton a week whether they smoked them or not. The price was a dollar a carton.

That Marty sold his cigarettes was something Yetta hadn't expected. "It's against the law, isn't it? Black marketing your cigarettes?"

Sam laughed. "It is, but everyone does it. Even the first sergeant. I even sold every bit of my ration while I was in the hospital, in isolation, no less. I couldn't even leave the room."

Sally Ann was impressed. Her raspy voice did not conceal her admiration. "How did you manage that, Sam?"

Pleased to be the center of attention, Sam rested his back against the lounge. "The Red Cross ladies bought them for us at the hospital PX. Then the German barber used to come around and buy all we had." As he now thought about the deals, they did seem to be an accomplishment.

Yetta came around with what remained of the cognac. "Just what were you in the hospital for?"

Sam suddenly seemed to be studying the pattern in the carpet. "I'd rather not talk about it."

Sally Ann said, "You don't look like the VD type." It was a flippant remark. Was she teasing?

Sam didn't know if there was any such thing as a VD type. How would Sally Ann define one? "No, nothing like that?"

Until then Sally Ann showed no particular interest in Sam, but now she was curious. Sam had a secret and she wanted to know what it was. "Was it psychiatric? Nervous breakdown? You can talk about it. We've all had our crises at one time or another."

"They thought I might have TB, but it wasn't anything."

Sally Ann seemed disappointed. Sam as a potential man of mystery was just a sick kid. "You look a picture of health, Sam. A little skinny, that's all." When she leaned back on the lounge she caught her reflection in the mirror above the sink and touched her hair to see if it was in place.

Sam noticed the movement and realized that her hair was bleached, bleached and in need of a perm and a touch-up of the color at the roots. She drank steadily when she wasn't smoking. Her glass didn't stay empty for long between refills. Sam was still nursing the wine she'd given him.

"Drink up, Buddy Boy," Marty said. "Remember, we have to be back by midnight."

"I almost forgot." It had already been late when he left the barracks.

Yetta sat on the floor next to Marty, managing the movement smoothly in spite of her tight skirt. "What happens if an enlisted man comes in late?"

"Get her," Marty said to Sam. "She thinks we're enlisted. She knows only the officers."

Yetta pretended to pout. "Don't tease, honey. I just wanted to know, that's all."

Sam was surprised by the tone of her voice, a genuine warmth he hadn't detected before when everything was superficial, artificial, and insincere. The false gaiety had disappeared.

"An enlisted man gets a delinquency report, a D.R.," Marty explained.

"Did you ever get one?"

"Me? I stay out of that kind of trouble. Sam and I stick to needling the NCO's and the officers."

Sally Ann again refilled her wine glass. "Don't you like the Army?"

Sam shook his head. "Nobody likes the Army."

Sally Ann hedged. "It's not that bad, is it?"

"Maybe not," Sam said. "Everybody bitches about it anyway. It's the draftee's privilege, the U.S. attitude."

Sally Ann didn't get it. "You mean American attitude?"

"No. U.S. That's the prefix on our serial numbers. It means Army of the United States— draftee. The real enlisted men are R.A. Stands for Regular Army."

"Jerks," Marty said. He looked at Yetta. "Not like us."

"Don't be so confident," she retorted. She patted his head possessively like he might a puppy.

The subtle suggestion of intimacy made Sam wonder what had brought about the change from the weekend before. That disaster had been nearly hostile. Maybe it had something to do with helping her move in.

Marty put his glass down and retrenched from his anti-Regular Army argument. "We have some good guys in the company. Old soldiers. We even have a guy who was in the First World War, if you can believe it. He must have been a baby when he joined up. Most of the RA's enlisted in the Depression. Couldn't get a civilian job, so they joined the Army. Then they got swept up in World War II. Anybody who made it through that deserves some respect."

"It's different now," Sam said. "I wouldn't give up my freedom as a civilian for the security of the Army. The new RAs don't have what it takes to make it as civilians." Sam thought about one of the men in the company. He was a borderline moron who had never held a job until he was drafted. In the Army he had his meals, a roof over his head, a uniform, and someone to tell him what do to. It suited him.

Marty must have been thinking about the same sort of enlisted men. "I ask them why they joined the Army. 'Couldn't you find a decent job?'"

Sam laughed. "The first sergeant hates him, but Marty's so efficient they can't get rid of him."

"Right." Marty glowered out from under his heavy brows. "And if they ever try to give me any trouble I've got plenty on them. AWOL. Forgery. Dereliction of duty." He grinned. "But I never say a thing to them about that."

Sam was uncomfortable on the floor. He got up, stretched. "We don't do anything out of line that they could get us on. No D.R.'s."

"That's why we're never late on a midnight pass."

Yetta handed him his untouched cognac. "We'll see that you're on your way on time. You have to leave the hotel by midnight anyway. Military rule. No guests after 2400 hours."

The conversation's serious tone hat had obviously made Sally Ann uncomfortable. She got up from the chaise lounge and paced briefly. "Imagine that. Me being told I can have a guest! Like an adolescent!" She stood stiffly, controlling her drinks. Her head was cocked to one side. The light glinted dully on her hair. "As if I weren't responsible."

There was a knock at the door. Yetta got up, opened it. "Oh, hello, Kay. Come in."

A sharp-featured girl with startling red hair came into the room carrying a bottle of wine. She was carefully dressed in a tailored suit. The collar of the blouse beneath it was unbuttoned, probably for comfort's sake. Sam remembered the pages of Logan Associates advertising copy for Marshal Field's ads. He had grown up reading *Women's Wear Daily* and recognized the quality of the arrival's suit. He could not help but notice the points of wear the girl did not hide, and the careful placement of a conservative pin to draw the eyes away from her ample bosom. She was a person of taste, he decided, who had seen better times and now lived on a smaller budget than she liked.

"I can't stay," the newcomer said. She apparently noticed that there were two couples and not a crowd that might absorb a fifth person. "I'm looking for a cork screw."

Sam reached into his pocket for his cheap imitation of a Swiss Army knife. "I've got one."

Yetta took his arm. "Kay, I want you to meet Sam Logan. This is Kay. She lives upstairs. Helped Marty and me move in today."

Kay looked at him and smiled a bit nervously, as if she hadn't been prepared to meet anyone. "How do you do?"

That was rather formal, and Sam was interested in her accent. It was English, but she didn't seem British. He hadn't heard any accent quite like it before.

Sam opened the tiny corkscrew that was part of the knife and attacked the wine bottle. "You a D.A. civilian, too?"

Kay waited patiently for her bottle. She smiled down at him as if she liked looking down at people. After a pause, she said, "No. Allied civilian. I'm from New Zealand."

The corkscrew was barely adequate for the job, but Sam pulled steadily, the bottle between his knees. It came out with a nice popping sound. He was relieved that the corkscrew hadn't broken. It was a cheap knife and the attachment little more than decoration. On some bottles it would just chew a hole in the cork. "That's interesting. How'd you get over here?" He had never met anyone from New Zealand.

"That's a long story," Kay said flatly as if the question had often been asked, but not often answered. She took the opened bottle from him. "May I have the cork, please?"

Sam handed it over.

She carefully stuck it back into the bottle, took a quick look around the room, smiled at Sally Ann, and left.

She hadn't thanked Sam for opening the bottle and had been little more than polite to Yetta. At first he thought she didn't want to intrude on the party, then decided she was a snob. His second thought turned out to be closer to the truth.

Sally Ann said, "Everyone knows she's been going out secretly with a brigadier general. They say she's just using him to get a better assignment. I wish I had a nice little brigadier."

Sam was aware of his own PFC status. "Does she think he exists for her own personal benefit?"

Yetta said, "She might be using him, but don't we all do that, even lovers?"

"I wouldn't know."

Sally Ann was drinking wine again. She teased, "Why Sam, haven't you ever had a lover?"

Sam blushed. He thought of that disaster with Betty. He wasn't about to get into that. One didn't kiss and tell. "If there's any doubt, you can try me."

She raised her eyebrows at the challenge, but said nothing. She raised her wine glass and nodded.

Sam didn't know quite what to make of her signal. Was it an acceptance of his invitation?

Marty grinned from the floor. If there had only been men in the room he might have said something about the blonde whore Sam had turned down.

Sam turned to Yetta. "I don't like the idea of using people."

"We use our friends most of all. They give us something in return for special services of our own."

"Those are contacts, not friends," Sam said. "You sound like my father talking." Hadn't he used Betty? But she had used him, too. She was ready for sex, or so she thought, and not how it turned out. He frowned at the memory.

Yetta patted him on the shoulder. "Stop looking so serious, Sam. This is a party, remember? Have a ball. I'll pour you some cognac, if there's any left."

Betty hadn't taught him anything about himself, but he hadn't been that introspective then, either. He hadn't known her except in the Biblical sense. Strange how you could sleep with a person and not know how they ticked. It was that long stint in the hospital that made him circumspect—who he was, where he was going, besides just aimlessly adrift in his own life.

Sally Ann had turned on the radio and was absently turning the dial. "I wish I had a little brigadier. They can do a lot for you."

"I suppose you'd have to play it pretty cool," Sam mused. He'd heard that the first thing a shatsie would ask for was cigarettes from the PX. At some point a casual request might tell a lover he was being used. With a brigadier, what other favors might one get?

Sally Ann touched her hair to see if it was in place. She looked trim in her dress but she seemed to have lost weight since its purchase. "We all have to be discreet. Remember that, Sam. Discretion is the better part of virtue."

Immorality concealed was still immorality, wasn't it? Sam turned to Yetta. "You go along with that?"

"I'm just here to have a good time, Sam."

"I was thinking about last Saturday." What about Saturday? Was it the fiasco with the girls, or his encounter with the blonde whore? He self-consciously rubbed the bumpy ridge of his once broken nose. On the floor Marty said nothing, was satisfied that Sam was doing the talking and he the drinking.

Yetta's round face flushed. "I'm not sure what you mean."

"Nothing. I shouldn't have mentioned it," Sam said suddenly discovering that his maroon sport jacket needed buttoning. He looked away, remembered the disappointment of the weekend before. He noticed a crack that ran down from the ceiling and disappeared behind the mirror at the sink.

"I hope I didn't spoil anything," Yetta said. Her usually loud voice was suddenly apologetic. "We didn't want you to get any ideas."

Sally Ann had found some music on the radio. It was Armed Forces Radio. "Is this alright with everyone? I want to dance with Sam." She put the empty glass down on top of the radio and came toward him. She was being deliberately provocative. Was she teasing him?

"Why not?" Sam was enjoying the way she looked at him, though he didn't know if she was serious or just playing a game. What the heck? Why not? But she was unsteady on her feet. He didn't know how much she had drunk. "You sure you can dance?"

"Sure I'm sure I can dance. You should have seen me two nights ago." She put her arms around him as he caught the rhythm of the music.

"Two nights ago?"

"We had a party for the office gang. You should have seen Captain Thomas. Really tied one on. Went home with the major's wife."

"That wasn't very discreet," Sam said, almost forgetting to dance.

"I guess not." Sally Ann danced closer, pressing her hips against his. He could feel himself getting hard. "Most people thought it was rather funny. You haven't seen his wife."

"Funny?" How could it be funny? "Doesn't sound very virtuous."

Sally Ann laughed. "Shame on, Sam. People don't believe in virtue any more. You aren't a prude, are you?"

"That's not the way I was taught. Maybe I was taught wrong. I've been puzzled lately. Just what do people believe in, anyway?" He thought about the First Sergeant and the letters from his girlfriend back in the States. If discretion was the better part of virtue, then adultery was excusable as long as it was discreet. But why bother to marry in the first place? To make the parties feel honest? If a woman exchanged sex for security, that wasn't honest, either. He guessed it depended on how honest people were about relationships. Sam didn't have much experience with relationships. What was genuine? What was real, and what was a charade?

Sally Ann had been puzzling over his questions. The lines in her face deepened suddenly and she pulled back. She must have felt his hard on. "I don't know. What do you believe in, Sam?"

Sam hid his discomfort with a self-conscious smile. "I asked you first." Concentrate on the music. He didn't want to think about anything, especially about things he was uncertain about. He was still traumatized by the long hospital stay. He tried to focus on the details of his surroundings, on the woman in his arms, the music, her body. She was holding him tightly, perhaps because the drink had made her unsteady and she needed someone to lean on. He felt her bra strap under her dress as he held her and stopped moving. This wasn't dancing. This was a stand up preliminary to intercourse. "Why dance?"

"Why not? I like to dance." She hugged him.

He noticed the dark shadows under her glazed eyes. She looked burnt out. A frown tugged at the corners of her mouth. Sam's stomach churned with wine and cognac.

Sally Annlooked at him. In her heels she was as tall as he was and her eyes were level with his. "What's the point of being in Europe if it isn't to have a good time?"

Sam had stopped dancing. "Supposedly we're here to occupy Germany and keep the peace, to show the Germans…" Here he almost laughed at the irony, "the American way of life." Like who do we think we are, telling other people how to live?

Sally Ann looked at him as if she were his third grade teacher. "Sam, you don't think the Russians are really afraid of us, do you?"

"I suppose not." As a lowly supply clerk he wasn't a threat to anybody. As for the US Forces in Germany, they were certainly outnumbered. It was common knowledge that in case of an invasion by the Red Army they didn't expect to hold anything of West German territory east of the Rhine for more than a few days.

"It's all window dressing," Sally Annsaid. "We've got nothing important to do, so we shuffle papers from one chain of command to another. I knew that when we came here. That's why Yetta and I came together. Why shouldn't we take advantage of it? Party time."

Sam didn't get it. He'd been casting about for something important, purposeful in his life. "I don't see the point of just having a party."

Yetta excused herself and left the room. The bathroom was shared, and down he hall.

Sally Ann kissed her finger, touched it to his lips. "That's what's so nice about you, Sam. You're so serious. That's because you're young."

He was defensive. "I'm old enough."

"You are." She agreed. She was unsteady on her feet. "You are old enough." Old enough for what? She broke away and returned to the radio to change the station. Armed Forces network had changed to news and sport.

Marty got up from the floor and whispered to Sam, "Like her?"

"She's drunk."

"It's getting late. We can't do anything on these passes. Make a date with her. She's the answer to your problems, Sam. One night with her...."

Sam watched her at the radio. How old was she? "I've never known anybody like her before."

Marty scoffed. "You've never known anybody at all."

"She's lots older than Fran."

"Oh, for God's sake, Sam. Here we go again. Forget about Fran, will you? You gonna date this girl here?"

"I don't know."

"Sometimes I wonder about you, Sam," Marty whispered harshly. "Take her out—for your own good."

"She must be around forty. Isn't that a bit old, for me, anyway?"

Marty gave Sam an exasperated look. "The rest of the outfit will get a big laugh out of what you did Saturday night. What would the first sergeant say, or Strycklan, the baker?"

Sam panicked. "You wouldn't say anything."

"Oh, no?"

"I just felt sorry for her, that's all."

"Bullshit. You chickened out."

Loud American music filled the room. Sally Ann had found a station. She looked at them, keeping herself steady from the drinks. "Shh. Mustn't wake the whole hotel. After all, Kay may be entertaining a friend with that bottle." She giggled and turned down the volume. "Maybe a major general this time."

Sally Ann stepped close to Sam, coming on to him. "Want to dance?"

Sam put his arms around her and moved to the music, but it wasn't dancing. Marty watched him sternly from the lounge. Sam's stomach wasn't doing well and he felt awkward. Should he or shouldn't he? Sally Ann held him tighter. *What the hell,'* he thought. He suddenly stopped moving to the music and kissed Sally Ann. She hadn't expected it, but in a moment her mouth was open. Surprised, Sam pulled away.

He had gripped her hard, one hand behind her head, and her hair was coming undone. She looked at him and covered her confusion by fumbling with a hairpin. What was she confused about? His surprise kiss or her surprise willingness? "Why, Sam..." She had obviously redefined him.

Sam blundered on. "Have you any plans for the weekend?"

"I... I suppose something could be arranged."

"Saturday night?"

She hesitated, then collected herself. "Call me here at the hotel."

"OK." Sam kissed her lightly on the lips, drew away before she could return it. "How about dinner, early, so we can drink later?"

"Sounds good to me, Sam." Sally Ann leaned her head on his shoulder and dug her fingers possessively into his back.

Yetta came back into the room and hesitated when she saw Sam and Sally Ann standing in a half embrace. "You people been behaving yourselves while I've been gone?"

"Sure." Marty got up from the chaise lounge. "Come on, Sam. Break it up. It's time to get back to the barracks. You don't want a DR do you?"

Sam separated himself. "Got to go, Sally. Thanks for the wine, Yetta."

Marty helped Sam on with his coat, not that he needed help but it gave him an opportunity to pat him on the back. "All set, Sam?"

"All set."

Marty opened the door for Sam, waited for him to leave, then turned and kissed Yetta smartly on the lips.

Sam saw it. "Maybe I'd better go back to the barracks alone."

Marty left Yetta and walked with Sam down the dimly lit hallway of the *Goldene Traube*. "Not tonight, Sam. Maybe some other time when I've fixed myself an overnight pass."

It was an advantage of being the company clerk who made out the passes for the Captain's signature.

Chapter Five

The Third Weekend—Youth and Age

Sally Ann put down her fork and lifted her glass of wine. "Now tell me your real age." She sipped Moselle and looked at him over her glass.

Sam raised his own, made a silent toast. "I told you I was thirty." It was a necessary deception.

Sally Ann's forty years had not treated her well. Her bleached hair had a lifeless, washed out look. Her eyes seemed filmy, not as if she'd been crying, but as if she'd been reading too much, or staying up too late, or sitting too long in a movie. Sam could see how those eyes and the broad cheekbones might once have been briefly beautiful, but it had been a fragile beauty, now gone. Makeup could not rejuvenate it.

She smiled uncomfortably as she set down her glass. "You didn't expect me to believe that, did you, Sam? After all, I'm a sensible person."

Marty had insisted that Sam claim to be thirty, more of a contemporary. So he was thirty, with a Master's degree to satisfy her interest in intellectual matters. He also inflated his rank to corporal. He could do that because she had never seen him in his uniform. He never wore it off base. Actually, he was twenty-one, and hadn't finished his Bachelor's degree.

Sam toyed with the wine menu which the waiter had not retrieved. They were in one of Munich's better restaurants where there were white cloths on the tables, waiters instead of waitresses, and the conservative respectability that went with antique furniture, authentic relics on the walls, dark mahogany. It was a pleasant change for him, used to Formica tables, cheap stainless steel flatware, and tile floors in American restaurants where the only tradition was eat and get out.

Sam didn't want to lie to her. After some hesitation he asked, "Is my age really important? What's important to me is you and what you think."

"Very sweet, but I don't believe you." She pushed back the sleeves of her dress, exposing her thin wrists. She always wore dresses or blouses with sleeves. "Do you know how old I am?"

It was one of those questions one never asks a woman. Sam estimated an age five years younger than he really thought, and in this case knew. "You're thirty-five, aren't you?"

She took a deep breath and answered firmly but a little too quickly. "I'm forty, and I know you aren't thirty, and I can't understand your interest in me."

"I don't think age is the important thing," Sam insisted, feeling foolish and defensive. "You shouldn't be pre-occupied with it." She made him feel like some little kid facing up to his teacher.

"That's true, Sam," she conceded. "Perhaps I am preoccupied." She picked at the remains of her wienerschnitzel, pushed aside the capers.

Sam desperately wanted to change the subject. "Let's talk about something else. How do you like it here in Munich?"

"It's all right, but I'm getting tired of this crowd. I've got to get away from here. Maybe I'll try Spain."

"Spain? Why Spain?" Sam hadn't been to Spain. It was farther away than he could get on a weekend, even a three-day pass.

"It's cheap, living down there. I'm tired of Germany."

"You've only been here two years."

"That's long enough, working in the same office."

Sam remembered that Yetta had stayed only a year in Wiesbaden. Perhaps their restlessness made them friends. "Do you like working for the Army?"

"There's too much brown nosing," she said, looking at him to see if he was embarrassed by her frank language. "I'm sick of it all. Besides, I have a chance for an embassy job in Madrid."

"Do you speak Spanish?"

She smiled and the small wrinkles in her face reminded him of an antique porcelain doll. "No, but I don't speak German, either."

Two years in a foreign country, Sam thought, *and she still can't speak the language. If you didn't learn the languages what was the point?* "Why did you want to leave the States? I mean, for temporary jobs."

She turned her head and spoke as if explaining something to a child. "I thought that working for the government would be a good way to see Europe."

Sam admitted that if she didn't know the language she could hardly work for a German company. "Was it?"

"In a way. I've seen something of Europe. I guess that's enough."

Sam tilted back in his chair. So Sally Ann was moving from one dead-end office job to another. She was already forty. What kind of a career was that? He admitted that he hadn't thought much about a career. He had been adrift but the hospital stay had made him think about his future. What was Sally Ann's future? "I guess seeing Europe is enough if that's all you want." He had thought Sally Ann was a woman of the world, as Marty called her, but now he saw her as a middle-aged woman going nowhere, marking time. Would a stint at the American embassy in Madrid be a step up, or just sideways?

Sam noticed that Sally Ann's glass was empty. He caught the eye of a passing waiter, held up his glass and ordered, *"Noch zwei, bitte."*

The waiter nodded and whisked away, a rustle of coat and tails.

"I don't know what you expect me to want, Sam. I've done about everything." She paused, obviously considering what she wanted to tell him. "I've already been divorced. I'm not going to get married again."

Sam didn't say anything. He could tell by her tone she had bitter memories. Sally Ann's divorce was none of his business.

Sam was embarrassed for having learned more than he should about her. He self-consciously rubbed the bridge of his once-broken nose and coughed. Still that peculiar rattle in his chest. Still that lingering doubt that the doctors' diagnosis had been correct.

He wanted to be looking forward, not back, and applied that concept to his here and now. Falling into a lame cliché, he said, "Been there, done that. So what's next?"

"There are things to do," she said. "I have friends at the hotel. We have fun. Three weeks ago I went to Rome with Kay. You met her the other night. You'd like her, Sam. Skis in Switzerland, climbs mountains."

"Are you trying to fix me up? You already said she has a boyfriend. What interest would she have in a… in a corporal, like me?" Again that hierarchy of the Army social order. He was no brigadier, not even a lieutenant.

"Oh, of course." She glossed over the rank business. "Then there was Berlin. I met Yetta in Berlin with some friend of hers."

He guessed it. "Fran." At once he remembered her face, her eyes that always seemed to be looking somewhere else.

"Yes, how did you know?"

Sam shrugged off the recollection of Fran's odd demeanor. He wondered what had brought her to Europe. "Yetta mentioned it once."

"And before that it was Paris," Sally Ann continued. "Four of us had a wonderful weekend. We…"

Sam didn't want to hear about her weekend in Paris. "Do you ski?"

"No."

The waiter returned with two glasses of Moselle. He deftly removed the empty glasses and placed the fresh ones on the table.

Sam lifted his glass and took a very small sip. Sally Anndrank more than he did. Marty had goaded him into this date. Marty said Sally Ann had been around the block a few times. She was, as the French said, a woman of a certain age who knew what she wanted in a lover and could teach Sam a few things he needed to learn, but Sam was so inept he didn't know where to start. He felt bogged down in meaningless chit-chat. At another time, or in another culture, there might be a direct, frank assignation: "Your place or mine?" He was caught up in a sort of flamenco dance of courtship, except he didn't know the posturing or the steps. He felt inept and stupid, but he was stuck in this conversation and didn't know how to lead it. He'd try this: "So you were married once?"

She didn't mind talking about it. "It didn't work out. I'm not looking. The officers around here that are old enough are already married, and the ones that are on the make are too young." She was watching closely for his reaction, almost as if she was testing his intentions.

Sam remembered her prospects for Madrid. "Will it be any different at the embassy in Spain?" He rubbed his fingers up and down the stem of his wine glass. He didn't want to get drunk, and Sally Ann could handle whole bottles. If he were drunk he'd be useless. He remembered that business with the blonde whore.

Sally Ann dodged his question about prospects at the embassy in Spain. She shifted uncomfortably in her chair. "Let's go someplace else. I know a nice bar on a street where the Americans never go. Excuse me for a minute." She took a gulp of wine as she rose, then walked unsteadily in the direction of the ladies' room.

Sam paid the check while she was gone. The waiter insisted on helping Sally Annon with her coat. He smiled at Sam and whispered, loud enough to flatter Sally Ann, "Allow me, sir. It is your duty, but my privilege." When they left, Sam looked back. The waiter winked at him, sharing his assessment of what a young man was doing with an older woman not his mother or his aunt.

Sam wanted to remember the old world elegance of good service, and would think long afterward of the subtle relationship of servants to those they served.

The fresh air was a shock to Sam's head, and the motion of walking churned the alcohol in his stomach, but he managed to steady himself and guide Sally Ann through Munich's evening traffic, through the crowd of pedestrians, and toward the side street she indicated.

The tavern was in sharp contrast from the white table cloth restaurant they'd left. It was intimate and warm, with thick oak tables scrubbed white and only one waitress. She wore a traditional black dress with a white apron that hid the change purse she wore under it. She came to the table and waited for their order.

Sam and Sally Ann switched to beer and drank in silence for some minutes. Sam concentrated on drinking as little as was polite. He didn't want to get drunk and make a fool of himself. Sally Ann, however, needed no urging to drink more, in fact seemed to want to get drunk. She studied his features, his black crew cut, still looking fresh, his clear eyes and bland, at times almost blank youth, a face not marked much by life experiences. His once broken nose was the only disfigurement in an otherwise soft-jawed face. Finally, as if she could no longer remain silent, she said, "You're a nice boy, Sam, but you're not thirty. So tell me, how old are you?"

Why was she asking? Why did she insist, unless it was to convince herself if he was of an acceptable age, she wouldn't be robbing the cradle.

Sam was defensive. "Does it make any difference? Now, if I lied to you and said I was older, or younger for that matter, would that make me some other kind of person?" Sam suddenly felt tired. He was tired of the verbal sparring. He wanted to get the evening over with, to escort her back to the *Goldene Traube* for a final drink in her room before going to bed.

But whose bed? Hers? Or his, back at the barracks?

Sally Anndidn't answer his question. He squeezed her hand, but she frowned and drew her hand away. She avoided looking at him, stared into the depths of her glass as if she might find some answer in the beer.

"It wouldn't change me, would it?" Sam insisted. He nearly laughed out of frustration at his own predicament. Change him? From what, to what? He had no idea and instead of laughing coughed instead, haunted by the trauma of being so long in hospital limbo.

Sally Ann still didn't answer. She looked at him with a sad, helpless expression. She lifted her glass. "Drink some beer, Lonesome Sam." She poured part of hers into his empty glass.

"You're making me sound like some B picture cowboy." He pictured himself, a ragged, unwashed cowboy on a swaybacked horse, contemplating a sterile desert, looking for some company. Perhaps Sally Ann and he shared a common loneliness. It was not the kind of commonality that bonds can be forged with. Was he any different when he was with Fran? Or with Betty, who had so suddenly shaken his self esteem? Sam wished he had drunk more. He raised his glass...

Sally Ann pulled herself together. "I like you, Sam, but...."

Sam was still on that issue of their difference in ages. "A person is only as old as he feels, and as he wants to be." But he couldn't even convince himself. He felt slightly sick.

"You're very nice." She patted him on the arm in a motherly fashion. "You can afford to say that, but I can't." Her fingers lingered on his wrist, drew away.

He persisted, lamely. "Does it make any difference?"

She looked at him sympathetically, reached across the table and touched his cheek. She finished her beer and smoothed back her bleached hair. The discussion was over.

Sam wondered, *What do I want her for?* Marty said he needed his ashes hauled, but would that do any good? For her? For him? It was all futile and foolish. He rose. "Come on Sally, It's time we got back to your hotel."

She was too drunk to protest.

They walked down the side streets, stumbled on the cobblestones, tripped in the dim light of the occasional gas street lamps. When she staggered against him Sam winced. He could feel how slim her body was. He could imagine how her ribs and shoulder blades must show, how thin she was. He drew his mind in on itself and almost persuaded himself that he must sleep with her if only to relieve her loneliness.

They climbed the steps at the *Goldene Traube.* "You're a nice boy, Sam," she said again. She kissed him with her mouth open. Sam could taste beer and lipstick. He pressed her close to himself, tried to forget their pointless conversation, tried to lose himself in the embrace. Her breath caught, but she kept on kissing him. Her mouth was fierce, hungry against his. "Sam, Sam," she murmured softly. "My thirty-year-old Sam."

"Good night, Sally." Sam pulled away from her. He didn't want to kiss her again. He knew now that she was willing, but he felt guilty at the opportunity to take advantage of her vulnerability and his own willingness. He would go back to the company and make up a story for Marty, some acceptable lie. He would have to learn to lie to others if he couldn't lie to himself.

"You've a nice mouth, Sam. A very nice mouth." Her coat had slipped back on her thin shoulders and her hair was mussed.

He suddenly felt ashamed and wanted to cry, to go back to the barracks and pull the blanket over his head. He wanted to bang his fists against the bed frame. "Good night."

Sam left her on the steps. He felt defeated and empty, still tasting her lipstick. He knew he was too young for her and wanted desperately to do something for her, if only to lead her back through the *Goldene Traube's* maze of hallways and put her to bed. But if he did, would he feel tempted to take advantage of her weakness and her need? Better not. He had led her on and then backed away and now he felt ashamed of himself, not because he had failed to seduce her, but because he almost had.

Chapter Six

Pie and Plans

Sam looked into the orderly room on Monday morning and found Marty lounging with his feet on his desk and leafing through the Manual for Courts Martial. "Morning, Sam."

Sam was thinking of their argument the night before about Sally Ann. He didn't answer.

Marty gestured with the manual. "You know, the penalty for forgery is seven years."

Sam pushed his hands deep into his fatigue pockets. "Maybe you and the first sergeant will get adjoining cells."

"That's friendly of you." Marty shuddered. "Imagine spending seven years in a federal prison with that guy." He leafed through the pages of the manual. "Ten years for disobeying a direct order. All kinds of little facts in here. I wonder what would ever happen if this pass business got out."

Sam was glum. Mondays were not his best days. "If they really want you they can always get you."

Marty dropped the book atop the clutter of papers on his desk. He sucked on his tiny pipe. "Like wasting food, for instance. I guess they've got us coming and going."

Sam turned to go. The supply room was across the hall. *Thank goodness this place is usually deserted*, he thought. *I couldn't stand it if those RA's were around all the time.*

"Sam?"

"Yeh?"

"Still mad about last night?" Marty took his feet off the desk and leaned forward in a fatherly manner. "Don't take it so hard, son. Let old Papa Vidal..." He was interrupted by the telephone. "Detachment A, Corporal Vidal, sir. Oh, hi, Steve. Get my morning report?"

Sam hung in the doorway, still sullen. He did not want to stay, but didn't want to go back to the supply room and the stack of paperwork there, either. The supply sergeant couldn't understand the new Army's paper work. Things had come a long way since the old Army days of "moonlight requisitions." Now there were inventories. So far the chair they'd put in their room hadn't been missed.

Marty had Morning Report trouble. "What? Eleven on leave instead of seven, and six master sergeants on duty instead of eight? Oh, for God's sake!"

Sam smiled to himself, took a paper clip from the disk on the first sergeant's desk, bent it open and started to clean his fingernails.

Marty hung up the phone. "My strength report's all screwed up. And I thought I had it fixed last week." He dipped into his desk drawer and took out a manila folder. "Oops. We still got a piece of apple pie left over from Friday." He held up an aluminum pan with one cut of pie drying in it. "Want this?"

"Not hungry."

"Maybe you can take this back to the bakers for a refill." He handed the pan to Sam, then leafed though the morning reports. "I've had enough pie for awhile, too. Hell, this strength report is a pain. Every time I enter a correction Sergeant Adams raises hell."

Sam enjoyed seeing Marty squirm. "Get it fixed?"

"You better believe it, shatsie. You know what the guy does? Takes my illegal corrections and then calls a buddy at Southern Area Command's Morning Report unit. That guy, a corporal, has a friend in Heidelberg at the USAREUR MRU. He'll let my faked report slip through. The next step is Washington, but the MRU at the Pentagon is still nine months behind. By the time they find the mistakes I'll be long gone from here, shipped out!" Marty chuckled complacently. "Nobody'll know the difference, right up the chain of command. Hey, didn't I tell you the PFCs and corporals run the Army?"

Someone came up behind Sam and snatched the pie pan out of his hands. "Private Vidal!"

Marty blanched. "Yes, Sergeant. I'm right here."

First Sergeant Adams was a short man with clenched, indignant jaws and a chest decorated with a display of overseas service ribbons including a purple heart. His uniform bore all the possible insignia of his unit and was tailored to fit around his bulging paunch. For all his neatness, he had a seedy look and pose that resembled a ham actor beyond his prime. He gestured dramatically with the pie pan.

"Something wrong, sergeant?" Marty asked innocently, sliding the folder of morning reports under the desk blotter.

Sergeant Adams gestured with the pie pan. "You guys opening a bakery?"

"No, sergeant." Marty put his pipe in his pocket, making sure it was buttoned.

"A tea room, then." Great, studied sarcasm, the sort only a seasoned master sergeant can produce.

"No, sergeant."

"Maybe we don't give you enough to eat around here?"

"The food is fine."

"Then there's no reason for you to have pie in the orderly room. Who told you you could steal pie from the mess hall?"

"It's not stolen, sergeant," Sam said. He wondered if the pilfered pie was a court martial offense. "Sergeant Stryklan gave us the pie. Lieutenant Green had some, too."

"He did?" If the lieutenant was a co-conspirator there'd be no likelihood of a court martial. "The orderly room is no place for pie. This isn't a tea room or a playground. This is the Army."

Sam said, "We were saving this piece for you."

Sergeant Adams was briefly tempted, but the pie was obviously stale. Here was a hint of mold on the edges. "Take that pie back to Sergeant Stryklan right now and tell him I want to see him."

"He's on pass, sergeant. Won't be back until tomorrow. He's the only one with a key to the bake shop."

"Leave the pan with the mess sergeant, then."

"You sure you don't want your piece?" Sam asked.

If looks could kill, Sam would be dead.

Sam dumped the piece of apple pie in the waste basket and handed the pan to Marty. Marty held the pan by the rim, like a nervous supplicant might with a hat. "I've some company correspondence to get ready for the captain's signature. Can I take care of that first?"

MSGT Adams stared at him briefly, then turned on his heel. "You *will* have no more pie in the orderly room. Goddamn college kids. Can't tell 'em anything."

Marty followed MSGT Adams into the hallway. "You're right, sergeant," he said with genuine humility. "That's what I told the draft board. I'm not cut out for this kind of work."

Adams took his overseas cap from a peg by the orderly room door. An exasperated expression made him look older, fatter, but he was, after all, a professional soldier, not a draftee. "You were drafted for twenty-four months, Vidal. Make up your mind that you're going to serve it, all of it. There's no way out." He seemed to be passing judgment on himself. "I'm going to the mess hall for coffee. You'd better give me that pie pan before you break it."

Marty watched him go, then returned to the orderly room for the morning reports. "No more pies, Sam."

Sam sank into the training sergeant's chair. "Shaft."

"Are you depressed again?"

"No. I'm not depressed. I wish you wouldn't go around asking me if I'm cracking up or something. I'd just like to get out of here, that's all."

Marty carefully smoothed the rumpled jacket of his dirty fatigues. "Easy, Buddy Boy. It's only Monday."

"This weekend's Christmas. What're you going to do on your pass?"

"Yetta and I are driving to Davos. She says her back is well enough to ski."

Sam chuckled and leaned back in the swivel chair. His fatigues still had some starch in the U.S. Army patch over his pocket. "That'll be the day. You ski with Yetta? She's an expert and you spend most of your time getting back up."

Marty smiled complacently.

Sam envied him. He hadn't made plans for the weekend, had visions of spending Christmas Eve in the caserne movie, then going to bed early. "I suppose you wouldn't want a passenger."

"Not if you were by yourself, Sam. Why don't you ask Sally Ann?"

Sam frowned. "I couldn't face her."

Marty had taken out the tiny pipe again, thoughtfully sucked on the stem. "You must admit, you disappointed her."

"How do you know? What's better, Marty? To be a gentleman and satisfy her in bed, or be a gentleman by declining to take advantage of her? She was drunk, for God's sake."

"You don't ride with me unless you have a date, and even then if you must stay in Davos, stay in another hotel. I want to be alone." He winked and added, "with Yetta."

"Davos at Christmas? Don't you think the hotels will all be booked?"

"There'll always be some little gasthaus with rooms above the bar."

That was possible. "I could call Fran."

"If you do, don't stay at the same hotel. I don't want the girls to team up and give us the same song and dance we got at the *Bahnhof* hotel. See her alone. You'll be rewarded."

Sam looked at Marty's knowing expression and remembered the afternoon Marty and Yetta had spent unpacking her stuff.

Sam crossed the hall to the supply room and dug out the thick book of the German railway timetables. He had bought it for five marks to save himself the trouble of phoning the RTO office down at the *Hauptbahnhof*. Besides train connections, the timetable had excellent, detailed maps. "I'd better have something specific to suggest if I call Fran. Someplace good for skiing." Just the signs of those train connections gave him a case of *reisefeber*, an itch to travel.

The orderly room phone rang and Marty moved to answer it. "Company business calls. Aren't they lucky someone competent is actually here to run the place?" He carried with him the sheaf of bungled strength reports.

Sam studied the maps in the front of the timetable. He didn't have to tag along with Marty and Yetta like some stray dog. What was a good place to see? Something as far away as a two-and-a-half-day pass could take him, away from the captain's awful dog and the first sergeant's bluster, the paper work and the indifferent stupidity of the officers who let him and Marty run the company for them while they were out doing God knows what. It was too late in the year for golf and fishing, but the CO drank and probably had a woman on the side. He couldn't always be "at the PX" or whatever excuse they used for his whereabouts when he was away.

His eye caught the name of a little Swiss town, Zermatt! The Matterhorn! Something about the peak had always fascinated him. If he could see it for himself... Sam quickly leafed through the railway timetables. Scanning the columns, the changes, the layovers, the length of time it took to get there, he saw that it was possible IF Marty drove them to Davos and saved a layover in Zurich. Sam wrote the figures on a slip of paper and carried both it and the heavy timetable to the orderly room and the class A telephone. The phone in the supply room couldn't be used for long distance calls.

"I'll go to Zermatt if you drive me to Davos. Saves a change in Zurich," he told Marty. "Done with the phone?"

Marty looked up from his heavy duty, German-made standard Olympia typewriter. "All right if you chip in for gas."

"As long as I don't have to buy you a week's supply. No more of my buying five gallons that you save for later."

Sam looked for Fran's number in his address book. Remembering phone numbers was not his thing. It took him three tries before he could get an open line through to Heidelberg military.

"Office of the Comptroller, Miss Wagner."

"Hello, there. This is Munich calling."

"Yes?" She didn't seem sure who it was.

"Sam. Sam Logan." What would he say to her? He hardly knew her, and he was about to ask her to spend a weekend in Switzerland. It was over a week since he'd seen her, and that was a fiasco. That romantic moment under the stars atop a mountain hadn't developed into anything, and he hadn't called or written since last week. He was feeling stupid and ineffectual.

It didn't help that she sounded like she was talking to a stranger. She asked him how he was, like memorized lines meaning nothing and delivered half-heartedly. He remembered her face, that disconnected look, and wondered *how can I ask a girl who's almost a stranger to go off with me for a weekend?* Before he went with Betty that time he'd known her for a long time, and even then was surprised that she accepted his invitation. He realized afterwards that she had her own reasons.

Perfunctory salutations over, Fran remembered him. "I didn't think you'd call again." She sounded pleased.

Sam found the paper clip he had used on his nails. "You underestimate my perseverance." He paused, not sure how to propose the trip to Zermatt or anyplace else for that matter.

"What do you want, Sam?" Her voice sounded far away. She was at work, of course. Maybe others might be overhearing her conversation, or she was in the middle of something.

"I wondered if you had anything on for the Christmas weekend?"

"I'm supposed to go to an office party."

Only supposed to go? Then maybe she'd be open to some other option. "Marty and Yetta are driving down to Davos. We can ride with them in that direction if we want. Would you like to go? Been to Switzerland?"

"To Davos with Marty and Yetta? Sound like a great party."

Sam bent the paper clip. "I… ah, I was thinking of going on from there to Zermatt. You know, the Matterhorn? They've got great skiing."

She was hesitant. "You mean, just you and me?"

"If you feel like getting away… I mean, it's a long way but there won't be another chance to go. Not for me, anyway. They won't let me take a leave. The supply sergeant says I'm indispensable." The reality was the supply sergeant was too incompetent to handle his job alone, had told Sam that the weeks in the hospital were enough leave time for anybody. Sam suspected that the truth was the sergeant was semi-literate and couldn't puzzle his way through military forms and regulations.

Marty was eavesdropping. "Yeh, me, too. You'd think that Master Sergeant Adams could do morning reports while I took a week off. No sir."

There was a pregnant pause at the other end of the line while Fran considered the invitation and the implications. "Alright, Sam. I'll go. I need to get away from here."

Sam was shaken. He hadn't actually expected an acceptance. Now that she had accepted he realized that he didn't have enough money to take her.

Now he felt really stupid. Switzerland was supposed to be expensive. "It may take some chipping in on expenses," he ventured. "End of the month, Christmas shopping, PFC pay, and all that." He almost added, "You can turn me down."

"Don't worry, Sam. I like to pay my own way. Then I'm not obligated, if you get my meaning." It was a warning that he shouldn't expect sex.

Marty suddenly stopped typing. A dog barked in the hall and the captain came in with General on a leash. Sam turned, saw them, nodded his head in recognition and stood at attention. The bent paper clip dropped into the waste basket. Sam pretended he was making an official call. "That'll be fine, sir."

"How can I meet you Sam? I'm a long way from Munich."

General, released from his leash, leaped around the room. Marty's fatigue cap was on a filing cabined marked "Fire Priority Two." The captain took the fatigue cap and teased the dog with it. Marty frowned but hesitated to protest.

Using his official voice, Sam continued his call with Fran. "I'll make all the arrangements and let you know, sir."

The captain disappeared into his office and closed the door. General, left in the orderly room, barked and tried to follow, dropping the cap. Marty quickly retrieved it full of dog slobber, and returned to his typing.

Fran understood that Sam had to disguise the call. "And the room reservations. Don't forget that, Sam. Two singles."

Sam swallowed. He might have had a fantasy about a double room, one of those cushy German beds with a cloud-like cushion of feather quilts, but that was too much to expect. "I'll fix it up." He leafed through the railway timetable. "You can probably get an early morning express." He gave her the details.

She was impressed with his efficiency. "That was quick."

"I have the timetables." He rubbed his once-broken nose with his free hand. "I try to be. I... I'll call you when I have everything fixed up."

"I've got to hang up now, Sam. Be good." There was a click and a few other sounds as the circuit was broken down the line. Then the dial tone came again and Sam, a bit dazed, put down the phone.

General had stopped scratching at the captain's door and looked up at Sam, his tail an invitation to play. It was amazing how fast the dog had grown.

Sam ignored the dog. "She'll go."

Marty pushed bask his swivel chair and took the tiny pipe from his mouth. He held it in an expansive gesture, his arms outstretched. "Ah, my boy finally shacks up." His face broke into a fatherly grin.

"Two singles, Marty, not one double."

"Don't tell me you're just going to ski?"

"Sure. Why not? She's no Sally Ann, you know. Fran's a nice girl." It was easy to be morally self-righteous when there was no alternative.

"The only trouble with Fran is she's too American," Marty said. "When she's in Europe a

131

little longer she'll realize she hasn't got something unique. Those damn American women. Professional virgins. They think that if they don't give it to you there's no place else in the world to get it."

"Fran isn't like that."

"What do you mean? She's spoiled, too. Why do you think Yetta was so mad at me? She gave me a cold shoulder, so I told her she didn't have anything I couldn't buy for ten marks on any street corner."

Sam remembered the blonde whore from the Dolly Bar. "Twenty marks."

"Anyway, it's time the women got put in their place." Marty clenched the tiny empty pope in his teeth and grinned. "And I know just the place."

Sam shook his head in disgust, gathered up the thick Deutsche Bundesbahn timetables. "I'm looking for something else." Oh? What was that? Girlfriend? Romance?

Marty grimaced and was about to say something when the captain came in from his office. General leaped up, looking for the fatigue cap again.

The captain asked, "Where's the cap?"

Marty quickly put it on, dog slobber and all. "Here, sir."

The captain hesitated. Taking the cap from the filing cabinet was one thing, but once it was on Marty's head, well... Being the CO of the company was not much of a challenge. In fact, there was almost nothing to do except sign passes and hand out cash on payday. He was bored. "Lieutenant Green said you boys had some pie."

Sam shuffled his feet. "Yes, sir."

"Got any left?"

"No, sir. Sergeant Adams made us throw out the last piece."

"Throw it out?" It sounded like a preliminary to an accusation for wasting food, a violation of the Universal Code of Military Justice.

Marty sensed the risk of trouble. Sergeant Adams had already blown his stack over the pie, but there was nothing to be gained by suggesting that Adams wasted food. "It was stale, dried out, sir. We'd had it since Friday. Might even have been moldy."

"I see." The captain paused, looked around. "You boys don't have anything that needs a signature, do you?"

"No, sir."

"Then I'm going to the mess hall for coffee. "Take care of General. And keep him off my carpet." The captain left.

Sam followed. He carefully closed the gate so General couldn't follow him. "Watch the dog, Buddy Boy." He barked softly, sending the puppy into waves of excitement.

Chapter Seven

The Fourth Weekend—Christmas Eve

Sam waited expectantly on the platform for
Fran's train to arrive. He was keyed up with what
the Germans call *reisefeber*, the excited anticipation
of travel. It had begun when he first looked up the
timetables for trains between Heidelberg, Munich
and Zermatt. Now, though he had not actually left
Munich, the excitement had reached its peak, fired
up by the act of packing, waxing his skis, and of
standing at last in the Munich *Hauptbahnhof* waiting
for Fran.

The atmosphere of railroad stations always
excited him. Munich was a hub for international
travel. Trains like the Orient Express left from
there for Istanbul, for Switzerland, Italy, Vienna,
Paris, Stockholm, Amsterdam. There were more
than thirty platforms at the station, with crowds of
people on the move, some greeting, others saying
goodbye, those returning home for a visit, others
departing for a Christmas holiday. Many were
laden with wrapped presents, adding to the festive
atmosphere.

Sam loved the trains, the echoing station
announcements over the loudspeakers, the hiss of
brakes and the clanking of the couplers. For the
Deutsche Bundesbahn it was a time of transition from
steam engines to diesel electric locomotives. The
mainline expresses were now diesel-electric, but the
locals were still steam. The steam locomotives were

more romantic, like huge, resting, iron beasts breathing steam and waiting to be awakened.

Sam felt he was back in good physical condition. The weeks in a hospital bed had atrophied his muscles. He felt he was in shape now but mentally there remained a residue of doubt. He had changed since he went into the hospital and was unsure about himself now that he was out. Marty said he worried too much. But Marty always had simple suggestions, like shack up with Sally Ann and get his ashes hauled, Marty's cure-all solution of choice. Sam had doubts he couldn't exactly identify or understand. A psychiatrist might have helped him dig through his confusion, but at this stage his thoughts were of Fran. What if she didn't come? Suppose she missed her train? Of if he lost her in the crowd? Of if he wasn't on the right platform? At least he had looked that up on the announcement board.

Sam compulsively cleaned his fingernails with the edges of his platform admission ticket. In grammar school his teacher had once shown the fifth grade class what fingernail dirt looked like under a microscope and he had been conscious of his nails ever since.

Out in the marshalling yard the locomotives came and went, probing their cautious paths among the signal towers, wheels clicking over the points as they were directed right and left until they were eased alongside the proper platform.

Days ago Sam had bought Fran's Christmas present. He hoped his gift for Fran was appropriate, but it was hard to tell. Something expensive would have been extravagant and beyond his meager Army salary. Flowers would have been awkward, for what would she do with them while traveling?

People could be suspicious of gifts. Was one expected to reciprocate? If not, was the recipient obligated? It had to be something simple, but not trivial and stupid. He had kept the little gift in his supply room office drawer, wrapping it and unwrapping it so often he finally had to find another bit of fresh tissue paper for it.

The snow-spattered, dark green diesel-electric pulling the cars from Heidelberg throbbed powerfully alongside the platform with a string of first and second class cars. Sam knew from his previous trips that third class pre-war cars with their wooden benches had disappeared. Before the express from Heidelberg and points north came to a complete halt, the doors were flung open and the platform filled with people carrying everything from shopping bags and gifts to skis.

All seemed in a hurry. The season when American tourists flooded Europe was long since over. The present crop were mostly Germans, men in new trench coats and women, some with fur collars, who moved toward the exits. Many carried Christmas gifts and new suitcases. It was an atmosphere of prosperity. The *wirtschaftswunder*, Gemany's post war prosperity, was apparent. The irony was that the factories destroyed by allied bombers had been replaced by modern, new equipment. Towns that had been reduced to shells of destroyed buildings had been rebuilt to the old specifications as if the war had never happened. Now there were modern railway stations and the *Bundesbahn* had new rolling stock and the diesel-electrics.

But there were still notices on the windows of newspaper kiosks and *anshlagssauler*, the pillars for posted notices, bits of paper seeking lost relatives who had disappeared in the confusion and chaos of war and never found.

Some of the people on the platform were carrying skis with the poles separate or bundled with the cable bindings. Essentially little more than a beginner skier himself, Sam felt a kinship with them. At the Kreutzek where he had met Fran, she had rented skis. His, checked out from the service club, would ride on the rack of Marty's Green Beetle for the first leg of their trip.

Like a trout facing upstream for something to eat, Sam searched the face in the crowd for Fran. Where was she? He was beginning to fear she hadn't come, that something had gone wrong at the last minute.

"Merry Christmas, Sam!"

He had not recognized her. She had been swept past him by the crowd and had to work her way back. Besides the zippered nylon bag he recognized from her Garmisch trip, this time she did carry skis. He hadn't expected that, and hoped that was the reason he hadn't recognized her.

"Where'd you get these?" he asked, relieving her of the load of hickory and Tonkin cane. They walked toward the exit, jostled by a fat man with a beat-up, leather briefcase and a determination in his elbows.

"I followed your advice and checked them out from the Special Services warehouse in Heidelberg."

"Good deal." Sam remembered the present he carried for her in his pocket, but the problem of getting the skis through the exit and showing his platform ticket, too, delayed him.

"Were you waiting long?" she asked as they were jammed and jostled through the gate.

The terrazzo lobby of the station was wet with footprints carried in from the snow and slush on the street outside. Probably a refugee, a stout, middle-aged woman in a shapeless, black coat and head scarf was mopping up, a fruitless task undone in moments. Once they got past her, Sam guided Fran out of the crush of people and stopped. "I've got something for you."

Her face with its pointed chin looked small, pushing past the collar of her hooded ski parka. In her trim ski pants she looked slim and even fragile, like a school kid who hadn't yet reached her full growth. Strange how she could look seventeen when he knew she was older than he was. Perhaps it was her innocent eyes and the naiveté of her posture that made her seem so young.

Sam handed her the gift.

She hesitated. "Well, I... Should I open it now?"

"Not until Christmas morning."

"Back home at North Creek we always opened ours on Christmas Eve," she said, sparring playfully.

Sam, an only child raised in Chicago, knew nothing of lumber camps outside children's books about Paul Bunyan and flapjack pans so big that the cook skated around on the hot iron to spread the butter. He imagined Fran and her brothers on a lumber foreman's Christmas Eve in the woods long ago, her father, when he was still alive, going about in thick socks and a heavy flannel shirt, the two sons, smaller replicas, doing the same. And Fran, and her little sister. How must it be now, with the father gone and the brothers married with their own children, and Fran's mother visiting one or the other? Did the brothers and their families sing Christmas carols in the snow like some Currier and Ives painting? But it was all his fantasy and might have nothing in common with reality. Fran had escaped that life, gone to the city, and how she was in Germany.

His own life in the Army was far different from Chicago with its filthy slush on the streets of the Loop, the big, almost empty apartment with the Gold Coast address that had to complement the Michigan Avenue business address and the office that would move to the Prudential Building when it was finished.

"I have a present for you, too," she said. "It's in my bag." She bent to unzip the little bag, hesitated. "But there's a lot of things... I'll give it to you in the car." The contents of her overnight bag were too intimate to open up in a public place.

Sam picked up her skis again and led her to the street outside the *Hauptbahnhof.* Marty was waiting by the Green Beetle under the watchful eyes of a traffic cop guarding the loading zone. Yetta was bundled up inside.

"Got another pair of skis," Sam said. His and Marty's were already strapped to the rack on the back of the Volkswagen.

While Yetta and Fran chatted on the pavement Sam struggled to stow Fran's bag in the already full compartment under the hood. Though Fran's bag was cloth, Yetta had a hard, American suitcase that took up most of the space. He tried without success to wedge Fran's in, finally gave up and put it in the back. The Volkswagen was heavily loaded, and the floor of the back seat even had a five gallon jerry can Marty had borrowed from the Army for reserve gasoline. It was not a safe arrangement, but gas from the Army fuel dump was cheaper than on the German market. The can was stowed like a chaperone between Sam and Fran in the back seat. He had to set Fran's bag on top of it.

With a wave to the traffic cop, Marty put the car in gear and raced the motor as he eased in the clutch and they crept into the Munich traffic. It was Christmassy cold and snowing.

Sam had "liberated" an Army blanket from the company supplies and Marty had it in the back seat. The VW heater didn't send much warmth to the back of the car, so they tucked themselves in to keep their feet warm.

Fran unzipped her bag and handed Sam a flat box wrapped much more elaborately than his gift to her. "Merry Christmas, Sam. You can open it now if you want."

The back seat of the Green Beetle lurching through its gears in the Munich traffic didn't seem the right place. "I'll wait until we get to Zermatt for the right atmosphere, but you can open yours now."

She did, fumbled with the tissue paper and tape. "Oh, Sam," she exclaimed with surprise and pleasure. "That's cute."

It was a small, stuffed teddy bear dressed in a Tyrolean pair of *lederhosen* and a little hat complete with a tiny feather. "That'll be our mascot," Sam said.

"My last boyfriend wanted to give me a ring," she said, remembering.

"Oh?" Sam felt a pang of jealousy.

"I wasn't ready," she explained. "Some men can be possessive, smothering, but at first he was funny. He was a businessman who sometimes came to North Creek to ski. I was working in a clothing store. He came in to buy a hat. He had lost his while riding the chair lift, so it was gone. He made me show every hat in the store and didn't buy any. He and his friends kept teasing me. I was terribly embarrassed." She fell silent. "But then he came back later on his own, bought a hat, and asked me out."

The way she told her story seemed more real to Sam than his almost suppressed memory of his brief affair with Betty. With the Volkswagen rear engine roaring and the road noise of the snow tires on the cobbled pavement of the autobahn, what Fran said couldn't be heard by Marty and Yetta in the front seat. Sam listened, half mesmerized by the steady tick-tock sweep of the little windshield wipers.

Fran continued her story, more for her own benefit of remembering than for his listening. "He came up every weekend he could, even spent his vacation at North Creek."

"In the summer?"

"He stayed in the city. He wanted me to join him there."

"Did you go?"

"I did and I didn't."

"I don't get it. What about the ring?"

"It wasn't an engagement ring, Sam. That's not what he wanted."

"I see." Sam thought he understood.

"I wanted to get out of the woods. I was ready to move in with him in New York. I'd always called him at his office, but I found out his home address and discovered he was already married. He just wanted something on the side—me."

"That must have been a shock."

"Not entirely. There were clues. But I'm not the type to be someone's mistress."

"Did you stay in New York?"

"I did at first, got a job, but he pursued me. He was persistent, insistent and possessive. I could see he could be abusive, so I wanted out. I didn't want to go back to the woods. By then I decided I didn't fit in in North Creek any more. I wasn't crazy about the big city, either. I'm basically a small town girl. But I didn't want to marry a lumber foreman like my dad and have two boys and a girl. So I decided to just up and leave the country, so here I am. That's my story."

"So you're born again," Sam said. But he wondered if people could run away from what they were. No matter where you moved, you brought your old self with you.

"I'm the new me," she said. "Like it?" To make her point she leaned across the jerry can that separated them and kissed him.

Sam was still trying to process her story. For fear of saying something stupid and immature he didn't say anything. Fran had kicked off her boots and wriggled into a position that allowed her to lie in the back seat with her head in his lap. He tried to get into a comfortable position that wouldn't cramp his legs, kissed her, and leaned his head against the window.

"We've got a long ride ahead of us," he said. "All mountains. Too bad we'll miss the scenery in the dark."

With her head in his lap, Sam could feel himself getting hard and was afraid Fran would notice. But what if she did? Could be an opportunity, but having sex in the back of a cramped Volkswagen with a five gallon Jerry can and baggage in the way and two people in the front seat was awkward, even though it might be possible. He hoped.

Marty called back over the roar of the engine. "You two all right back there? Getting enough heat?"

Before either could answer they heard Yetta laughing knowingly.

...

Sam awoke with a dull throbbing in his ears. The continuous whine of the Green Beetle's four cylinder rear engine seemed engraved on his skull. Fran was awake, sitting jammed in her corner and staring blankly out the window. The car had stopped moving.

Sam asked, "Where are we?"

"Swiss border," Marty answered. "Got your ID card?" The Army did not permit them to have US passports, perhaps to make it difficult for them to go AWOL.

Sam struggled to get his wallet out of his hip pocket while Fran reached forward and nudged Yetta. "Wake up. We're at the border."

Yetta brushed the hair out of her eyes and dug into her purse. Only Marty was fully awake. He was staring out the partly steamed window. He had driven fast and recklessly in spite of the snow. Perhaps the stress of that kept him alert, but he was a capable driver and no one was worried enough to stay awake. Marty rolled down the driver's side window.

A German border guard in a military overcoat looked in. Snow had collected on his shoulders like white epaulettes. *"Passkontrol. Amerikaner?"* He had recognized the license plate as being from U.S. forces in Germany. A gust of cold wind blew in with the snow-hushed sounds of the world. The guard took off his gloves and blew on his fingers while Sam held out the identification cards and passes.

"*Heute bin ich Dolmetscher*," Sam said, knowing some German and that a joke or two would relieve the boredom of the guard's lonely Christmas and make the crossing go easily for the Green Beetle and its illegal, unsafe can of gasoline in the back seat, which Sam carefully covered up with the filched Army blanket

The guard nodded, grateful for the language. Not many English-speaking tourists passed at this part of the border, especially in winter. "*Alles Militär?*" He asked, nodding at the girls.

"*Ja.*" Sam winked. "*Die damen auch.*" The guard would know from the girls' AGO I.D. cards that they were employees, but not wives. Wives and civilian family had passports. "*Noch ein Wochen ende.*" Meaning a pleasant regular weekend with the girls. Shared with the border guard who probably had the average one track male mind, the remark was intended to make the guard a co-conspirator to a tryst and helped them avoid a time-consuming car inspection. If they were not permitted to carry extra gas in the car, what then? They weren't exactly smuggling contraband, but there was no point in bringing on trouble if it could be avoided.

"*Viel vergnügen*," the guard said, handing back the ID cards and waving them on. "*Frohe Weinachten.*"

"*Gleichfals.* Merry Christmas to you, too," Sam said.

A single headlight slowed in the darkness of the roadway and came to a stop within the circle of light cast by the bright windows of the toll house. To Sam's astonishment, it was a German motorcycle with a man so bundled up in a Wehrmacht style helmet and leathers he looked like some apparition. His legs were also protected by canvas chaps. Sam noticed that the motorbike was equipped with metal pads like skis so the driver could put both feet down on ice and snow and avoid falling. You had to be crazy or determined to be out in that weather on a motorcycle at night, in the snow. The man dismounted and brushed the caked snow from his leather jacket and legs. His face was wrapped in a scarf up to the edge of his goggles.

The motorcyclist had drawn the guard's attention, so Sam and his friends were already forgotten. Marty threw the Volkswagen into gear and moved on toward the Swiss side of the border where the guard, more friendly than the German, drew the same remarks from Sam. At the Swiss border Marty had to show his car insurance carnet and was reminded that the policy was nearly expired. Marty got out to wipe snow from the headlights and they moved on into the night.

The Volkswagen suddenly lurched. "Time to gas up," Marty said. The car didn't have a gas gauge. When it got down to the last gallon, he had to pull a little knob to access the last gallon. That gave them about twenty miles to find a gas station, but at night, what might be open? It was time to get out the jerry can and pour in the reserve fuel they carried. Marty pulled off at the next rest stop and they wrestled the heavy can of fuel out of the back seat, opened the hood, and took off the gas cap. It took both of them to hold the heavy can steady in the freezing cold while they poured in the gasoline. Once empty and no longer likely to leak, the can could be stowed on its side in the back seat.

They pressed on into the Swiss night.

Sam studied Fran's face. In the dim light her skin was drawn and she looked older. "Tired?"

"Awfully."

"Try to get some sleep. We'll be driving all night and then there's the train in the morning." Sam yawned. As usual, in his determination to escape from the Army and go as far as possible in his limited pass time, he was overextended. He had once rushed off all the way to Milan on a weekend, and his stomach had churned the whole next week from cheap Chianti. Yet when the trips were over he always remembered what a great time he had had. Even if something went wrong he could call it an adventure.

"Do you always have to go so far away?" Fran asked.

"Always seem to."

She curled up against his shoulder. "The Army can't be as bad as all that."

"It's not just the Army" He thought of Betty and his failed romance. He and Fran had something in common in that way. She had fled a bad relationship. He had been inept, misunderstood, a jerk beyond all apologies. "I guess we actually don't have a bad deal in Munich, even though Marty and I are the only ones in the office who do any work. It's just the basic situation that's so dumb."

"What do you mean?"

"Why we're here, for instance. Occupation troops. To defend Germany, really. From the Russians? What a sad joke. Everyone knows we couldn't stand a chance of holding out if they drove their tanks through the Fulda Gap. We're supposed to be here to intimidate, but how can we do that if we aren't even a threat?"

Fran didn't know anything about military tactics and strategy, not that Sam did, either. Supply clerks weren't supposed to know anything. They were just supposed to follow orders. That was the Army way.

"If we had to fight, I wouldn't even know what we were fighting. I mean, we defeated Germany, didn't we? Are we supposed to defend them?"

"I guess you're supposed to fight for freedom and the American Way of Life," Fran said.

Sam laughed. "And apple pie and motherhood." He patted her on the shoulder like she was a child. "There's a German way and a French way, and an English way. These are all perfectly good ways and the people are just as free as Americans are."

"What about the Russian way?"

Sam had no idea of the Russian way, but he didn't think it was apple pie. Maybe black bread and vodka. "You'd think we had a corner on the freedom market the way they talk about it at I and E." There it was, the military jargon of his draftee status.

"What's that?"

"Troop information and education," Sam said glumly. "The Army's propaganda system."

They rode on in silence. Finally Sam spoke again. "What do you actually do in Heidelberg? You never said."

"I'm just another file clerk. Not like Yetta. She got herself a job as secretary, but then, she's had experience in a lot of things."

It sounded to Sam like envy, but experience could be defined in many ways. He didn't think he had job experience in anything, unless pushing supply room forms and taking inventory counted.

Yetta was asleep in the front seat. Marty, intent on his driving, did not seem to be listening to the whispers behind him. "Have you nice people to work with? I mean, do the D.A.'s get the same crap we do?"

"I don't know. We're civilians, but because we're technically part of the military we fall under the Universal Code of Military Justice. We can actually be court-martialed."

"Can't be too different from our situation, then," though he couldn't see Fran being locked up in the stockade for insubordination. Fired, maybe. He recalled the court-martial look that so often came over sergeant Adams' face, like his anger over pilfered pie.

"It doesn't happen often," Fran said. "I've never heard of a case in Heidelberg."

"It's an easy way to dispose of someone you don't get along with." He told Fran about the pie incident which sounded funny now. Maybe it was just a way to needle the college boys in a cadre full of grammar school graduates with battlefield commissions, or at least with extra stripes on their shoulders, the Army's caste system at work, regular Army versus draftees. Did that happen in Fran's office? "What kind of atmosphere do you work in?"

"No squabbles over pie," she said, "but the officers are scrambling for rank. Heidelberg is all brass, you know. We have about thirty generals. You can imagine how many captains."

"They must get sore arms saluting all the time," Sam said.

"That's not the problem," Fran explained. "We're not actually at war, so ranks are pretty static. If a captain gets passed over for major the third time, he's demoted to master sergeant. End of career."

"Sounds like a dog eat dog rat race."

Fran's legs were cramped from sitting so long in the back seat of the Green Beetle. She wriggled for a new position. "If not scrambling for promotion, the officers do a lot of drinking at cocktail parties. They're all on the make, married men, too, and some of them right in front of their wives. It's disgusting."

Sam thought about the officers in his company. The captain's wife was so unpleasant, so he said, that she drove him and the dog out of the house. Maybe it was just the dog she couldn't stand. Then the sergeant first class who got love letters from another woman. And the executive office who complained, too, about being married to a wife who never stopped shopping for German junk. Then the training sergeant who spent his evenings trolling for German girls and rejoicing that his wife had not yet been shipped overseas to join him. Just what was marriage supposed to be, anyway? Not one he had observed in the Army had been satisfactory.

"How about you? Sam asked.

"You wouldn't believe it, but in the controller's office, because I don't jump in the sack at the first invitation I'm known as the frigid bitch. Not a very nice name, is it?"

"I guess not."

"I suppose it's true," she admitted glumly. "It doesn't pay to be too different when you work for the military. Just because I don't sleep around." She sat up and looked him in the eye. "In that office everyone knows what everyone else is doing, and everybody talks."

"I'm not talking," Sam said, and hugged her, kissed her on the cheek. "Doesn't sound very discreet to me. I'm told that discretion is the better part of virtue. Why don't you transfer to another office like Yetta did?"

"Would it be different somewhere else?"

Sam thought a moment. There were WACs at regimental headquarters and rumors that they were dykes. "I guess not. Not if what Sally Ann says about her job is true."

Fran had her hand on the inside of Sam's thigh. It dawned on him that the reputation for being a frigid bitch was only because, as the saying goes, you don't shit where you eat. Better to make love with someone with no connection to her Heidelberg office,

"So you met Sally Ann?"

What was she hinting at? She couldn't know that he nearly put Sally Ann to bed drunk. Had the women been comparing notes? Talking about him? "Yes."

"She and Yetta are the only really nice people I've met over here… present company excepted." She gave him a reassuring kiss. "The rest are, well it's like they're all wearing masks."

"When you came over here you signed a contract," Sam said. "I didn't have a choice."

"I know now. That's why I want to get away from it." Her act of getting away was to lose herself in his kiss and his embrace. Sam slid his hand between her knees….

Then her breath caught and she shook her head, trembling and whispered, "Please, Sam." She pushed him away. "Stop."

Disappointed, Sam sat up and worked his feet into another position beside the empty jerry can.

His disappointment faded when she added, "Not here." The back seat of Marty's speeding Green Beetle with Yetta in the front seat, too, wasn't exactly private.

Fran's face was turned away and he couldn't see her expression. "It's all right, Sam," she whispered. "I mean, you're all right. It's me, that's all." She folded her arms and leaned down with her head rested on his knees.

Sam tucked her into the Army blanket. "I didn't hurt you, did I?"

"No."

Sam cleared his throat. "I mean, because I don't want to hurt anybody, especially not you."

"You only did what I should have expected. I just don't think clearly all the time."

Sam remembered her often distracted expression, looking into space.

She continued. "I get carried away and forget sometimes what's really happening."

Marty called, "You two all right back there? Getting enough heat?"

"We have to make our own heat," Sam said. "I think you're using it all for the defrosters."

That was true enough, for in spite of the engine heat diverted to the windshield, there was still condensation on the side windows.

Sam coughed—that nagging lung problem again—and rubbed some of the steam off the side window. Outside snowflakes swirled by. Marty slowed down as they were passing through a village somewhere. He had expected to be rejected. He even wanted to be, like he deserved nothing.

Fran moved back to his end of the back seat. She put her arms around his neck. "I'm sorry, Sam. My fault." She kissed him. "I'm really glad you asked me to come along on this trip. I wanted so much to avoid that crowd in Heidelberg at the colonel's party."

Sam returned the kiss. Conscious that Marty might be watching them in the rear view mirror he suggested, "Let's keep Marty from falling sleep. Let's sing him a song. That'll keep him awake."

Marty turned briefly to look at them, then turned back to his driving with the little pipe between his teeth. "No Christmas carols, kiddies."

"How about a drinking song? That's more your style." He turned to Fran. "Repeat after me. *In Muenshcn steht's ein Hofbrau Haus...*"

„*In Muenshcn steht's ein Hofbrau Haus...*"

'Right! *Ein zwei, gsoffe!*

Fran repeated the lyric, raising her left hand as if it held a stein of beer. Her other hand was around Sam's neck.

Outside the Green Beetle the snow swirled thicker and the road signs marked off the kilometers. There was no north or south or Switzerland, only the mountains lurking, huge, craggy, heavy with snow beyond in the darkness and the whining of the four cylinder Volkswagen engine.

„*In Muenshcn steht's ein Hofbrau Haus...*"

Chapter Eight

The Fifth Weekend—Zermatt

The next afternoon Sam and Fran were among the passengers on the Zermatt train, a short string of old-fashioned cars that moved briskly along the level valley floor between Brig and Visp and then ground on its cogs up the gorge to leave civilization behind.

"I guess that's the end of the road," Sam said as he pointed across the snowy gorge that had been a valley, got narrower as the train climbed toward Zermatt.

Fatigue seemed to have made Fran's face a stiff and expressionless mask. Her ski pants and parka were rumpled from sleeping in the back seat of the Marty's car, and her hair had come out of place so often that she no longer did more than pluck at it in tired irritation. She looked out the train window and managed a nod.

"Imagine trying to build a road here," Sam continued. "The higher you go, the longer the winter is, and the steeper the cliffs. Seems almost impossible."

Fran tried to find a comfortable position on the old-fashioned, hard wooden seat, finally gave up. "They built the railroad, didn't they? I should think they could build a road if they really wanted to."

Sam admitted, "You're right, I guess you can do almost anything if you really want to… except make a train if you're late. I'm sorry we missed our connection. It doesn't matter. I couldn't ski now if

I tried. I'm too stiff. It'll be dark before we can get to a ski run."

But in spite of his fatigue, the higher the train climbed, the more excited Sam became. He peered through his camera viewfinder. "I wish it hadn't started snowing again. I can't get a picture."

"When we get to Zermatt I'm going to take a nap," Fran said.

"I'm sorry," Sam apologized, fearing he had wasted her pass. "I suppose we should have gone to St. Moritz. It would have been much closer."

So far as he was concerned, the trip would not be a waste even if they had no time left to ski at all. The Swiss scenery was enough of a reward in itself, an adventure that made him feel like he was part of a slide show of endless picture postcards.

To the left were a few chateaus heavy with new snow. On the right, reaching up beyond the view visible through the train windows, stretched the alps which had finally closed in almost completely on the ever-narrowing gorge. The train ground to a stop. "This is it." He stood up to get their skis down from the overhead rack.

They shouldered their way through an international assortment of tourists as they stepped down off the train. Taking up a position on the platform and balancing his skis against his shoulder, Sam took out the hotel information he had obtained from the Army travel office in Munich. Normally he would gamble at finding a room at the last moment, but this was the Christmas holiday, and though most people spent it with their families, there were still tourists. "We're at the Gornergrat Hotel."

"Isn't that way up on the mountain?"

"No. That's the Gornergrat itself. The hotel with that name is supposed to be close to the station."

Fran pointed across the narrow street. "There it is. I hope they have a nice hot bath."

Sam shouldered both pairs of their skis and followed Fran as she picked her way over piles of snow and across the street. It was a skiers' paradise. There were no cars in the town. Even the railway ended there. Everything was decorated for Christmas. In spite of the fatigue of driving all night crammed in the back seat of the Green Beetle, and then the train, Sam felt rejuvenated and excited.

The manager of the Gornergrat was a tall, robust man with a large, almost handlebar mustache. His eyes were dark and deep set with a glitter that was partly cheerfulness and partly the shine of shrewd Swiss business success. His cheeks were red and a first Sam thought he might be wearing rouge, but then remembered that some Swiss were supposed to have taken small amounts of arsenic to give themselves a ruddy look. With one glance at Sam, Fran, Sam's white-painted skis and their luggage, he sized them up as American and military. Speaking in English he said, "You can leave your skis here." He indicated a vestibule with a laden rack.

"I didn't think we were so obviously American," Sam commented.

The manager's eyes twinkled above the bushy mustache. "That's not so difficult to recognize."

Sam wondered sheepishly if it was also obvious to the manager that here were two lovers who had come to Zermatt to find privacy for their affair, not that he and Fran were exactly lovers, might be, might become. Probably the manager was a better judge of that than he was. Sam showed his reservation confirmation papers. "I believe you have reservations for two single rooms for Sam Logan?"

"Of course." He pushed two police registration forms across the counter to him. "I will need to see your passports, of course."

Sam was familiar with the routine. At European hotels you always had to fill in the police registration card indicating your nationality, identification, how long you were staying, home address, and so on. But of course, he didn't have a passport. He got out his wallet and showed his laminated military ID card.

Fran was standing, exhausted and hesitant. She had withdrawn a few feet and stood as if wondering whether Sam would say something she wasn't sure of. She seemed glad he was speaking English and not his halting German as he had to the border guards and later when they bought their train tickets.

Sam turned to her. "You need to fill out the registration."

Fran stepped forward. At least they weren't registering as Mr. and Mrs. Sam Logan, which might have been the situation if they'd booked a double room.

The manager had no doubt seen all manner of couples, and, being Swiss, knew how to accommodate the hotel guests. "The rooms are adjoining." Had he winked? No, he was too discreet for that.

The manager handed the room keys to a young porter, a kid in a tailored jacket that had sleeves too short for his growing arms. He led the way up the stairs, carrying both their bags.

Adjoining rooms? Sam wondered, were they next door to each other, or did they have a door between them for private visitations?

It was an old hotel. The thin carpet in the upstairs hall only partly covered the wide, rough floor boards that creaked under Sam's feet.

Sure enough, the rooms were side by side. Sam knocked at the connecting door, which Fran opened. He could see that she had opened her zipped bag on the little stand. Like other old hotels, it had an amoire, not a closet, and she had hung her parka on a wooden hanger. On the dresser which doubled as a night strand, she had set out minimum toiletries, makeup, hair brush, and—he was pleased to see it—the Christmas gift Tyrolean teddy bear in his lederhosen and hat with a little feather.

Fran handed him a flat package which he had almost forgotten. "Here's your present. And the picture."

"Thanks. I guess I can open it now." He fumbled with the fancy ribbon.

They were woolen gloves with brilliant knit patterns. The fingers were a little short for his long, thin hands.

She saw that they weren't a perfect fit and apologized "I wasn't sure of the size. I hope they're all right."

Wearing the new gloves, Sam took her by the shoulders and forced her often averted eyes to look at him. "They're perfect. Thanks." He kissed her gently.

She was tired and withdrawn, but the kiss aroused her. They clung together, but she was aware of the bed beside them and as a diversion reminded him, "Don't forget the picture."

The Christmas package also contained a framed photo of her. It was taken in a studio and brought out the best of her otherwise angular face and sharp chin.

Her diversion had almost succeeded. "I'm too tired to ski, Sam. What I really need after the long night is a nap."

Was that an invitation? Apparently not, for she gently maneuvered him to the door that connected their adjoining rooms. She asked, "Do you have an alarm clock?"

He did, a little travel alarm that didn't keep very good time, but worked. "Yes."

The dreamy, withdrawn expression was on her face again, this time with a faint smile as though something far away had pleased her. "Set it for an hour and knock at my door, will you?"

That sounded like an invitation. At least, that's what Sam was hoping for. Like a good Boy Scout he always carried a condom in his wallet, just in case he got lucky. Maybe she needed an hour to 'slip into something more comfortable.' He hoped. "What time should I set it for? Five-thirty alright?"

She nodded, already plucking at the buttons of her cardigan. He was about to close the connecting door when she came up to him and kissed him quickly on the mouth. He was uncertain, should he turn away, or stay, but she turned away.

As he stood in the doorway he saw her standing at the night stand and holding up her little stuffed bear as if consulting it to make up her mind.

"See you at five-thirty," Sam said, and closed the door.

Sam's room was cold, but someone, probably the boy who had brought up their luggage, had turned on the radiator. It snapped, popped, and gurgled and even managed to give off some heat from its inadequate coils.

He took off his ski boots. Like all such footwear, they had flexible soles so could be used when skiing cross country or climbing the slopes. The only features that distinguished them from other stout winter boots were the grooved heels and toes squared off to fit in the cable bindings. He lay down on the single bed, found the mattress hard and probably as old as the hotel itself.

She sure is hard to figure out, Sam thought. He studied Fran's features in the framed photo she had given him. It seemed to him that she had told him the important, main features of her life, but there was nothing truly intimate about what she said. It was as if she had recited her own resume to him, though no resume would have said she left the States to avoid being pursued by a controlling lover. He sensed that she was lacking something, and he wanted to put his arms around her, to hug her, as if a hug could cure whatever in her spirit ailed her.

She said she wanted to take a nap and rest up after the exhausting night of travel, but was it an invitation? Did she really want a cuddle, but was too shy to say so? Did she really want sex? He didn't know about that, either, and he was too respectful of her need for privacy to simply barge into her room like some hero in a romance novel. He was not that aggressive.

On the other hand, the door connecting their adjoining rooms was not locked, at least not from his side, and if she wanted to join him here he was, ready and willing. He wished.

Sam undressed quickly, hopping around the cold, wooden floor in his stocking feet. The floor boards, as in the hall, were wide and knotted, much more primitive than the parquet floors with scatter rugs he had seen almost everywhere else in his weekend jaunts. The runner in the hallway was worn thin. It was a one star hotel which may have been why he had been able to secure a reservation during the holiday season.

Zermatt was a special place, at the end of a local railway, no highway to it, and cliffs and mountains with their cornices of hanging snow looming over the small town. As the jumping off place for climbing the spectacular Matterhorn, it was a town for mountaineers. Davos, where Marty and Yetta were, was more popular, a playground for the rich and famous.

Sam looked out the window at the breathlessly close mountainsides laden with snow. It would soon be dark. The excitement of being there almost dispelled his fatigue. The town was decorated with Christmas lights, and had a fairy land atmosphere. It was romantic and lacked only the romance of Fran sneaking in to join him. But that was a fantasy.

In his underwear and socks, Sam crept between the bed's icy sheets and curled into a small ball. The hotel didn't have the expected cloud of feather quilt, just a heavy, coarse, wool blanket. Who had slept there before? Skiers? Mountain climbers who set off and never returned? He had read about the early climbers who fell to their deaths, but since then the mountain had been tamed by fixed ropes. Even a ninety-year-old woman had climbed it. Now there were greater challenges, like the Geiger. Still, for Sam, Zermatt, at the narrow end of a gorge in the Alps, was the end of civilization. Considering the time limits of his pass, he had come a long way from the company supply room in Munich, perhaps too far....

...

The ringing of the alarm clock was familiar, but the room was not. Sam lay in the bed for a few moments, exhausted and puzzled, before he remembered where he was. He sat up, swung his legs over the edge of the bed, and stared at the floor where the tiny travel alarm clock's lively jangle gradually lost its intensity and stopped with a final, weak tinkle. Sam stumbled out of the bed, turned off the already silent alarm. He rewound the alarm spring.,

He knocked at the connecting door and announced "Five thirty!" and went to the wash stand. They'd traveled all night and he needed a shave. Should he bother? Yes, why not?

His American electric razor had burnt out the first time he plugged it into 220 volts, so his toilet kit now had an actual shaving brush and safety razor equipped with cheap blades good for only one shave at most before their edge was gone. The hotel had not provided soap.

Fran was already up. She opened the connecting door, catching him standing at the wash stand in his underwear and shaving. "Oops, sorry. I couldn't have gone another step without a nap," she said. She looked fresh and neat and her hair was in place. I'll wait for you downstairs."

Sam was startled. He wasn't used to be seen in his underwear by a woman he hardly knew. But she wasn't embarrassed. Well, nothing to do about that now. She had seen him in his skivvies. So what? Maybe that was a good thing. She might want to see more. Then again, maybe not. He wasn't exactly Mr. America. He considered himself more of the wimpy guy who got sand thrown in his face in the ads for Charles Atlas's Dynamic Tension that were always displayed in the back pages of comic books along with the Rosicrucians.

But she hadn't left. She seemed to enjoy his shyness.

He said, "I think I could sleep another eight hours."

Fran laid her hands on his shoulders. "Poor Sam. I bet you never get enough sleep. You look like you could sleep your life away." Was she teasing or flirting?

Sam put down the razor, quickly wiped his face with a towel. He tried to put his arms around her but she held him off, glanced at the front of his GI undershorts, saw a bulge beginning to form. "I'll see you downstairs."

"Not yet." He gently moved her back to his unmade bed until she was lying on her back with her long legs hanging over the edge and her feet still on the floor. Sam lay down beside her, his head on her stomach. He listened with curiosity to the rumbling sounds in her stomach.

Fran twisted Sam's black hair between her fingers. Then the muscles of her abdomen suddenly tightened and she pushed him away.

Sam thought she was ready. He was, for sure. He was already thinking of the condom in his wallet. Where had he hung his pants? "What's the matter?"

"Nothing," she said. But she was trembling and when he looked up at her face she turned away. She extricated herself from his embrace and stood up. "Not now." She kissed him quickly, before he could react, then said, "I'll see you downstairs. Time for dinner."

She escaped from his room. He couldn't very well chase her down the hallway in his underwear. Even a jaded Swiss hotel proprietor wouldn't approve of that scene. Sam dressed quickly and followed her downstairs. He hadn't tied his boots and nearly tripped on the laces as he hurried down the stairs.

They found a little café on the main street and had an early supper of wienerschnitzel and spaetzle, a Swiss favorite. Sam had a glass of beer and Fran some red wine.

The bill made him cringe. Fran snatched it away from him, made a quick calculation, and added some of the Swiss franks she'd exchanged for at the Davos railway station when they left Marty and Yetta. "My share," she said. She was sticking to her policy not to be seduced by a little dinner and wine.

"If you insist," he said, a pro forma answer. He knew that she knew he didn't have much money. In her job she earned a whole lot more than he did. Much as he wanted to be the provider in spite of his meager Army pay, he was grateful for her consideration. He conceded it was best that they stayed independent. He guessed that when the time came that she let him pay for everything she'd have accepted him as more than just a traveling companion. She was not like Yetta, who he guessed was happy enough to let Marty pay for everything. But then, Marty liked to be the big-shot spender.

They left the café and saw that the snow had stopped falling. Outside the hotel, the kid who had carried their bags was sweeping the sidewalk with a stiff broom. He stopped to let the Americans pass and then went on with his job.

As they trudged through the snow, Fran held Sam's hand tightly. Again she seemed preoccupied and distant. Occasionally she studied his face as if she were looking for something in it that gave her the answer to something. He didn't think he was handsome, and his once-broken nose didn't help any. On some faces it would look like he was a tough guy who survived brawls, but on him it looked like he was a wimp, the guy who lost the fight.

He didn't want to think about that. They were in Switzerland! Zermatt! It was exciting. They ,must look like honeymooners, or at least like lovers. Didn't he wish. But they had little time. Taking skis along on this quick trip was foolish. Their train the next morning left at 10:30. Even if they got up at a god-awful early hour, it would not be light enough in this December time of the year. When would the sun come up, if it penetrated at all into the Zermatt gorge? Nine o'clock? That hardly left time for anything.

It was too bad he couldn't get a longer pass, or a real leave. He thought glumly about getting some leave time. He was entitled to thirty days a year but his boss, the supply sergeant, depended on Sam as his clerk. Sam suspected that the sergeant was concealing illiteracy. Only Sam was adept at all those inventory forms, so he was stuck.

"I still haven't seen the Matterhorn," Fran said.

"The guy at the hotel said you can see it from the end of the street." He had forgotten his gloves, even though he now had two pair. His hands were cold and he shoved them into the thin pockets of his lightweight parka.

"Look at this quaint church," Fran said. She mounted the two steps of a little, simple church on the single main street.

Sam wasn't terribly interested in churches. American tourists were invariably led to cathedrals financed by hundreds of years of tithes of poor people who lived in thatched huts. Sam, more interested in seeing quaint Zermatt, reluctantly joined Fran at the church door. It was unlocked. When they looked in they saw a dazzling display of yuletide decorations. They didn't go inside, however, and as they turned to go he looked up.

There it was, what he had come to see: the Matterhorn. Though far from the tallest mountain in Switzerland, it was an impressive pinnacle that made his knees weak. It might be tamed now, but many had died in early attempts to climb it.

Sam was not a mountain climber, not a long distance runner, not even a hiker. His lung condition had precluded that kind of activity. His idea of getting to the top of a mountain was on an aerial tram. To him the Matterhorn was a symbol of the unattainable. At one time he had thoughts of being athletic, but the football injury was a setback. He realized there were physical things he could never do. In spite of his years, it made him feel old.

Fran had not noticed it yet, but did realize he was transfixed. The sight of the Matterhorn left him speechless. Though there are many mountains on planet Earth, and some are recognizable, like Gibraltar, and Devils Tower, the Matterhorn stands out like a trade mark, suitable for labels on bars of Swiss chocolate. Think Switzerland, and you have the Matterhorn.

Above the town and to the south, it base hidden by a ridge, stood the blue-white pinnacle of the mountain shining in the moonlight. The last shreds of cloud that had carried the afternoon's snow were passing slowly to the west. A few wisps of mist clung briefly to the sheer face of the mountain then blew away, leaving a sheer, icy finger of rock thrusting cold, naked, and brilliant into the night sky.

Sam didn't understand why, but he had a romantic fascination with the Matterhorn. Some people might be moved to tears by a beautiful sunset. For Sam it was the sight of this mountain. For him it represented the magical idea of Switzerland, land of yodelers, cowbells, chocolate, watches, Heidies in pigtails, maybe even secretive Zurich banks. It had been a neutral refuge during the war, and unlike the ruins of Germany which he encountered on his travels, Switzerland by contrast was undamaged, unspoiled.

Fran said, "It doesn't leave much to say, does it?"

"It's beautiful." With a humility you might experience in church, they walked slowly down the street, their feet treading carefully in the already trampled snow. Though there were other people out for an evening's walk and the sound of carols came from one of the Christmas-decorated hotels, Sam and Fran seemed alone.

Sam remembered travel brochures he had read. Pointing in the direction of the mountain, now hidden behind the buildings of the village, he said, "It's much more impressive than the Zugspitze in Garmisch. You know why?"

Fran had taken his arm. "No."

"The Zugspitze is domesticated by a tunnel to the top for a funicular train and the tourists. It takes away some of the stature as a mountain. The Matterhorn has its virgin beauty. It's been climbed often, but from here it doesn't seem used."

Fran stiffened at the mention of virginity. She studied his transfixed face again and smiled as though she had found in what she saw the answer she had been looking for.

If Sam had noticed her change of demeanor he attributed it to the scenery, not what she saw in him. "There's no train to the top of that. To get up there you need ice axes, ropes, and crampons. It's a different world up there." He was reminded of his own physical limitations and sighed. "A different world. I wish I could climb it."

"Not me," Fran said. "I'm no alpine climber."

"I've been afraid of heights." He remembered his weak knees when looking down from the Kreutzek's precipice.

"I'm glad we came, even though it's awfully far."

At an opening between the buildings they could again see the mountain. A crowd of tourists had stopped to look at it in the moonlight. Sam stopped and sat on the snow bank shoveled to the side of the street.

"I'm glad you came with me," he said. He knocked one foot against the other to shake the snow off his ski boots. He thought about those foolhardy macho guys who climbed mountains alone, without ropes, just their bare hands. He was reminded again that he had forgotten his gloves, the new ones Fran had given him. "It's better to travel with someone. On my own I guess I get lonely. Maybe that's why I go places with Marty even though he can be a pain in the ass."

"With his silly pipe," Fran agreed.

Sam chuckled. "I don't think he has any tobacco for it."

Fran understood. "It's a phony act he puts on. Not like you, Sam. You're genuine. You're the real thing."

"Thanks. You are, too." Sam kissed her on the bit of cheek not covered by her ski parka. "You're a very understanding person."

Fran looked down at the snow. "I don't try to understand myself. I just try to get along with people."

Sam thought about her Heidelberg circle and the nickname, "Frigid Bitch." "But you don't sacrifice yourself to them."

She held her head proudly. "I don't think here's a sacrifice to be made."

Sam had begun to feel uncomfortable. They had never talked like this before and he had no idea where it would lead. "You don't need to sacrifice, I guess. You can stand for yourself, like that mountain."

"People aren't mountains, Sam. They don't stand alone. They need something." Her dreamy look was gone and her eyes focused sharply on his.

Sam avoided her eyes. "I guess." He didn't know what he needed. Since he had no goals and was more or less adrift in his life in spite of mulling over it so long in the hospital, he was undecided. "If they know what they need." Maybe what he needed was to get laid, but he sure wasn't going to tell her that. She probably already knew that anyway.

This time she looked away. "That's not always easy to find out."

Sam was dejected. He didn't know how to handle this. He got clumsily to his feet, found it necessary to cough. It was a reflex, not necessarily something in his lungs, but something psychological. The mountain he had come to see looked more distant now, like the pictures he had seen in the travel folders. From somewhere nearby he heard the turbulent splash of a mountain stream, still not quite frozen, tumbling and hurtling toward the valley. "Let's get back to the hotel. It's cold out here."

He took a last look at the Matterhorn glinting icily in the moonlight. He would never forget that sight, though at times he would not be sure why it had been so important or why it made him feel inadequate and lonely.

They walked in silence back to the Gornergrat. Sam held Fran's hand tightly, and though they said little they seemed to be bound by the experience they had shared. Whenever he glanced at her he found her looking at him as if she had just met someone new she was trying to size up.

He liked her. He did not know her very well, but he was drawn to her. She was what the Italians called simpatico, sensitive, but tentative. He found himself trying not to think too much about it for fear of spoiling things. Sometimes just the wrong word or remark could spoil everything.

The hotel steps were clear of snow and the dining room was filled with latecomers. Sam nodded cheerfully to the hotel manager and went upstairs with Fran to their adjoining rooms. No need to go into hers, since they were connected.

Sam took off his ski jacket and dropped it on the only chair, but Fran took charge, picked it up and hung it in the armoire.

Sam followed her through the connecting door into her room and watched as she slipped off her ski parka and, as she had done with his, hung it up in the antique armoire. He then pulled the heavy drapes aside and stood by her window. The lights across the narrow street caught the corners and scalloped edges of the typical Swiss chalet architecture. The snow absorbed much of the sounds of Christmas music.

Fran stood beside him, moved closer when he put his arm around her. "You wouldn't think we were in Munich yesterday, would you?"

She smiled and nodded. She let him draw her close and kiss her on the forehead but didn't wait for him to work his way down to her lips. Her mouth tasted sweet and was abruptly passionate, her tongue finding his. Then she pulled back, as if surprised at herself, as if her own passion was unexpected, not her normal, restrained self. "I like you, Sam." Well, why not?

They were standing near her bed and he was figuring how they would get into it. Now, as Marty put it, was the time for the old college try Marty had insisted was all Sam needed and what Sam also wanted. While he kissed Fran he backed up against the bed and awkwardly fell into it with Fran on top of him. She didn't try to get up.

He could feel her trembling, her shoulders and thighs. "Oh, Sam…"

Now is the time, he told himself. But he was awkward. He had no practice in getting a girl's clothes off or unhooking her bra. He was trying to figure out what to do next, but suddenly Fran was in a hurry and he couldn't think fast enough to keep up with her. If only she would give him time to arrange things the way he thought they were supposed to be, except he didn't know.

Before he could figure it out, she had pulled her sweater over her head. "Sam," she said, kissing him again. "Oh, Sam." His face was flushed and wet from her kisses. She shuddered and buried her face in his neck. "I don't want to be lonely," she cried. It was like the far away whimper of a child lost in a fearful darkness it did not understand.

Sam slid out from under her. He switched off the light, leaving the room lit only by moonlight and fumbled awkwardly in the near dark for the condom he kept in his wallet…

...but when the moment came something went wrong. They lay in her bed under the coarse, wool blanket. They were not naked, Sam in his GI Issue underpants and tee shirt, Fran in just her panties, close together but not actually touching. She seemed to fear the warmth of his body and the touch of his skin as he tried to caress her. She lay there stiffly, staring at the ceiling. Under the blanket, Sam knew that her arms were extended stiffly along her sides, ready to push him away if he approached her again.

"Fran?" He was ready now. His Midwestern, puritanical rejection of Marty's argument for sex had faded with his own erection. As the Latin phrase went, *penis erectus non conciem habet,* or, plainly, an erect penis has no conscience, or morals or inhibitions, or brains. He was ready. He had no more questions, no more reluctance, no fear of consequences. He slipped off his GI undershorts. All that remained now was for him to get Fran to relax and accept him, but she lay there unresponsive. When he tried to touch her, even on her shoulder, she pushed him away with a swift, firm motion.

Almost choking on a sob she said, "I can't, Sam." She sat up, hiding her small but perky breasts with the blanket, and reached for her sweater. With a swift motion, she turned her back to him and slipped it on. "I'm sorry, Sam. I just can't." She started to cry. She murmured, perhaps only to herself, "It wasn't right for me in New York and it isn't right now."

Deprived of the blanket, Sam was embarrassed to show himself. Why couldn't she simply make up her mind as he had and let it go at that? Why did everything have to be so complicated? He was sure she wanted him, and he was ready, and now she didn't want to.

Fran glanced at him, saw his erection, and quickly turned away, faced the window as though she didn't dare look at him.

"Fran?"

"Go to your own room. Please leave me alone."

Damn, Sam thought. He remembered the cruel nickname she was called at her office in Heidelberg. Frigid Bitch. But he didn't think she was that. She was, well, confused maybe. He was no psychologist. He didn't understand women. He didn't understand himself. He thought that when you were ready to do it, you just did it.

He wasn't ready to give up yet, even though she got back into her bed and pulled the wool blanket and sheet over her, shivering. "I can't. I'm sorry. I just can't."

Sam stood beside her bed, trying to understand their situation. He was always mulling over things, trying to find meanings that might not be there at all. Marty had said he worried too much. Maybe that was it. He was hamstrung by his own indecision.

Sam felt compassion for her. She was shivering, perhaps from the cold, perhaps from something else. Surely she wasn't afraid of him. He wasn't that aggressive. She should probably change into warm pajamas but maybe she didn't want to show herself or give him the chance to get close enough to embrace her, an embrace that might break down her last resistance.

He'd make one last try. "Mind if I sleep here? We wouldn't have to do anything. It's nice to have company. You wouldn't feel lonely."

Being lonely was her hot button weakness, but she laughed. "I don't think so."

"I have very warm feet," he suggested. "No cold toes in the small of your back."

She looked fearfully at his foot.

"Don't you trust me?" Perhaps, after a little while, she'd change her mind.

"I don't trust that," she said, pointing at his penis as if it were a dangerous weapon with a mind of its own, which wasn't that far from the truth.

He was embarrassed. He felt like a fool, naked and impotent.

Fran sat up, wrapped the blanket around her shoulders. "Please leave, Sam. You can't sleep here. The bed is too narrow."

Now he was feeling ridiculous. He had been taught that no meant no and that was it. He had to respect her rejection even if he didn't understand it.

She reached down to where he had dropped his pants and his shorts on the floor and tossed them to him. "Now put on your pants and get out of here."

He did a little dance and flaunted his maleness at her. "Chicken."

She shook her head. "I don't think you'd do very well as a male stripper, Sam. Now if you don't get out I'll call the manager."

Would she? Would she dare? Sam laughed. That was suddenly funny. "You'll what? How would you explain that you're half naked and I'm...?" He bent to pick up his undershorts. It was ludicrous. It wasn't supposed to go this way. They were supposed to have hot, orgasmic sex and fall asleep in an afterglow of satisfaction and love. He lost his breath and suddenly started to cough again.

"Please leave, Sam. Please. If you love me you'll just sleep in your room tonight."

Love? That put another light on it. Sam looked at the room. In the pale moonlight there were bits of clothing, his pants, his shirt, his ski boots, all scattered about like the debris after an explosion.

Silently, he gathered up his clothes and went to the connecting door where he paused and looked back. Fran said, "I'm sorry."

"I'm sorry, too."

"You shouldn't be sorry, Sam. It's not your fault."

He shrugged. "All right. Then I'm not sorry. No hard feelings?"

She shook her head. "No hard feelings, Sam, honey. I just respect you more."

Sam, not knowing what to say, nodded, and closed the door. Back in his own room, he tried to gather his thoughts. He was disappointed, but he was almost glad. By leaving as she requested, he had gained more of her confidence and trust than he could have if he had stayed. It was hard to leave, but tonight was just not the night, not yet.

Self-styled man of the world Marty had said if you didn't make it by the third date, you wouldn't make it at all. On the other hand, if it were a one night stand, that's all it would be, ever. Bam, bam, thank you ma'am. Fran wasn't that kind of a girl and that wasn't the kind of relationship Sam was looking for. Though, if he were honest with himself, he didn't know what he was looking for.

He lay in bed listening to the pop click of the ineffective radiator and watching the beams of light on the carpet as the moon drifted on its passage. Hell, he was just a PFC, a draftee, with only a two-year obligation and then he would go back to Chicago and finish his aborted college degree. This was just an interlude. He wasn't committed to anything or anybody. In his confusion about his situation he almost forgot about Fran lying there in the next room.

What did it all mean, anyway? What were his intentions, aside from getting laid? Was she just a sexual object? He compared his relationship with Fran with Betty, back in Iron Mountain. He had seduced her, or maybe she had seduced him to satisfy her own agenda. He'd thought at first that he was being manly and persuasive. The whole thing turned out to be a fiasco. He told himself he was more considerate and understanding with Fran that he had been with Betty. If was all very confusing. He didn't want this affair with Fran to be another failure, yet so far it seemed that it was.

Maybe not.

He heard the connecting door open and Fran was there, now in her pajamas, standing beside his bed to apologize. "I'm sorry I disappointed you, Sam."

He looked up, pulled himself up on his elbows. Had she changed her mind? "I've disappointed myself. Why don't we just forget about it? You haven't hurt my feelings. I hope I haven't hurt yours." Still, it wasn't pleasant to be rejected. No rejection was pleasant. He was sure that Marty wasn't being rejected by Yetta up in Davos this weekend. But Yetta was a party girl; Fran wasn't.

Fran touched him on his bare shoulder to comfort him, but that touch might be a risk that ignited passion or turned into a promise. "Why don't we just forget the whole thing?" she suggested. "Maybe I shouldn't see you again."

"Is that the way you want it?" If they broke it off, it would be another failure. He didn't want that, either. Sam took her wrist, pulled himself up and kissed her. "Whatever you want." He did not agree or disagree with her decision, nor did he have any idea where this relationship would go if given a chance. If she wanted to break it off, he had no hold on her. It was her decision.

She kissed him on the mouth and made a quick retreat to the connecting door. "Goodnight, Sam."

If that was it, that was it. His thoughts turned to what was next. He remembered the ever-present railway timetable that ruled over his precious hours of escape from the Army. "Want to get up early tomorrow? We have to take the early train, but there's time for an early walk. We might even be

able to ski up and down the street a little." He
admitted that hauling their skis all the way to
Zermatt had been wishful thinking.

"Knock at my door. I'll be up."

"We'll probably have to take separate trains
from Bern, but we'll be together until then."

The room was chilly. Sam pulled the blanket
around his shoulders. If she didn't want him, what
did she want? He didn't think Fran was a frigid
bitch, and he didn't think she was what some guys
called a prick teaser. But how many times would
she reject prospective lovers before they stopped
showing an interest? Would she always be alone?

Would he? He didn't have an idea of a dream
girl, some imaginary perfect woman, if such
existed, and he didn't think he'd fit the part of
some woman's perfect man. I'm Sam Logan,
private, here I am, broken nose and weak lungs
and all. What you see is what you get, if that's what
you want, if that's what you'll settle for. He didn't
see himself as much of a bargain. It was
depressing.

Even though, by their own standards, Sam and
Fran were both up early the next morning, by the
time they got to the dining room they were almost
the last ones. They ate breakfast in silence in the
hotel's dining room, coffee, rolls, cheese, jam, and
a skimpy plate of cold cuts. She avoided looking at
him, didn't mention what had happened the night
before.

It was Sunday. Though the church bell rang its
summons, it was ignored by the tourists. In the
crisp, early morning air small parties were heading

for the ski tows or the mountain paths. Some carried only their skis. Others were laden with great rucksacks bulging with loaves of bread and bottles of wine as they climbed toward some distant mountain hut.

Sam and Fran were not among them. Probably other tourists had a week to spend, but Sam and Fran had only a long weekend. Their free time was over and all that remained was the complicated connections back to Germany. They walked beside each other, not arm in arm. This time Sam had remembered his gloves, the colorful ones Fran had given him.

The snow was more brilliant than the day before, for this morning the sun was on it. The Matterhorn still showed white and imposing beyond the ridges. On Saturday the mountain had been a symbolic moment of truth in Sam's romantic imagination. Now that memory was becoming no more than a picture postcard like those that turn up in an old shoe box of souvenirs.

As they prepared to leave Zermatt, they had different destinations. Each lost in their own thoughts, Sam and Fran had not spoken for some time when Sam finally said, "We have to see about our schedules. There's not much time before the train leaves."

They walked down the street through the snow toward the station, answering the Christmas greetings of skiers starting out for a morning's sport.

Only a few travelers were in the station. Most of those who were leaving would be on the afternoon train. Sam asked, "Is your bag packed? I guess we'd better not forget our skis." Remembering that gear he felt foolish. It was like the guy who brings along a fishing rod on an ocean liner, as if one might stop the Queen Mary in mid ocean to throw out a line. He told himself it might have worked out if they hadn't missed a connection.

Fran said nothing but turned back to the hotel while Sam consulted timetables at the station. Having missed one connection on the way south, he didn't trust his notes.

In a few minutes he rejoined her in the hotel lobby. He had two slips of paper and gave one to Fran. "Here's your connections."

"Thanks."

"Your schedule worked out fine. Brig to Bern to Basel and then on to Heidelberg or Mannheim."

Fran looked at the last notation and sighed. "I won't get much sleep again. Don't get in until two in the morning. It's a long ride."

Sam paused, hesitant and apologetic. "I'm afraid I can't be with you past Brig. There's only a couple of trains, and if I go with you as far as Bern I miss my connection to Munich."

"We both have to be back on time."

"Yes," Sam admitted. "Duty calls. Maybe we should have gone to Davos with Marty and Yetta."

"I can't stand your friend Marty."

"He's just my roommate. He isn't hard to get along with." Sam tentatively took her hand.

Fran shook her head. "He isn't serious about anything."

"I'm too series about everything."

"I've nothing against that, Sam. It speaks well of you." She looked up the street. "We've had a nice trip."

Yes, Sam thought. *We've had a weekend's worth of scenery and trains, even if we didn't ski as planned.* He indicated the camera hanging on its strap around his neck. "I'll do the pictures during the week." As usual he would develop the weekend's film on Monday at the service club, then make prints on Tuesday or Wednesday.

"Will you mail me some at the Schrieder?"

"I thought I might give them to you personally, maybe next weekend?" Sam's tone was hopeful, but lacked conviction or enthusiasm.

"I'm going to Garmisch with some friends from Heidelberg. Big New Year's Party."

"I see."

Sam had expected something like that. She might or might not have plans for New Year's. Her tone and expression convinced him that she hadn't changed her mind since the night before. She was going to keep on running away as she had from the man in New York.

Sam coughed self-consciously. He zipped his jacket and pretended to check their skis in the vestibule rack. "We didn't get to use these after all. Sure lugged them around." He looked nervously at Fran but she averted her eyes, looked down at her boots.

He had to touch her arm to get her to look at him, and even then there was an embarrassment in her eyes. Often she was unfocussed as if she weren't looking at anything at all, but now she avoided his eyes, as if she had seen something and didn't like what she saw, or was ashamed. He had to say something. "Take it easy, won't you?"

For a moment she did look at him and forced a smile. "I'll be all-right."

Their intimate knowledge of each other brought them together, but their embarrassment kept them apart.

She seemed to get over it on the leg of the journey to Brig where they had to take separate paths. On the funicular train down from Zermatt they had a compartment to themselves and cuddled as they looked out the window at the spectacular scenery, each lost in thought. It had been an emotional weekend, Sam thought, and he didn't know when if he ever would see Fran again. She'd rejected him, but then again, she hadn't. He didn't know where he stood.

When the train pulled in at Brig and they had to change, taking different trains from there, they stood together on the platform ignoring the other tourists and held each other in an embrace. Her kiss was warmer and wetter than he expected.

As they parted, she said with a smile, "Be good, Sam."

Had she started to cry again? He didn't know. He would think about that all the way back to Munich. "Be good" sounded to him like good by forever.

Chapter Nine

Monday Morning Interlude

Sam was in the supply room, typing a letter to his father on a beat up Olympia standard manual typewriter when Marty stuck his head in the door and waved some yellow forms. "Hey, Buddy Boy, how about going with me to the personnel office while I deliver the morning report?"

Sam took the letter out of the typewriter and put it in the pocket of his fatigues. He didn't like to leave letters behind even though he didn't think the supply sergeant was much of a reader. "Alright. He took his field jacket down from the hook where it hung.

They walked down the hall and out of the building before Marty said anything. Finally, unable to restrain his curiosity any longer, Marty asked, "How'd you make out in Zermatt?"

Sam buttoned his jacket. It was an old one he had borrowed from stock while his was at the quartermaster laundry. "Not so hot. We missed a train connection and then it was too late in the day and we were too tired to do any skiing."

"I'm not asking about the skiing," Marty said. He shifted his morning report to his left hand as an officer approached. His snappy salute didn't satisfy.

The officer was a stranger in the caserne and looked suspiciously at the sloppy soldiers in fatigues and low quarter shoes instead of regulation combat boots. He sneered, but said nothing.

Sam waited until after the salute before continuing. "Let's just say I didn't make out and leave it at that, shall we?"

"Allright."

"I suppose you and Yetta spent all your time in bed." Sam's tone was bitter and tinged with jealousy.

Marty's shoulders were hunched. "She was in bed, but I wasn't. We tried skiing and she hurt her back again."

"Serious?"

"I don't know how bad it is. She's going to the hospital this morning to see if anything's cracked. The long drive back in the Green Beetle didn't help any."

"That's too bad." Sam put his hands in the pockets of the faded jacket. His Army issue gloves were lost somewhere... yes, must be in his overcoat. The knit gloves Fran had given him were too colorful to be worn with an Army uniform and were in their flat box in his wall locker. The Christmas ribbon was there, too, but he had set up the framed portrait of her on the four drawer dresser they shared.

"Yetta's a real nice girl," Marty said, as if surprised.

"I'm surprised. I didn't think you'd be interested in nice girls."

Marty opened the door to the personnel office. "I'm not as bad a guy as you think, Sam." He dropped the morning report in the tray on the counter. "Let's go get the mail."

Sam smiled. So that's why Marty wanted him along. The Christmas rush of mail was still on and the mail bags were bound to be heavy. Fetching the bags was Marty's responsibility, though Sam sorted the mail.

They walked in silence for a few yards. Then Sam asked, "How do things stand between you and Yetta? I mean, besides her back."

Marty's heavy brows bushed together. "She's got me worried about her. You know me, Sam. I never worried about anybody."

"That's a change for the better. How'd it happen?"

"I learned a lot about her and her life. We had a long talk on the drive back last night." They had reached regimental headquarters. The mail room was in the basement.

"Oh?"

"Did you know she's thirty-five years old?"

That was about ten years older than Marty. Sam asked, "You didn't find out Fran's age, did you?"

"No. She's younger, though."

Their age difference was something Sam had not thought about. His relationship with Fran was tenuous enough without adding another disquieting factor. "Old" was ten years older than you were, so to a fifteen-year-old twenty-five was ancient. The French had an expression—a woman of a certain age—which meant they were experienced in love, knew what they wanted, and how to get it.

Marty didn't know Fran's age. Sam hadn't thought about women's biological clocks, their critical window of opportunity if they wanted children. He wasn't thinking about marriage or making babies, only about avoiding making a baby by accident. He hadn't finished college, and if he knocked someone up that would force him to reset all his plans, such as they were, which wasn't much beyond getting out of the Army. He had no clue about what Fran's plans might be, if she was seriously looking for a husband, or if she saw him as a possible candidate. She was in Europe to escape her past and to have fun, at least, that's the way he saw it. He assumed, rightly or wrongly, that she was in Europe to have a fling. He was in the Army because he had no other viable choice, and Germany was a heck of a lot better place than Korea.

They'd reached the mail room at regimental headquarters. At the mail room window Marty asked, "Anything for Detachment A?" The clerk nodded and disappeared. Marty continued, "Yetta's nice. She thinks a lot of me," something which seemed to surprise him.

Sam smirked. "How'd that happen?"

Marty missed the sarcastic insinuation. "You'd be surprised. We have a lot in common."

"I wish I could say the same about me and Fran."

The mail clerk, a skinny blonde kid who didn't look strong enough to lift a heavy mail bag, returned with four small bundles. Two were letters held together by a rubber band which Marty stuffed in the pockets of his field jacket. He gave

Sam the others. "Is that all? No late Christmas packages?"

"They all come by troop ship," the kid explained. "Must have been delayed."

Sam already had his Christmas present, a very nice lambs wool men's sweater his father had sent. It was too large for him, and he realized it had to be from one of the men's clothing stores whose advertising account his father had. The sweater had arrived with no note and the tag intact. It was stamped "sample."

Leaving the mail room, Marty asked, "What about you and Fran? Something go wrong?"

Sam peeked at the return addresses on the letters Marty had handed him. He hadn't gotten a letter from his father in weeks. Christmas was always a busy time for the advertisers. For some, if they didn't have major sales over that holiday, they didn't survive. Then his father might have trouble collecting bills for the advertising. Sam didn't want to talk about his aborted evening with Fran. "I think she decided to give up men and be an old maid."

Marty didn't believe that. "No kidding? Well, any American girl who's still single at twenty-five thinks she's going to be an old maid. Yetta was married. She's divorced now."

"She never mentioned that."

"And don't you, either. Discretion." Marty winked. "When she was laid up with her bad back she was feeling pretty low and told me. Her marriage was an unhappy deal." He sounded sympathetic.

Since Sam's hands were full of mail, Marty opened the door for him and they stepped out into the Munich cold. "Yetta tried to hide her disappointment. I guess that's why she laughs all the time. Talks about having a ball and all that crap."

Sam hadn't been able to put up a false front. After the Zermatt fiasco he didn't laugh muich.

Marty was suspicious of Sam's silence. "Just what did happen with you and Fran in Switzerland? Someone steal the Matterhorn? You told me you didn't get to ski after all. So did you spend the whole time in bed? Sounds good to me."

"No, wise guy." Failures were bad enough without having to talk about them. "I just flubbed the whole thing. I don't know what went wrong."

"Well, things between me and Yetta look fine. She as much as said that when her back gets better we'll take off for a weekend and make up for lost time."

"Next weekend?"

"If she's well enough." Marty grinned.

"You sound more like a shack rat than a nurse maid."

"No, Sam. For once it's not just another shack job. I've get better interests in her than that."

Well, that was new. If it were true, Sam would have respect for Marty. It sounded like Marty was serious, a change for the better.

"You seeing Fran next weekend?"

"No. She's going to Garmisch with some friends."

"Someone cutting you out, eh? Going to try to run into her there? Sort of like, by accident?"

Sam didn't want to admit that. "She's putting me off. I don't think she wants to see me again."

"Did you have a fight?"

"Not exactly." Sam fussed with his shapeless fatigue hat and seemed to be busy trying to position it just right on his forehead like Beetle Baily.

"What then? Attempted rape? Remember what it says in the Universal Code of Military Justice. Rape means life imprisonment." Marty raised a menacing finger, but he wasn't serious. He seldom was serious. His talk about Yetta was an exception.

Sam coughed. "I wish you wouldn't pry into my affairs, Marty. One minute she says we shouldn't see each other again; then she gives me a hot kiss goodbye. I don't know where I stand."

He wanted to see Fran again, if only to redeem himself. At first he had fantasized about a night of sex without attachments, but that would be too easy. He realized he was too serious to indulge in what some might call casual, recreational sex. You didn't just hop into bed unless you cared about someone. He hoped Fran cared about him. If it was going to be a brief affair, at least it should end amicably, no hard feelings, no anger, and no disappointment. As things stood, it was an unfinished chapter, not even *coitus interruptus*. He would have to see Fran again for clarification. One minute she'd been rejecting him; then they necked and snuggled on the train to Brig. What the hell?

"Why not forget about it?" Marty asked.

"Maybe you're right. She's going to Garmisch and I'll go somewhere else. Maybe I'll ski. Maybe I'll get drunk."

Marty scoffed. "You never get drunk. You're afraid to loosen up. Now you sound like a little kid who runs off in a corner to feel sorry for himself. No whining, Buddy Boy."

That hurt. "Can't I do anything without you twisting my reasons? How many times have you gone off to get drunk?"

"Only on occasions when I have nothing better to do."

"I suppose that's an honorable enough reason for getting drunk. "

Marty taunted him. "Just because you didn't make out you're going to run away and cry. Be a good little boy, Sammy, or Mommy will make you sit in the corner."

His mother had called him Sammy before she died, years ago. He usually remembered her with joy, but now that name for him, Sammy, made him feel childish and angry. He took a deep breath and gripped the bundles of letters to keep his hands from shaking. "Do we always have to fight?"

Marty shook his head as they approached their building. "You know me. I'm too much of a coward to fight. That's why I'm just a company clerk." Marty reached inside his jacket and took the tiny pipe out of his shirt pocket. He sucked on it thoughtfully without filling or lighting it. "Tell you what. To make you feel better, I'll drive you to the station to catch whatever train you're taking this weekend. Save you some cab fare. OK?"

"Thanks." Sam immediately forgot their argument. He shifted his thoughts to the New Year's weekend. Plans had to be made for the next escape to freedom from Detachment A.

"And I won't even charge you," Marty added.

"Miracles, miracles." Sam wondered where he would go next weekend. Military rail tickets were dirt cheap. The dollar was still worth four Deutsch marks and you could get a nice meal for about five marks if you didn't need a tablecloth and wine. It was a three-day pass, but he didn't have much money left after the Zermatt trip even after that one star hotel. It would have to be someplace close and cheap, someplace in Bavaria where he could ski and have a quiet New Year's by himself. He told himself he could have a good time on his own.

Chapter Ten

The Fifth Weekend—Sam and the General's Girl

By 11:25 on Saturday morning Sam was already in Immenstadt to change trains for Obersdorf in the Black Forest. Exploring the system of the Deutsche Bundesbahn was an adventure. Though the distance between Obersdorf and Munich was not great, the town was so set off in a corner of the Black Forest that Sam had to change trains twice to get there, lugging his skis, poles, and bag in and out of compartments.

He preferred being able to settle down in one seat for an entire journey, but conceded that if he were going to tuck himself away where he would not be reminded of Fran he had to be content with the inconvenience of and the risk of getting stranded if he'd made a mistake looking up his connections in the thick, complicated book of timetables. Puzzling through the codes of the timetables was fun, but one could make a mistake, like when certain trains didn't run every day of the week. On most weekends it would be a mere inconvenience if he missed a train, but the error he'd made on the Zermatt trip had caused him and Fran to arrive too late to ski. It was a fiasco and was his fault.

It was quiet and the temperature would be just right for skiing, in the Fahrenheit twenties with bright sunshine reflecting off the snow. He expected that when he got to Obersdorf some people would be skiing without their shirts on.

Aside from the little railway station there didn't seem to be much of a town at Immenstadt. He stood with some apprehension at the small *bahnhof.* There were only three platforms, widely spaced, and ample sidings and ancient trackside buildings. The real marshalling yards were on the main lines, but the atmosphere here was that of a small, provincial station where trains were slow and so infrequent that the novelty of seeing them come in was about the only excitement for the local children.

Just when he was beginning to think he'd made a mistake in his timetable, the train, powered by an old locomotive that wheezed with a sigh of steam to a clanking stop, pulled in at the station. Besides the locomotive there were only three passenger cars, one first class, two second. Sam was about to reach up for the handle of the door to the second class car when he saw a girl struggling with her skis and a suitcase trying to board the other end of the same car. Sam wanted someone to talk to and leaned his skis against the car while he opened the door for her. "*Darf ich?*" he asked politely.

She was wearing a bright green ski jacket with a hood. A pair of goggles with dark lenses was jammed into a breast pocket. She looked at him a little breathlessly. "*Dankeschoen.*"

After helping her on board, Sam picked up his skis and followed her into the train. Up to now he had been tired. He had stayed up to watch the typical New Year's fireworks display. He helped her stow her skis on top of the luggage rack and followed his usual practice when traveling alone in civvies to speak German. He needed the practice. He asked in the best German he could muster, *"Fahren Sie nach Obersdorf?"*

The girl had pushed her hood back, revealing red hair. She gave him an uncomfortably long look as if he had said something impertinent or inappropriate in his schoolbook German. Finally, she said, "I must say, your accent is horrible."

Sam laughed, embarrassed. He had thought for sure she was German. If she were, her English was perfect and she completely fooled him. On the other hand, her accent almost sounded like British English, learned in school. Yet, it wasn't quite right for that, either. He said, "You didn't answer my question."

"Yes, I'm going to Obersdorf. Why?"

"I heard there's good skiing there, not alpine, of course. I've been to the Zugspitze. A bit more than I can handle."

She told him, yes, she'd been to Obersdorf before and the skiing on the Nebelhorn was very good, but her answers were clipped as if she didn't really want to talk to him.

He got the message and shut up. He looked out the window. The train was starting. A few children in snow suits stood on the platform and waved. Sam waved back. Then they were out of sight.

The roadbed was not in good repair and the car swayed. The main line tracks were all welded, but not this old spur. The wheels bumped and clicked on the joints in the rails and began to get louder. Wheels clicked against the joints.

"Hear that? Sam asked.

"What?"

"The click-click. You may have noticed the sound is different in the United States." He realized it was because the car had single axles, not four wheel trucks. In the States the train wheels went clickety-click. In an old Shirley Temple movie the starlet had pronounced the sound "honeymanoosh."

"I've never been to the United States," she said.

"American passenger rail cars have four wheels at each end of the car, but here, these old cars have only two. The American sound is clickety-click, but here it's just click-click, unless you're on a main express line. American rails are laid down in sections. The German main lines are welded. The German expresses just scream along."

She was obviously bored and could hardly wait for the train to get to the destination. Sam realized that his interest, not an obsession, in the German railways system was not everyone's cup of tea, or glass of beer, or whatever. He was being a jerk. He shut up and watched Immenstadt fade in the distance as the mountains loomed ahead. He was sitting across from the girl and stretched out, careful not to kick her. Like him, she was wearing flexible-soled ski boots you could climb in.

Her face seemed familiar. That red hair. He felt compelled to ask, "Didn't I see you when I changed trains at Buchlos?"

"You might have."

This was going nowhere. Where had he heard that accent? "Then you must have come from Munich."

"That's right."

This wasn't the tourist season. She must live in Germany. "Say, you're not from New Zealand, are you?"

She laughed. That was a good sign.

"Staying at the *Goldene Traube*?" It was a guess.

That clicked. Now she was curious. "How did you guess?"

Now he remembered. Sam fumbled in his pocket and took out the imitation Swiss Army knife with the corkscrew. "This. I opened a bottle of wine for you. Remember? Couple of weeks ago at Yetta's room. She'd just moved in."

"Yetta?"

"A friend of Sally Ann's."

"Oh, of course. Now I remember. You're a friend of Yetta's private—Marty Vidal I believe his name is. I've forgotten yours."

"Sam Logan. Marty's my roommate. And you're Kay." That she remembered Marty's full name was remarkable. He was trying to remember what was up with Kay. It was such a brief meeting.

The conversation died again. The train wheels click-clicked.

"Yetta hurt her back pretty badly. She's been in bed all week," Kay said.

"Oh?" Marty hadn't mentioned that. Sam knew she hadn't been well on New Year's but he thought she was back to work all week.

"He's been up to see her every night, nursing her. Didn't he mention it?"

"No." Apparently Marty didn't talk about everything he did. Usually he insisted on Sam's hearing all about the latest liaison, always in detail. "He only said he was going out."

Kay seemed cannily interested. "The entire *Goldene Traube* has been talking about that private of hers."

"Marty? He's a corporal."

"Corporal then."

Sam nearly shuddered at the thought of all that gossip. What might people be saying about him and Fran? So much for discretion.

"Yes. He's a regular nurse. Faithful as a St. Bernard."

"More like a sheep in wolf's clothing. I never thought he was that serious about anything." So much for gossip. Now he was doing it.

"Perhaps you know him better than I do. Perhaps you don't know him at all, even if he is your roommate. Sally Ann says he's a gem, but she's partial. He's always making her bicarbonate of soda for her hangovers. I will say it looks like he's in love with Yetta." The way she said 'love" gave the word a peculiar quality. Was she being ironic? Sarcastic?

Sam hadn't seen Marty as a loving sort of person. "I suppose that's possible. I can't imagine him mooning about and love struck."

"Just because you live with a person doesn't mean you really know them," Kay said. She paused, thinking about the situation. "He was with her when she fell. Skiing, wasn't it? At Davos?"

Sam felt he was being quizzed. Marty hadn't filled him in on he details, and even if he knew, was it any business of Kay's? All that gossip made him nervous and he didn't really want to be a busybody. "I guess he was… with her when she fell."

"He certainly sees a lot of her." Kay seemed aware of his reluctance to talk about it, but she persisted. "I'm generally not interested in things like that, but everyone has noticed their, er, affair. I've seen him in the lobby a few times myself."

Sam was equivocal. "Marty's full of surprises." He might put on a front with his tiny pipe and that outrageous cigarette holder, but there was more to him than that. Sam hadn't seen it before. For a change, Marty seemed actually sincere and unselfish.

Apparently satisfied that Sam wasn't going to give her any more information, or didn't know any, Kay was quiet. They rode along in silence, listening to the click-click of the train.

Sam finally broke the silence. "Funny, meeting you on the train like this."

"Not really. Half the people I know in Munich I meet on the trains. When else am I out of the office?"

"Do you go to Obersdorf often?"

No answer.

"This is my first trip."

Kay's expression clouded. What did he want? "So?"

"I was wondering if you could recommend a hotel."

"There are several good ones. But this weekend you'll be lucky to get a room anywhere."

"Where do you stay?"

"I'd rather not say." She evasively looked out the window at the passing forest, or maybe at nothing at all.

Sam exhaled slowly and waited. You never knew. He had a brief fantasy about a room shortage and sharing one with her, a thought he dismissed as foolish.

"I'm meeting someone."

Well, that might explain her hesitancy. What was it the other women had said about Kay? He'd forgotten. "You're getting a late start. Someone as interested in skiing as you are would have left last night. You've missed a morning on the slopes."

That was easy. "Last night was New Years Eve," she explained. "We had a party."

She couldn't have partied very late and still be up bright and early for those train connections. Sam leaned his head back. The old-fashioned wooden bench cut into his neck. Marty had gone to a party at Yetta's last night. Sam had been invited, but had felt that the "party" was for two. Sam stayed in the barracks to save money and to avoid being a third wheel. He'd had nothing to celebrate, stayed up until the midnight fireworks, then went to bed. Marty had been out most of the night, but true to his word had got up early to give Sam the promised ride to the station.

"I looked in on your friend Yetta. The corporal—Marty—was there. Seemed to be having a good time."

Sam chuckled. "I'm sure he did, judging from the shape he was in when he got up this morning to drive me to the *bahnhof*."

"Hangover?"

"I should say so." Sam was picking up on Kay's accent. He liked the sound of her voice but he didn't want to appear to be mimicking her. The New Zealand accent was more clipped and precise than the redneck drawl of his supply sergeant boss.

Sam was painfully aware of the awful American accents some people had when trying to speak German. Kay had noted his flat, Midwestern accent. Even when he was in civvies his accent in German gave him away.

Thinking about Marty, who outranked him by one stripe and enjoyed a few dollars a month more in pay, Sam admitted a twinge of envy. "Marty likes his brandy."

"I know."

Just what did she know? "Being a corporal Marty can almost afford a car, that Green Beetle Volkswagen, though he scrimps on the gas."

He recalled sitting with that jerry can full of Army fuel in the back of the car on the way to Switzerland. It was too bad payday wasn't until Monday. End of the month and he was pretty much tapped out. Lucky the train tickets were cheap. He figured if he couldn't afford the lift ticket at Obersdorf he'd just climb the hill like the other cheapskates. "I'm lucky if I can buy a beer."

Kay looked at him sharply. He detected a hint of that British class system. "Perhaps you just aren't officer material." There were the officers, and then the non persons, the noncoms.

Sam didn't think much of the officers he had seen. His CO was a drunk who hardly came into the office except to sign the passes and on payday to dole out the cash. The exec wasn't much better, a battlefield commission. Neither of them were West Point types. There were hierarchies among the officers, too. And of course, he was at the bottom. "The officers I've seen were no models of integrity. I think the Army attracts a certain type. They're not even warriors. Just a bunch of bums in uniforms who couldn't survive in the business world."

"And what world do you come from?" Kay asked, obviously bristling as if his disparaging comments reflected on her.

"My family's in advertising. My father has a pretty successful firm in Chicago." He didn't say he had no desire to go into that business, coming up with ads for end-of-year sales, 'fifty percent off and don't miss this deal.'

Kay was a civilian and not even an American. What did she care if he had a bad attitude toward U.S. Army officers? But then he remembered and realized he had put his foot in it. Someone had said, was it Yetta? that Kay was a general's mistress.

He had better keep his mouth shut and avoid trouble. He realized that gossip could travel. His views of the Army might well trickle up to the general, whoever he was, and trickle back down to his company, distorted at every repetition like that old party game of telephone. God knows what rumors he might be setting off. One word from the general and he might be transferred to some patrol on the East German border, facing down a bunch of nervous Russian peasants with machine guns.

He'd better sidestep this chance encounter with Kay. "Is the party you're meeting going to be at the station?" If the general were meeting her at the train he'd better become invisible. Sam squirmed uncomfortably and self-consciously rubbed the bridge of his broken nose.

"No!"

She said it with such vehemence he was reassured. "Then, since you've been there before, maybe you could point me in the direction of a cheap place to stay in Obersdorf."

"You might get a berth in a dormitory."

Click-click.

The sound of the wheels was slowing down. They were arriving in Obersdorf.

The train jerked to a halt. Arriving on the platform Sam saw that the single platform, under a long, low roof, was the end of the line. Beyond were nothing but mountains, high, but not as spectacular as the rugged Swiss Alps. The Black Forest mountains were more like Appalachia.

Zermatt had been the end of the line, too. Sam hoped this weekend would not end with the same indecision and frustrated hopes.

There was no one waiting for Kay on the platform and Sam followed her, having difficulty keeping up with her brisk walk. The skis on her shoulder were like an integrated part of her body. Sam's had come on loan from the service club and were, he had to admit, a little too long for his size. He had put on a couple of pounds since he got out of the hospital, but that long in bed had caused his muscles to atrophy, and he was clumsy. No wonder he kept falling down on the ski slopes. He kept tripping on the thick soles of his ski boots.

A few hundred yards up the single street Kay stopped and turned. "There's a nice hotel a few doors on. You can't miss it. I'm afraid I have to leave you here." She pointed to a building on her left, the *Gasthof zum Traube*, which Sam translated as Inn at the Grape. It seemed half the inns in Germany were named after stags or grapes.

Sam nodded and when he turned to look up the street he saw a banner hung across announcing a ski club meet. That plus the New Year's holiday meant he might not find a room at all. It was the risk of taking off on an impulse without planning. That and the risk of getting the train connections wrong like he did in Switzerland.

Obersdorf was too small a place to have the typical *Zimmernachweiss* tourist office like you found in the railway stations of big cities. The first hotel he tried was booked solid. So was the second. If he were to avoid encountering Kay and her general, he'd better not look for a room there. He exhausted all the other possibilities, then turned back to the *Zum Traube* after all.

The sprawling *Gasthof zum Traube* looked to be the biggest hotel, several stories high. General or no general, Sam needed a roof. He entered the lobby, racked his skis inside the entrance, and approached the registration desk before he realized Kay was there, talking on the phone. She spotted him.

Sam shrugged sheepishly. He didn't want her to think he was dogging her. He apologized, "Full up down the street."

Kay frowned at him and turned away as she got her connection.

The clerk at the registration desk was dressed in a formal jacket in a regional style, something he had seen in a *Heimat* film, the typical south German movie that ended with a clop dance, girls in dirndls, the men in lederhosen. Sam asked *"Haben ein einzelzimmer?"*

Again his accent gave him away. "I'm sorry, sir, but our rooms are fully booked."

Shit, Sam thought. If he didn't get a room he wasn't going to sleep in a snow bank. He might have to take the next train out again.

Seeing his disappointment, the clerk offered, "We have beds in the dormitory on the top floor."

That was his last option. Sam filled out the pink registration form and showed his military ID card.

He overheard Kay saying, "But Bill. We had plans for this weekend. Yes, I know, but... what? Not coming? After I..." Kay looked over her shoulder at Sam and gave him a murderous look.

Sam turned his back and remained defensively hunched over the registration form but he still heard her say, "I can't talk now. There's someone here... some GI ... No of course he's not with me. I'll call you later... not at home? Where then? Now don't get excited. I'll see you on Monday and... but you took this chance before."

Sam finished filling out the registration form and retrieved his government ID He didn't want to hear more. It was none of his business.

Kay's quick anger abated and was crushed by something she heard on the phone. "Is that it? All our plans? You promised... Hello? Bill?" Kay hung up the phone and pushed it back across the counter to the clerk. Her expression was blank and her eyes dull. She turned to look at Sam and bit her lip.

Sam held up the form and said, "The rooms are all booked, but they can get me a bed in the dormitory."

Kay's eyes were stony. "You can go to hell."

She must think I'm following her, Sam thought.

Kay spoke briefly to the clerk. "Have my bag sent up to my room. I'll be back later." She surged across the lobby, retrieved her skis from the rack, and left.

Sam watched her go. He exchanged the registration slip for a key attached to a polished wooden ball with the hotel's name on it and followed the clerk's directions to the stairs that led to the top floor dormitories, one for men, one for women and a couple of unisex bathrooms, plus a single, separate shower with a sign *Dusch*. There were a dozen cots, most of them already occupied. He picked the last one near a little window that looked out on the ski slope and the street below the hotel terrace. He thought he saw Kay's green jacket among the people lining up for the T-bar tow.

The dormitory cot reminded him of his Army basic training barracks. It was a bare mattress with a folded blanket, sheet, pillow, and a rough-looking towel all stacked neatly at the head of the bed. This was the minimum, but the price was right.

He'd get a bit of lunch before skiing. He unzipped his bag and realized he'd made a mess of packing. He had brought a heavy, wool sweater, a white shirt but no tie, had forgotten extra socks and even his razor. Usually he packed automatically for a weekend, depending on habit. Now he felt aimless and ineffectual.

He washed up and went down to the ground floor hotel restaurant for lunch. The dining room was crowded with skiers and local characters. Sam liked the rustic atmosphere. The local people wore work boots, leather knickers, jackets decorated with horn buttons and leaf designs. Like cowboys who never take off their expensive hats, these wore floppy hats characteristic of this part of Germany. Under the rough, cord hatband of each was a carefully pinned *Gämsbart,* sticking up like a little whisk broom. Those who had not killed an antelope or bear for a souvenir to mount on their hats simply stuck in a sprig of evergreen.

At one table with a sign that said *Stamtisch,* reserved for the regulars, there were five locals drinking out of their personal steins, no doubt commenting about the tourists who had invaded the town.

Sam found an empty table and sat down. The hotel, he realized, was relatively new, and though the designs of the wrought iron decorations were traditional, they had a sameness that testified to a decorator, not a collection of bits accumulated over the years. Unlike older places he had visited, there were no historic initials and names carved into the wooden table top.

Sam picked up the menu and wistfully scanned the list. The Zermatt trip had been expensive and he was at the end of his last month's pay. His pocket was his bank. Being in the Army, he had no check book or savings account. He might tuck away a few bucks from time to time, and he could have amassed a significant stash while in the hospital, but he had spent most of that on his new camera. The cost of a bed in the dormitory was reasonable. At least he had his return tickets back to Munich, but his meal money was pretty limited. Obersdorf would be W*ürstchen* for lunch, the same sausage for supper and, thank God the Germans didn't serve it for the continental breakfast.

He ordered a sausage and, because German restaurants never did the automatic glass of ice water typical in the United States, he ordered a glass of light beer, *ein hellas*. The waitress in her black apron had just brought his order when Kay came into the dining room. As she passed his table, Sam said, "I thought you were going skiing."

"The lift doesn't run during the lunch hour," she said, pausing briefly at his table. She was clearly not eager to talk to him.

"Take it easy. Relax. Have a *würstchen.*"

Kay gave him a drop dead look and searched for a place at a table on the other side of the dining room.

Sam shrugged. It was just as well. He couldn't afford to buy her even a sausage for lunch anyway. He could see that she was upset for having been stood up, he presumed by her "general," and he was sympathetic. He knew how rejection felt.

He shouldn't have made those remarks about officers. That had put her off. Even though they had gotten off on the wrong foot, he didn't know anyone else at the hotel. He and Kay were both stationed in Munich. They had friends in common. It wasn't his fault that her date hadn't shown up. Maybe he could just happen to be on the ski slope at the same time.

But then he remembered how, as little more than an intermediate skier fresh off the bunny beginners run, he had not been able to keep up with Fran or Yetta. He was slow and kept falling down.

Well, even if Kay were an expert skier, she would have to return to the hotel at some time. He nursed his single glass of beer and the sausage as long as he could, waiting for Kay to leave, then tried to follow her. But he was delayed extricating his skis from the tangle of gear on the rack in the vestibule. When he did get outside, he saw Kay in her green jacket disappearing up on the T bar. He couldn't afford a lift ticket, so shouldered his skis and poles and started the long trudge up the beaten track used by others who were as broke or as cheap as he was.

At the base of the track he checked his camera. He had shot several pictures already, had only a few negatives left on the roll. He hadn't brought an extra roll of film.

He had not proceeded very far when he saw Kay pass him on her way down. She was a pretty good skier. Maybe she had learned in the mountains of New Zealand. He had not reached the top of the hill when she passed him on the T bar, going up. At this rate she would make several runs before he managed one. He did not catch sight of her again.

When Sam finally reached the top he found the snow a powdery dream, the air sparkling with clarity and cold. A few brave souls, macho guys, were skiing shirtless in the sunshine. Sam hesitated at the top of the run. It was really much more fun to be with someone.

Setting his camera for a picture of the scene and of the people coming off the lift at the top, he spotted Kay's green jacket. She must already be on her second or third run and he had only managed to climb to the top once. He was quick enough to snap a photo of her as she got off, but she didn't see him.

He started down the run, tried to concentrate on his turns. Those long ski trooper skis were hard to control, and he skidded too much when trying to go to the right. He knew he should put his weight farther forward, but his knees weren't very strong, and after falling several times he was beginning to lose confidence altogether. He'd fallen on his butt so often that the wallet in his hip pocket was going to leave a square bruise.

Finally, near the bottom of the hill he gave up, took off his skis, and walked the trampled snow down to the hotel. Time to take a break. It was already late afternoon and he was bruised and exhausted as much from picking himself back up as from trudging up to the top while others slid past on the T-bar.

The hotel had a terrace facing the ski hill. There, sitting at little tables in the waning sunshine and waited on by girls in local costumes and aprons, tourists were served coffee and hot chocolate. Sam checked his supply of Dmarks. At least he had enough for a cup of steaming hot chocolate. He settled down to watch the action on the hill and to recover.

He was pleased to see that he wasn't the only one prone to spills. He spotted Kay sliding to an expert stop at the bottom of the run, only a few yards from the terrace where he sat. She caught his eye and waved.

In a couple of minutes she had jammed her skis and poles into the snow bank, came to the terrace, and to his surprise came up to his table. "Mind if I join you?"

"I thought you were mad at me."

"Not mad at you. It's Sam, isn't it?"

"Yes. Sam Logan." He remembered the general. "I hope you don't mind sitting with a PFC."

"Why should I?" She apparently remembered his comments on the train. "You're the one with an attitude about rank."

"Sorry." Sam concluded that she was as much in need of company as he was and, not being a total stranger, it was OK to join him.

"You're not much of a skier," she said. "I watched you on the hill."

"I do it as an excuse to get away from the office. I'm not interested in visiting cathedrals or museums, and I like to ski, even though I'm not very good at it. I don't hang around in bars like most of the guys."

"Or go out carousing and picking up whores," Kay added.

Her frankness embarrassed him. He remembered the blonde he and Marty had picked up. "Well, not really my style." Was he blushing?

"I think you're shy, Sam."

Now he really was blushing. Marty might have retorted, "Try me," but that wasn't Sam's style. He struggled to respond, finally admitted, "I'm trying to get over it."

The waitress brought Kay a menu but, without looking at it, in her perfect German she ordered a coffee and *Schwartzwalder kirschtorte*, which Sam translated as Black Forest cherry cake.

"I saw you climbing up the Nebelhorn. Why didn't you take the tow?"

"Too broke," Sam admitted. "End of the month."

"You did find a room?"

"I'm in the dormitory up in the attic."

"I thought you'd be with someone this long holiday."

"You mean Fran?" In that billet those women must all know everyone's business. "She's gone to Garmisch with friends. What about you? On your own?" He already knew from overhearing her phone call, that her date wasn't coming.

"I was supposed to meet someone, but he's a no show."

"Too bad. That leaves you and me." He looked closely at her. She didn't avert her eyes.

"You're flirting."

Sam chuckled. "Why not?"

Her coffee and cake arrived. The sight of the cake and coffee and the handsome table setting was worthy of a souvenir photo. Without asking permission, Sam shot a picture of the cake, and sneaked a second one of Kay.

She didn't notice the second. Whatever she was thinking about she hid it while she stirred cream in her coffee from the little silver pot that was part of the elegant table service. When she did finally speak it came as a surprise. "Are you in love with Fran?"

That was a tough one, totally unexpected, but then that grapevine in the women's billet was pretty intrusive. Did everyone know everything? Did they all know what happened in Zermatt? Were there no secrets at all? Whatever happened to discretion?

Sam almost said yes, but if he did, that might short circuit anything that might happen right now between him and Kay. Instead he stammered, "I… I'm not sure. I haven't really thought about it. Are you in love with…" Sam was going to say "Bill" but remembered he wasn't supposed to have overheard her phone conversation or know anything about Kay's alleged affair with the general. "…your friend?"

Kay brightened, as though happy to have the opportunity to deny having any emotion. "Of course not. I don't believe in falling in love with anybody. It doesn't pay."

Sam remembered her obvious hurt when she made that telephone call. He didn't think her denial sounded sincere. He didn't want to think she could believe that love "didn't pay." In his romantic, Midwestern culture, Sam still thought, hoped, that love was something beautiful, ideal, wonderful.

Fran had said, "If you love me." That was using love as leverage, intimidation, even a threat. Was love a misconception? Did it have a definition at all? What did he, Sam Logan, know about love anyway? Nothing. Still he clung to the romantic idea even if he couldn't define it.

Coming from a Midwestern even Puritan ethic, Sam had been disappointed to find that much of the idealism was based on false premises. The land of the free and the home of the brave was OK if you were white. There was that American ideal one sang about in those patriotic songs. Kate Smith, the fat lady, always sang "America the Beautiful," and that was the flag one wrapped oneself in. But Sam saw fear of H-bombs, the iron curtain, the fear of atomic attack, and the sense that America was slipping in the estimation of the rest of the world. Fear bred a kind of hysteria about communism. Scandinavian, French and German socialists were not much less than communists, weren't they? It was all kind of crazy, all over, everywhere. Why else was he, Sam Logan, stationed in Munich as part of the occupation so long after the end of the war, with the East German and Russian communists right at the border? Was he supposed to preserve the American way of life for Germany? Sam Logan— supply clerk?

But Sam already knew there was a German way of life, a French way, a European way, and in spite of occasional labor strikes, everybody seemed to be content, even prosperous. The German *wirtschaftswunder*, thanks in part to the Marshall Plan, had rebuilt the industry American bombers had destroyed. There was no mass migration to the USA from Europe as there had been from Ireland during the potato famine. He was beginning to see past all the propaganda and speeches and found much of it to be, like Shakespeare said, full of sound and fury signifying nothing. He didn't believe any of it.

So what was left?

Well, maybe love. What really mattered to the individual was love. Except Sam didn't have it.

Mulling it all over at the table with Kay he asked, perhaps foolishly, "Don't you think love is important?"

Someone else might have ignored the question, perhaps because there was no easy answer. Kay was willing to engage. She spooned a bit of the whipped cream off her chocolate cherry cake and stirred it into her coffee. "That depends on your psychology. What do you think love is?"

Sam looked hungrily at the cake, regretting that he couldn't afford a piece. She noticed and took a bit of it on her pastry fork and held it across the table to him. It wasn't a tease. "Want to try some?"

"Well, I…"

Before he could protest she fed it to him. He savored the bit of chocolate cake and was self-consciously aware of that act of intimacy. "Very nice."

"We could share it," she offered.

"No. That's all right. You go ahead. It's getting close to dinner time. Wouldn't want to spoil my appetite." It was a lame excuse. His dinner would be another sausage. If he were flushed it would be wild boar chops or *rumpsteak*, good reason to ask the first sergeant what it took to be promoted to corporal. The few extra bucks would go toward some better meals.

The sample of cake had effectively dodged the issue of what love is and what it meant. The moment of psychological probing had mercifully passed. Asking an almost stranger for the meaning of love was, well, weird. Sam changed the subject. "What made you leave New Zealand and come to Europe? It's a long way. Must be expensive."

"I came to see the coronation in London."

"That's a long way from Munich."

"New Zealand is so far that when we do travel, we stay away for a long time. It's like the Grand Tour. I ran out of money and got stranded."

"But the job in Munich?" Sam didn't see the connection. "I thought just Americans worked for the U.S. military."

"It's NATO. New Zealand is part of the British Empire, so we qualify."

"So how long will you stay in Munich?"

"Depends. When I get bored I'll go back to Wellington."

Sam remembered the business with the elusive general. "You might get married." He said it as if it were a question. Wasn't marriage what all women wanted? Did he?

He didn't know about marriage. That was far from his thoughts. Being drafted put his life on hold for the duration.

It was getting colder on the terrace as the sun was setting behind the Nebelhorn. Most of the skiers were quitting for the day. Kay shivered. "I'd have to fall in love first," she said, smiling at him as if it were an invitation. She had unzipped her green jacket when she came out on the terrace sunshine. Now she zipped it up again. "I'm cold. Let's go inside."

She signaled, *"Fraulein?"*

The black-aproned waitress who brought the bill must have thought they were together for she had combined their orders. She started to hand the bill to Sam, but Kay snatched it away. "I'll get this one," she said.

"Gee," Sam said, gratefully. "Maybe I should have ordered some cake, too."

"Don't press your luck, Sam," she said with a teasing grin. "Let's go inside and you can tell me what love is."

Perhaps she wanted his answer for her own enlightenment. Perhaps she was as curious about Sam's views as he was with her disbelief. If Kay didn't believe in love, what did she believe in?

Sam didn't know. Dodging the bullet he joked, "We've hardly met and you're already talking about love!" He grinned. Was this a line Casanova might have used?

Kay refused to let him embarrass her. "I said I didn't believe in love, but you seem to. You should be able to say what it is." Perhaps, instead of being merely curious, she couldn't bear to see another person believe in something she denied. To destroy Sam's vague idea of love might reinforce her own disbelief.

It was like arguing with a determined missionary or a prosecutor determined to break down a witness. She was making him very uncomfortable, standing in the lobby while skiers coming off the slopes moved past them to stack their skis in the rack. "Is there some other place where we can talk about this?" Certainly not up in the attic in that dormitory.

"Let's go up to my room."

Oh.

Sam didn't know what to expect next. He watched while Kay asked the clerk to fetch her room key from its hook behind the counter. The hotel didn't have an elevator. Anyone who could ski the Nebelhorn had to have the legs for a couple of flights of stairs. She led the way and he followed, feeling obedient. It was like climbing the thirteen steps to the gallows. Won't you come into my parlor, said the spider to the fly?

Immediately Sam had fantasies of a seduction, except he was not prepared. He had not replaced the condom he usually carried in his wallet. He had put that on in Zermatt, though it was never used for its intended purpose. He dismissed the fantasy as foolish. They were just going to have a private conversation, nothing more, right? It was dumb to expect anything else.

Kay's room had an excellent view of the ski slopes and a double bed. It even had a private bath. Sam's own accommodation in the attic dormitory had unisex toilet facilities in a cramped space under the slanting roof. Kay's room was luxurious in a rustic, Black Forest sort of way. He almost expected a cuckoo clock, but no hotel guest would want to be cuckooed every hour. A painting on the wall of a snow scene looked to be an original. The window had double curtains, one set intended to block all light for people who liked to sleep in, and another, frilly curtain with a lace edge. At a small table by the window there were two chairs. It was a fine room with a view, a reminder that Sam was only a PFC at the end of the month's pay. He felt inferior with a twinge of envy.

This was where she had expected to have her tryst with the general, except the general hadn't come. Was Sam to be a substitute? Or was she going to have sex with him to spite the general for standing her up? That and all manner of unsubstantiated fantasies churned through his imagination.

Kay wasn't going to let him escape from the discussion. She took off the green jacket and dropped it on the bed. Then she sat on one of the chairs, complained about her ski boots, undid the double laces and took them off. She was wearing heavy, wool ski socks. Was she undressing, or just getting out of those ski clothes?

Sam was rather bewildered. She had fed him cake, now she was undressing. What next?

"So?" Kay asked. "What's love?"

She was not going to let him escape. "It's, well, needing someone, I guess. Didn't you ever need anyone?"

"Surely. My mother." Kay's New Zealand accent was crisp. "But she left me when I was young. I was raised by an uncle, a sheep rancher. Did you know there are more sheep in New Zealand than people?"

Sam didn't know that. A sheep farm in New Zealand was another world from Chicago's Gold Coast. Still, they had something in common, and he saw a connection. "Sounds like the story of my life, except for the sheep. I had just my father." He realized there wasn't much love in that relationship. His father wasn't a sports fan, and when Sam had his nose broken playing high school football his father told him it served him right. Sam wasn't big enough or tough enough for football.

"Just needing someone is a rather weak definition of love," Kay said.

"And having someone need you, I suppose." Sam sat on the chair opposite her and wished he were someplace else.

Not satisfied, Kay shook her head. "I think you need a glass of wine to loosen your brain." There was a telephone in the room and she called room service, ordered a bottle of Liebfraumilch and a platter of bread and cheese. Then she turned back to Sam. The interrogation continued. "Surely just needing someone isn't love. If you're sick you need a nurse. That doesn't mean you love her. You can do better than that, can't you Sam?"

Sam could see that Kay could be a pretty devastating partner, one of those who always has to be right, no compromise. Like a chess player facing inevitable defeat, he was ready to capitulate. "I'm afraid not. Not at the moment. Maybe you can teach me a definition of love."

"I told you I didn't believe in it. You forget easily."

"Then maybe you can show me how to live without it. I don't seem to be doing very well with my own definition."

"I'll drink to that," Kay said and, as if on cue, there was a knock at the door. A porter delivered a tray with a bottle of wine, two glasses, slabs of heavy *fulkorn* dark bread that looked like it had been sliced off a brick, butter formed into cunning little balls, and slices of assorted cheeses.

Kay, in charge, poured the wine. Sam raised his glass. Like Sally Ann, he said, "Cheers" and sipped.

"*Skål*," Kay said, sipping her own.

Sam was thinking of Fran. She was much different from Kay. Fran was a warmer, congenial sort, simpatico as they said, more fun to be with, though she could be withdrawn and tentative. Kay was anything but that. She was more like a sparring partner, waiting to get in the next punch. Of course, that might be fun, too, if you were the combative type. Sam wasn't. "Here's to you," he said, taking another sip.

"You can do better than that," Kay insisted. "Drink up. I can always order another bottle."

"Thanks." Sam spread some butter on one of the pieces of heavy bread. He'd only eaten a *bratwurst* since he arrived in Obersdorf, and that had been many hours and three train rides since a quick breakfast in the mess hall. He was afraid he might get drunk and make an ass of himself. He was also hungry. The cup of chocolate and taste of cake on the terrace was hardly a meal.

"This will help you forget that affair of yours," Kay said.

Damn. Those women knew everything about him. What had Yetta told her? Was Kay being malicious, sympathetic, or what? He didn't understand, but he could muster a reply. "And I'll help you forget the guy who stood you up."

"Touché." Now Kay was solemn. "To the affair that never was." She drank her wine slowly, sadly, and deliberately.

They succumbed to their own thoughts and ate in silence. When the first bottle was empty, she ordered another. Sam took off his own boots and jacket. It was warm in the room, and he took off his heavy, wool sweater, the one that was fine on a ski slope in a chilly wind, but not in a warm hotel room.

His image of Kay blurred, and he saw Fran, but then it wasn't Fran. Fran was in Garmisch with friends, whoever they were, maybe with some other guy. Sam never drank more than two of those strong German beers, and wasn't accustomed to wine. He drank beyond his limited capacity. He was forgetting where he was and who he was with.

He remembered Fran and her threat to call the manager and throw him out. But what would have happened if the hotel manager had come and found him naked? What if he was naked here in Obersdorf? Would Kay call the manager and throw him out? In his inebriated state he was no longer able to suppress the question that had been dogging him since Zermatt. Did he love Fran? But Kay said there was no such thing as love. Kay was the general's girl, or maybe she wasn't. Maybe that was just a rumor, more gossip.

What would it be like to sleep with the general's girl? He should try it. She seemed willing, even egging him on to test him, like it was a game and if he slept with her Kay would win. She would prove that there was no such thing as love, only sex, and if there was no such thing as love, maybe the sex was enough...

Chapter Eleven

The Fifth Weekend—The Morning After

When the morning light came into the room through the gap in the blackout drapes, Sam looked up at the ceiling. He remembered the hospital green of the ceiling, that long period of limbo when he didn't know who he was or what he wanted to be.

He gradually realized he was not in the dormitory bunk, but in the big double bed in Kay's room. He was naked, but he didn't remember anything else, and he was certain when Kay... where was she? In the bathroom?... came back, she wouldn't tell him what had happened. He would be afraid to ask, or too embarrassed. That would be her secret, her revenge on the general, Sam's defeat. It was like a war. There had been a battle, and he didn't understand the outcome, except love had been the loser.

Sam swung his feet off the bed and onto the floor. He felt awful. His head ached and he was afraid if he drank even a glass of water he would throw up. He needed a shave and remembered that he had forgotten his razor. All his gear was up in the men's dormitory. He also suddenly needed to pee.

Kay came out of the bathroom with a towel around her head and a big bath towel tucked around her body. He had not seen her except in bulky ski clothing, and realized she was not thin like Fran, but athletic and voluptuous. He had a vague recollection of attractive, ample breasts, now covered with the towel, but maybe that was just his imagination.

"So you're awake."

"More or less." He looked around, wondering where his jockey shorts were, saw them hung carefully on one of the two chairs by the window. There was no way he could get them without exposing himself. Well, obviously she had seen him naked, so what? "I need the bathroom."

"Help yourself," she said with a nod of her head.

As he passed her, she added, "You've got an awful bruise on your bottom."

"Kept falling on my wallet." He went into the bathroom, was impressed that it was also equipped with a bidet, something he had only seen once before in a Paris hotel.

Kay's taking a shower had steamed up the mirror. He wiped it with his hand, but didn't like what he saw. He looked like, how could he describe it? Not spent, but used.

But he had no recollection of having had sex with Kay. Maybe he had, maybe not. But he didn't think he had undressed himself. Maybe she had unwrapped him like a Christmas gift to see what was the surprise.

When he'd done his business and washed his face he returned to get dressed. He was embarrassed to look at her. He asked tentatively, "Was I good?"

Kay laughed.

He had not expected her to laugh. Was she laughing at him, standing there, feeling foolish, or was there some private joke he wasn't privy to?

It was a thoroughly amused laugh. She suppressed it only long enough to come up to him, put one hand on his shoulder while holding onto the bath towel, and give him an affectionate kiss. "You're something else, Sam. Now you'd better get back to your dormitory before the management discovers you. Take the back stairs."

Sam dressed quickly without tying the laces of his ski boots. Carrying his parka over his arm he went to the door and first peeked out into the hallway. There was no one there. He was being dismissed. There was no suggestion that there would be another night in Kay's hotel room. "See you at breakfast?"

"Sure."

At least she wasn't going to pretend she didn't know him.

He sneaked up the back stairs of the hotel to the top floor. He didn't have a key to the men's dormitory, but the door was open and there were quite a few Germans getting ready for breakfast and a day on the slopes. One was waxing his skis.

Sam's zip bag was on the cot where he had left it. His toothbrush, tooth paste and deodorant were there, but of course no razor and he had forgotten his soap holder, too. He didn't think the German hotel would provide, like some American accommodations, an emergency toilet kit.

He picked up the coarse towel and, barefoot in just his ski pants, waited his turn outside the only shower. It was a long wait. When he finally did get his turn at the shower there was only a feeble spray of water and it was cold. At least someone had left the tail end of a little bit of soap and he made do with that.

Back at his bunk, he put on his fresh set of underwear, his ski socks, and the white shirt, no tie. What was the weather going to be? He looked out the window, wondering about the ski conditions and the temperature. The sky was overcast, but there was no fresh snow on the spit, as the well-packed and sometimes icy ski area was called.

Down on the snow-covered street below the terrace there were a couple of cars parked, a black Mercedes and a new-looking orange Volkswagen. While he watched, an olive drab American Cadillac pulled up. Attached to the chromed front bumper was a little U.S. Army flag with a single star. Sam realized at once that Kay's general had arrived after all.

When Sam got down to the breakfast room Kay was already there, sitting with a beefy-looking man in his late forties with a buzz haircut. He was in civvies, a brown suit that was too tight for his heavy body, but his bearing was enough. The general didn't have to be in uniform with service badges and medals to exude his rank and authority.

Sam didn't come any closer than ten feet from their table. Kay looked up, saw him, and gave him a troubled glance.

Sam nodded that he understood, and turned away. No introductions were in order. How could a PFC meet a general? Say what? "Hi, Bill?" In civvies he wouldn't have to salute, and he wasn't supposed to know that this was the general. It would be awkward at best and lead to questions he didn't want to answer, even if he knew what the answers were.

Sam was wearing his heavy, twin lens reflex camera around his neck. He opened the viewfinder, set the distance for ten feet, and, letting the camera hang by his hip, snapped the shutter without obviously looking through it. It was the last frame on the roll of film.

It was best to be discreet. Like they always said, discretion was the better part of virtue.

Chapter Twelve

Sam in Kay's Room

Sam didn't know what to make of his encounter with Kay. He didn't know if he'd had sex with her or her with him in his drunken state. What the hell? Imagine finally getting laid, if that was what happened, and not having any memory of it. Then, when he saw her general show up after all, he felt like he was just a substitute or surrogate. He was confused and feeling used and humiliated.

He was also broke.

He was out of film, so no more pictures that weekend. Without money for a lift ticket, he made one more attempt at the Nebelhorn, trudging up the foot path to the top of the run, but he was so exhausted by the time he got to the top he'd had enough of skiing. He was also bruised from repeatedly falling down the day before. He knew that most accidents on the ski hill usually happened late in the day when people were tired. He was afraid that next time he might even break a leg, and he didn't want to risk another stint in the hospital.

He decided to pack it in and not stay a second night at the *Gasthof zum Traube*. He boarded the late train out of Obersdorf. His connections to Munich were poor and he didn't get back to the barracks until two in the morning, exhausted and drained emotionally.

He didn't know what to make of Kay. Her quizzing him about the meaning of love was like a third degree in an interrogation room, as if she might be unsure herself. It was like an agnostic challenging a person of faith to prove the non-existence of God. The discussion had led to no conclusion, unless whatever happened in her bed was an affirmation of some kind. He simply didn't understand. It was all speculation.

As soon as he could get into the darkroom he developed the film he exposed at Obersdorf. Studying the wet negatives as he held the film strip up to the light, he saw that the picture of the cherry chocolate cake was sharp and in focus, and the shot of Kay was OK, too, even the one of her at the top of the ski lift. The picture he sneaked of her with the general at breakfast wasn't clear, for the bright sun outside the window turned the people at the breakfast table into mere silhouettes. But there was another on the film strip before that, badly underexposed and not well focused. What the hell was that?

It didn't look like it would be possible to get a decent print. What he did see in the negative was a bed, and someone in it. He hadn't taken that. Had he somehow accidentally hit the shutter at some time? Not possible.

He would have to wait until the negatives were dry and make the prints when he came back to the lab next time. It was a mystery.

In the meantime, it was back to work in the supply room, back to roommate Marty with his tiny pipe. There was a change. Marty had become reticent about talking about Yetta. When asked how she was doing, bad back and all that, Marty said she was better, but did not elaborate. Was it all over? Or was their relationship serious and private?

Sam did admit he had run into Kay by accident and they had stayed at the same hotel, but he didn't want to say any more. If he told Marty he had waked up naked in Kay's bed, there would be more demands for details. Sam didn't kiss and tell, and he didn't know what to say anyway. He certainly didn't want to feed the gossip mill. He didn't mention that Kay's general had shown up. She was alleged to be the general's mistress, but Sam didn't know if the general were married, or anything more about her relationship. It was none of his business. It was all just talk.

When he returned to the photo lab the next evening he made sharp, glossy prints of the pictures, except for the one that was underexposed. The roll consisted of typical tourist shots, plus the ones of the *Schwarzwalder kirsch torte*, Kay, and Kay on the ski tow. He made 4x5 glossy prints of all except the portrait of Kay, which he did as a handsome 5x7. The shot of Kay at breakfast looked like any snapshot of a hotel restaurant. It would have been better with a fill-in flash, but he didn't own or carry a flash gun and bulbs.

The mysterious negative was so underexposed, that he had to consult the German darkroom attendant for advice. The suggestion was to use #4 paper and force the development. The picture was taken in subdued light and not in focus. The twin lens reflex camera was not easy to use. First, one had to take a light meter reading, get a number, and then set aperture and shutter speed in the right combination. If the shutter had been wide open, the camera on a tripod, and maybe a longer exposure with a cable release, it would have been possible. After several failed attempts, Sam finally got a murky print that was recognizable. What was clear enough was it was Sam in the bed, naked, sprawled out, vulnerable, and available, like the presentation of a nice meal on a platter.

Why had she taken it?

It wasn't her camera. It was his. There was only one way to find out her intention: ask her.

On Friday evening Sam phoned the *Goldene Traube* billet. The rooms did not have individual phones. You called the receptionist and left a message or got someone to call a person to the telephone. He left a message for Kay that he was coming by to drop off some photos.

Dressed in his German overcoat and hat, Sam took the Army bus from the caserne downtown and walked to the *Goldene Traube.* Kay's room was on the fourth floor. No elevator. He was out of breath and coughing nervously by the time he got to the top of the stairs.

Sam was rather uncomfortable as he went from door to door looking for her room number. It was like being an intruder in a college girls' dormitory. He didn't want to surprise someone going to the bathroom while dressed in only a robe or a slip. He could look like some prowler in that overcoat and hat.

He knocked at Kay's door. She was in.

"Come in."

Sam took off his hat as he opened the door. He was surprised to find Kay in her pajamas and bathrobe. "Sam!"

He stammered, "Sorry to bother you. I phoned and left a message downstairs. Maybe you didn't get it."

Sam looked quickly around the room. The covers of Kay's bed were turned down. A small Grundig radio was playing soft, classical music. He already knew that, though the bathrooms were down the hall, each room had a wash stand. There were wine bottles under the sink, empties in a waste basket, and a collection of perfume bottles and makeup on the dressing table which had a mirror and lamp. The somewhat seedy billet was a far cry from the luxury of the room at the *Gasthof zum Traube* in Obersdorf.

She was standing close to him, but no welcoming hug or anything like that, no hello kiss, which might have been appropriate if they were friends. They were not friends in spite of the intimacy in Obersdorf. "I haven't been well for a few days."

Sam stepped back "Got the flu?" After that long hospital stay Sam didn't want to catch anything.

"What they call a bit of Spanish tummy. There was another office party. One of the lieutenant colonels was promoted."

Sam knew the eagle epaulet insignia. "Full bird." Not everyone made full colonel, but you had to be really something to make general. He had little respect for anything less. And of course there was *that* general, the one who turned up in Obersdorf after all. He couldn't compete with *that*, not a PFC versus a general. Sam was a nobody.

"Any excuse for a party," Kay said with a grimace and her hand on her stomach. Her face looked drawn. She seemed tired, but of course, she was ill. Her hair was mussed and she looked like the morning after, but after what?

Sam saw a bucket under a towel beside the bed. "Maybe I'd better go," Sam said, but he was conscious of the envelope he was carrying with her photos.

"No, Sam. Stay awhile. I could use some company. Would you like a glass of wine? There's an open bottle of Liebfraumilch and a clean glass over there." She gestured toward the three -drawer bureau next to the small closet.

"I'll pass." Sam remembered his hangover in Obersdorf. He didn't want a repeat performance, at least, not if he weren't sober. "I brought you some pictures from Obersdorf."

He opened the envelope and handed her the prints one at a time. "This is the cherry chocolate cake. Nice picture of you. Here's one of you getting off the T-bar."

She studied them, pleased. "I didn't know you'd taken that."

Sam took out his piece de resistance. "How about this one?"

"Oh."

What did that mean? "Oh."?

"Souvenir?"

Kay smiled, but her expression was apologetic. "Something for you to remember."

"Trouble is, I don't remember," Sam said. "I was hoping you'd refresh my memory."

Kay sighed as if she regretted taking it. "Just put it in your scrapbook as one of your conquests."

Though Sam had recent pictures of Fran and some snapshots of Betty when he still used a simple Baby Brownie camera, he didn't consider them to be trophies. "I don't have conquests," Sam said. "No brag book."

"You're not that kind of a guy."

"No. I'm not." He didn't know what kind of a guy he was.

He still didn't know why she'd taken the picture. If it were with her own camera and she kept a scrapbook of conquests, it might have made sense. She didn't look to him to be a trophy hunter like some guys were.

Maybe the picture of him was a souvenir, like the picture of the cherry chocolate cake, something that was savored and not to be forgotten. What mattered was what had she done to him, if anything? Maybe nothing.

Maybe the picture was just Kay's idea of a joke, a practical joke to play on him and make him feel like a fool. That did make sense, considering their argument about love and whether or not there was such a thing. Maybe she was saying by taking that picture that there was no such thing as love, just sex, and he was sprawled there on the bed like the remains of a meal.

Just thinking of what she might have done while he was drunk was giving him a hard on. Had she given him a blow job? Or got him stiff and climbed on while he lay there like a piece of meat? That was ironic. What if he finally got laid and didn't even remember?

"I saw that your date showed up after all in Obersdorf." He had decided not to give her the picture of her at breakfast with the general. That wouldn't be tactful.

"Yes." She didn't elaborate and he hesitated to pry.

"Was it OK?"

She cocked her head. "Maybe."

That could mean anything. He didn't want a blow by blow description. He didn't like it when Marty bragged about his exploits with women. It would be tasteless to ask Kay for details. That might be what happened in the gossip mill at the *Goldene Traube*, but he was not in that loop and didn't want to be.

"I've got to go," Sam said. It wasn't true, but he made up an excuse. "There's a French movie down the street. Cocteau's *Orphee*. Story of Orpheus and his lost love Eurydice. I thought I might see it."

"Orpheus looks back and loses her forever. How appropriate," Kay said, leading him to the door. "Thanks for the photographs."

He didn't give her the print of him in her bed. Not that he thought she would show it around. Kay was too discreet for that, but if anyone found it in that nest of gossips, well, he shuddered at the thought. He'd heard that a porter at the temporary billet for officers' wives in Heidelberg had taken pictures of his conquests and gone to Federal prison for fornication.

Feeling bitter, Sam made his way down the old stairs. He heard some activity on the third floor and saw Marty and Yetta laughing in the hall. She was obviously feeling better, recovered from her back injury.

"Sam!" Yetta called.

"Hi. Feeling better?"

"Thanks to Marty, here. He's a fine nurse."

Marty said, "Maybe I'll go to med school when I get out of the Army. What are you doing here?"

"I was visiting Kay. Gave her some pictures. Turned out we were at Obersdorf at the same time. Even stayed at the same hotel."

Yetta raised her eyebrows. "Really?"

"Just a coincidence," Sam said. "She's sick. Maybe the flu or something."

Yetta gave him a knowing look. "Not the flu, Sam. Maybe she didn't tell you. She's pregnant."

Sam was stunned. "No secrets in this building. I see." *My God. Now what?*

For the time being, because he couldn't yet fathom his own consequences, Sam thought only about Kay, the girl who didn't believe that love existed. What of the general? Sam didn't know if the general was married, and what a pregnancy would do to those relationships. What a mess.

But then it dawned on him that maybe, if Kay really was pregnant, he might be the father.

Chapter Thirteen

The Sixth Weekend—nexpected Visit

It was Saturday, January 8th, and an unseasonable drizzle had turned the snowy Munich streets into rivers of slush. Marty drove the same as always, whipping the light Volkswagen around the corners in a half skid, as deftly and seemingly unconcerned as he had in the fresh snow on the way to Davos two weeks before.

Sam clung to his seat, ready for the crash if the brakes weren't enough at the next intersection.

Marty was calm. "Relax, Buddy Boy. You know the Green Beetle and I haven't had an accident yet."

"Yeh? We'll be lucky if we get to the *Bahnhof* at all."

Marty smirked at him. "I told you I'd get you there in time to meet her train. We still have fifteen minutes."

Sam looked at his watch. It was two-twenty-five. "I hope so."

"I thought you were going to the Zugspitze this weekend. Oops!" Marty hit the brakes and, seen by frightened faces behind the windows, stopped barely a foot from a street car.

"I was, but I changed my plans. Maybe next weekend." He hadn't explained that the news of Kay's alleged pregnancy had so rattled him with what ifs that he couldn't focus on another getaway. What if she really was pregnant? What if by some fluke he was the father?

Sam was in his second year of the two-year draft. He had eleven months left. If he got an early release to go back and finish college, he would be back in the States before Kay's baby was born, if there really was one.

Of course, it was more likely that if she was actually pregnant, it was the general's kid, not his, and he was out of it. If it was his, would he marry Kay? In the long run, her take-no-prisoners way of grilling him about love would make her a hostile partner. A marriage with someone like that could never last.

Since that revelation about Kay, Sam had been worried and dejected. He had moped around the supply room, picking absently at the neat stacks of equipment. Sam had issued a new man a shelter half, the Army's term for half a pup tent used on maneuvers, without the necessary wooden pegs. Sam was not usually careless.

In the afternoon he slipped away to the linen room and lay down on a stack of mattresses. He had relapsed into the same lack of direction and purpose he had suffered from when he was released from the hospital.

On Friday the letter had arrived. Mail in the afternoon was usually light. The parcel post, second class, and most of the first class mail came from the APO in the morning. The afternoon mail included a letter posted in Germany.

Sam looked at the return address. "It's from Fran."

Marty was curious. "What's she say?"

"I have to open it first." Sam opened the blade of his imitation Swiss Army knife and slit open the envelope. He had never had a letter from Fran and, thanks to the military phone system, had not written to her. The letter was on a single sheet of paper.

It would have been nice to get a love letter, but all this said was, "Am going to Munich on Saturday with a friend you might be interested in. Would like you to meet her and show her the points of interest. Our train will arrive at 1442. Can you meet us?" It was signed simply "Fran." Not "Love, Fran" or "Yours, Fran."

Well, that took care of any other weekend plans he might have made if he'd been able to get his head together.

Marty grinned at him like a malicious gargoyle. "So now you're chief tour supervisor? What's that, a consolation prize?"

"For what?"

"She's trying to palm you off on someone else, Sam."

"Could be."

"Could be this is your big chance. You could do a lot better than Fran. She's no raving beauty."

"Neither am I." He was conscious of his broken nose.

Sam had read and re-read the note. It was in his pocket along with his tourist map of Munich when they left for the *Hauptbahnhof.* So much had happened in the short time since Zermatt. With that business with Kay, Sam's situation had changed.

He thought about that encounter in the hallway with Marty and Yetta. "You and Yetta seem to be getting along pretty well. It is serious?"

Marty didn't answer. Maybe he didn't know the answer to that one himself, or hadn't decided. He changed the subject. "We had a party with Sally Ann. Got drunk as hell. She kept calling for you, Sam. You made quite an impression on her."

The Green Beetle skidded around a corner, throwing up a splash of slush. It was still drizzling and the wipers were ineffectual, spreading road grease and filth on the glass.

"She's a sad case."

Marty shifted gears, released the clutch with a lurch. "She's moving to Spain, you know."

"She said something about that."

"Got an embassy job. Seems she likes the price of wine down there."

Sam wiped some of the steam off the windshield. "You're a cynic."

Marty stopped at a railway crossing just barely in time as the red and white gates came down, dangling wet, bent pieces of fence like hangings in front of the car. "We're having a farewell party for Sally Ann next Friday night. Care to come? It'll be at Yetta's. You can bring your new girl-friend, Kay."

Was he being sarcastic? "She's not my girl-friend."

Sam had shown Marty the photographs, but not the one of himself in Kay's bed. "She's not my girl-friend. We just happened to run into each other at Obersdorf. She was with some general."

"You didn't make out with her?"

"She fed me a piece of cherry chocolate cake. The one in the picture I showed you. That's all."

"Come on, Buddy Boy, I saw that photo of someone in bed. That was you, wasn't it?"

"You saw that picture?"

"You left the envelope on the bureau. I peeked. Naughty, naughty Sam. You didn't tell me about that."

"Don't go through my stuff, Marty. I'd appreciate your discretion, for God's sake. Don't say anything to Yetta."

Marty didn't answer. Maybe he had already blabbed.

Sam continued, "Next thing the whole damned billet will be saying I knocked her up. If that rumor got to the general I might be sent to the East German border. You know how the Army is, how vindictive some people can be. She is not my girl-friend."

"I hear the general broke up with her."

"Where'd you hear that, I mean, about the general?"

"Nobody in that hotel makes a move without everyone knowing it." Marty laughed. "Any one of those women can tell you who is going out with who and who is making out."

Sam frowned. "Not very discreet is it?" So much for discretion being the better part of virtue.

Marty glanced at him. "In a buddy-buddy sort of way. They look out for each other in a sisterly sort of way. You never had a sister, did you?"

"I guess you and Yetta must be the subject of a lot of conversation."

"She's a nice girl, Sam."

"That's what Sally Ann said about me, 'You're a nice boy, Sam.' Yetta isn't exactly a girl."

"She's still nice."

Sam didn't know if Marty's intentions were serious. Marty was a draftee like himself. Marty was already a short timer. He'd be discharged. What then? "You seem to be making out all right."

'Making out' had several connotations, but Marty didn't take the bait. "I'm seeing her this afternoon. Tonight, too." It was convenient that, as the company clerk, he could issue overnight passes for both of them. "Why don't you meet me afterwards if you're so curious? I'll tell you all about it, say, midnight or so. We could go out for a beer if you're finished showing Fran and her friend around. We can compare notes."

"Sounds all right. Where?"

"In front of the *Goldene Traube*. If you can't make it, just leave a message with the receptionist."

"OK. Midnight."

They had arrived at the Munich *Hauptbahnhof*. Marty pulled up in front of the RTO, the military rail ticket office. Sam got out and slammed the door.

"Keep a cool tool," Marty called, gunned the motor, and sped away.

A cool tool. That reminded Sam that he had never replaced the single condom he used to carry in his wallet and tried to use in Zermatt. He didn't expect to need one. He had learned in his brief stint as a Boy Scout, one should be prepared.

Sam jumped back to escape a shower of slush thrown up by the Green Beetle's rear wheels.

The Munich railway station was full of people in motion, people saying goodbye and others greeting. This time Sam was not a traveler and felt out of place. He didn't buy a platform ticket, but stationed himself at the gate for the Heidelberg-Munich express.

His anticipation about Fran's arrival was tempered by their separation, the fact that she had turned him down in favor of some party last weekend. He had, instead, gone to Obersdorf with unanticipated consequences that might alter his whole life. And now she was coming with a friend who wanted him as a tour guide. Nothing romantic about that.

Was she intending to fix him up with someone else so he would feel bad?

The deep, enunciated voice of the loud speaker system reverberating in the station hall announced the arrival of the Heidelberg train. "*Actung, achtung. Schnellzug aus Frankfurt, Heidelberg, Stuttgart führt ein. Bitte vorsicht beim ankunft des Zuges.*" The dark green electric locomotive rumbled alongside the platform and stopped.

This time Sam recognized Fran. She was alone. There were no skis or ski boots this trip. Fran wore a stylish grey wool coat gathered at the waist with a belt. The small suitcase was familiar. The hours on the day train had not tired her. There was decisiveness in her walk he had not seen before.

Sam was ready for a welcoming embrace, but that did not materialize and, for fear of being rebuffed, he didn't move to hug her. "Hi," she said, not waiting for his greeting. "My girl-friend couldn't come." She hesitated as though she had rehearsed her speech on the train and had momentarily forgotten how to say it. "She decided to go to Basel at the last minute."

But she's come anyway, Sam thought. He was puzzled about her intentions. His own confused relations with women and the business with Kay made him more hesitant, worried, and reflective than ever. He had tried to give up Fran as a failed encounter, and Kay… well, that was even more troubling. Yet, here was Fran, smiling, self-assured, not what he had thought was her usual self.

"But you came. I'm glad you did."

"I have a reservation at *Hotel das blaue Haus*."

He knew where it was. "It's not far. We can walk," Sam said, and picked up her suitcase. "It's a bit sloppy out. Mid-winter thaw."

As they left the station Fran asked, "So what have you been up to these last two weeks?"

"A little skiing in Obersdorf in the Black Forest, but I always kept falling down. I almost went to the Zugspitze this weekend. Since the thaw, it's the only place with good snow."

"Then you stayed in town just for me." Fran was pleased. Apparently the "girlfriend" was only a ruse.

"I'm glad you came. I missed you." In reality he'd been so befuddled, worried, and confused over the situation with Kay he didn't think much about Fran at all.

"I talked to Yetta. She said you'd been at Obersdorf. I thought you might go again."

"There's a thaw in Obersdorf, too." Now Sam was suspicious. Was she expecting him to confirm whatever blabber had circulated at the *Goldene Traube*? Had Yetta also mentioned Kay? Worse, had Marty told Yetta about the picture of him naked in Kay's bed? And of Kay being pregnant?

If so, was Fran determined to get him back? Was jealousy a factor? He had no idea.

Maybe, just maybe, she had plans for sex. He'd better be prepared. Remembering Kay also reminded him about the condom thing. In the 1950's the American concept of drug store had not taken hold in Europe. Condoms weren't sold at an *Apotek*, which was for prescriptions. There was a *Drogerie* just ahead where one could buy toilet articles. Sam invented an excuse to go inside. "I just remembered I'm out of shaving soap. I'll be right out."

Fran followed him in, saying something about something cosmetic.

While she shopped Sam picked up a tube of shaving cream and looked for condoms, but condoms were always sold under the table, never put on display. Hoping Fran didn't see him, Sam approached the clerk, hoping it would be a man. No such luck. She was a very pretty blonde in a white coat. *"Haben Sie kondomer?"* he asked, confident that Fran, if she did overhear him, didn't know German.

The clerk, seeing them come into the store together, sized up the situation immediately. Amused by his obvious embarrassment, the pretty clerk launched into a teasing litany about condom types, reservoir ends, lubricated, and whether he liked colored ones. Sam didn't know much about condoms, and had never heard that they came in various colors.

Feeling desperately out of his depth, he ventured, *"Normal."*

Did he want a dozen? Or a package of three?

A dozen? Swallowing, Sam said, *"Drei."* He was handed a small packet, paid her and turned to go.

He was relieved that Fran hadn't been standing right behind him during that exchange, but she was aware of the conversation. She asked, "What was that all about?"

"She was trying to sell me something." Hoping Fran wouldn't ask what, he changed the subject. "A shame that you've only got a weekend to see Munich. I haven't done much touring in the city myself. I usually take off on the weekends. It's like New Yorkers who never see the Statue of Liberty."

They crossed Bahnhofstrasse, using a streetcar platform as a safety island in the traffic. Sam carried her suitcase and she took his other arm. They must look like a young married couple on holiday.

"I didn't go to Garmisch after all. Couldn't get a reservation. Too many GI's on pass."

Fran seemed relaxed, confident, happy to see him, while he was uncertain, even suspicious. She had, after all, invited herself.

They reached the hotel. Fran let go of his arm while he opened the big glass door for her. He waited while she went up to the reception desk to check in.

The clerk was an older man with grey hair and a bland expression. "*Ein doppelzimmer?*" Observing Sam's low quarter GI shoes, he saw through Sam's overcoat and German hat disguise and corrected himself. "A double room, miss?"

"No. A single. I have a reservation. Fran Wagner."

She filled out the police registration form, showed her government ID

The clerk, now suspicious, required payment for the room in advance.

If she had been expecting to travel with a friend, why didn't she reserve a double? If he had made the reservation he'd have gambled on spending the night with her and asked for a double, a step up from the adjoining rooms they had in Zermatt.

Sam was getting mixed signals. She obviously wanted to see him, but spending the night with him was not on her agenda.

As they stepped up to the elevator, the elderly clerk reminded him in German, "It is a room for one person only. This is a respectable hotel. We have a curfew for gentlemen in the room."

Sam reassured him. "*Ich verstehe. Ich bleibe nicht hier.*"

As the elevator door closed, Fran asked, "What did you say to him?"

"I said we could find the room without any help."

"Oh."

The room at *Das blaue Haus* was modern, almost Spartan, and reminiscent of the old Bauhaus school of architecture. It lacked the antique feel of the hotel in Zermatt or the elegance of Kay's room in Obersdorf. Unlike the somewhat dingy quarters of the *Goldene Traube* billet, it had a small private bathroom with a drain in the middle of the floor. Taking a shower meant getting the entire room wet. "Sort of minimalist modern," Sam commented.

"It's only for one night," Fran said. She took her suitcase from him and set it on the only chair.

She had said she wanted to be shown around the city, and he had his map, so that's the direction he was thinking. "If you want to see something of Munich, I have my visitors' map."

"The weather's too nasty for walking around in all that mess."

"No problem. We can take a streetcar. Cheap and easy way to see the city. Sit with the city map and get a good sense of the place as we ride around. I did that in Paris."

"Well, alright."

As they went back out into the drizzle and melting snow, Sam realized that riding a streetcar around town was not her real intention, but he was committed.

They did one circuit. The passengers, all damp, steamed up the windows of the old streetcar. With the doors opened so frequently, it was a chilly, uncomfortable ride, and once around was enough.

Back near her hotel, they found a small restaurant. It was early in the month and Sam didn't have to scrimp on a single sausage for supper. They ordered two Hungarian goulash dinners. Fran had a glass of red wine. Sam, leery about getting drunk again, had a bottle of carbonated *sprüdel.*

Then it was back to the hotel and the disapproving eye of the desk clerk as Sam followed her into the elevator. The intimacy of the small, private space gave him an opportunity to steal a kiss but Fran was not ready. "Not here, Sam," she said.

Once in the room Fran took off her wool coat and hung it over the back of the only chair. She was wearing a pretty, pale blue blouse with ruffles that hinted at her cleavage.

Rebuffed in the elevator, Sam felt awkward, not knowing what to do next.

Fran sat down on the bed, tested the mattress, noted the feather quilt. "I thought I'd just relax a bit. Catch my breath."

That reminder caused Sam to cough, something he often did when he was uncertain. He could not think of anything to say. He stood with his German trench coat unbuttoned. He was still wearing the black hat and his arms hung irresolute at his sides.

Looking at Fran he remembered her without her clothes, in just her panties, nearly naked, small, perky breasts, as she had been in Zermatt when, at the crucial moment, she rejected him. Now he realized how glad he was to see her and how much, in spite of the confusion about Kay, he wanted to be with her. He was reasonably sure that she had not made the five-hour train trip just to do some casual sightseeing.

If Yetta had told Fran about his seeing Kay in Obersdorf, maybe Fran had made the trip to make sure he was still hers. Was he?

Her next move affirmed that assumption. "Don't just stand there, Sam. You make me uncomfortable. Sit down."

He sat on the bed beside her without taking off his coat.

She put her face close to his and studied him. "Are you all right, Sam? You're preoccupied. It's me, Fran."

"I didn't think I'd see you again." Now he was no longer hesitant. He slipped his overcoat off his shoulders and tossed his hat across the room. He put his arms around her.

Fran kissed him firmly on the mouth. "I couldn't stay away. I had to see you once more to find out something."

"About what?"

"About myself."

"So did I."

"About me?" She sounded curious and pleased.

"About both of us."

"Both of us. That has a nice ring to it." She hesitated. "I've been asking myself a lot of questions lately, Sam. You've been helping me answer them."

"Me?" He remembered her struggle with herself in Zermatt. It didn't seem to him like he was helping. Maybe he'd made things worse for her.

They embraced, suddenly passionate. Her lips were soft, her mouth wet, and her tongue sought his. "I want you, Sam. All of you."

Sam didn't know what she meant by 'all of him.' Every inch of his now stiff erection? Or more than that? Body and soul? But an erect penis has no conscience, no brains, and does not pause to reflect. "I want you, too." Whatever that might mean.

Her eyes were clear and her vagueness that sometimes pulled her away from reality was gone. She kissed him on the neck and held him closer.

He still hadn't slipped off his overcoat, though it was down off his shoulders. He took it off and got up to hang it in the little closet.

"Don't forget to lock the door, Sam," she reminded him. He turned off the overhead light and laid her down on her back on the soft feather quilt. Only the brass table lamp glowed.

This time she did not hesitate. This time she was ready and willing. Remembering the condom in his trench coat pocket, Sam got up to retrieve it and went into the bathroom, naked, to put it on. He dropped the wrapper in the toilet and returned to her bed.

He slid in under the quilt and caressed her, luxuriating in the touch of her smooth skin, thrilled by the firmness of her breasts. Her vagina was dry and tight, and he had hardly penetrated and thrust once or twice before his excitement got the better of him and he ejaculated.

Damn!

She was not satisfied and he was embarrassed and ashamed. "I can try again, he said. I promise it will be better the second time around."

The telephone rang.

While Sam sat on the edge of the bed, lamenting, thinking that now he would have to wash and put on a fresh condom, Fran answered the phone. She didn't understand what was said and handed it to him.

Who could be calling? What was this about?

It was the hotel manager speaking in crisp, angry, accented by unmistakable English. "Ziss is a respectable hotel, Mr. GI Ziss is not a whore house. You have overstayed the curfew."

"*Sie ist mein verlobte*," Sam said, hoping that telling the manager they were engaged would be an adequate justification for him to be in her room.

"*Das ist mir egal*," the manager said. "If you do not leave by midnight I will call the police." He hung up.

Fran had sat down on the bed again, her shoulders hunched. "What did he say?"

Sam apologized. "He says they have a curfew and men are not allowed in the rooms after midnight." This was no way to leave a woman's bed. "I told him you were my fiancée. He didn't care. I have to leave."

Fran's eyes were open in surprise. "You told him that?"

"I thought it might help."

Now Fran reverted to her old, uncertain, even frightened self. She started to cry.

That she was crying caught him by surprise. He didn't understand it when a woman cried, whether it was from anger, disappointment, frustration with herself, anxiety. He didn't know how to react or how to comfort her, or even if he should, and what should he comfort her for other than to show some sympathy for whatever it was that caused her sudden unhappiness. He felt helpless and uncertain.

Putting on his pants, Sam took out his clean pocket handkerchief, handed it to her and took her in his arms in an awkward embrace. "Here."

She wiped her eyes, saw the mark on the handkerchief. "What's this? L-1101?"

"It's my laundry mark, My initial and the last four digits of my military ID number, US55-393-1101. The U.S. stands for the Army of the United States. Draftee. We mark everything, even our socks and underwear."

She started to hand it back.

"Keep it," Sam said. He was now putting on his shirt. It was nearly midnight and he was sure the manager would follow up on his threat. That's all Sam needed, to be arrested. What did the Army call it? Fornication. It was an actionable offense. You could go to prison for it. But everyone in the Army, it seemed to him, was a fornicator, the first sergeant, the officers, the non-coms, even the general if rumors about Kay were true.

At her door, they embraced. Teary-eyed, Fran looked up at him. "Fiancée? What is that in German?"

"*Verlobte*. It was just an excuse. I shouldn't have said it."

"It's all right."

From the inflection, it wasn't clear what she meant by that. All right. That could mean anything, like it didn't matter, was acceptable, or was good.

Sam's hasty remark was unfortunate. They were not engaged. No one had proposed. Sam hadn't even thought about anything so serious. Fran obviously thought the idea sounded appealing.

Sam put on his trench coat, picked up his black hat from where he had tossed it. "I'll pick you up in the morning. How about nine-thirty? I'd better wait in the lobby, just to be safe from that damned manager."

They kissed again, tenderly and regretfully. "I wish I could stay," Sam said. He didn't want to leave her unsatisfied, and he wanted to last longer at sex next time, if he could have another chance. That wasn't so certain.

He made his way to the elevator. In the lobby he saw the watchful manager who seemed to have decided that Sam's girl was not a pick-up off the street. He actually smiled at Sam and said without being sarcastic, *"Verlobt? Gratulera."* Congratulations, without sarcasm. So much depended on how you said it.

Sam nodded. *"Danke."* But *danke* could also mean, 'no thanks.'

The drizzle had stopped and the temperature had fallen. Munich was cold and damp, freezing again. The sidewalks were slippery. Out on the street, Sam looked at his watch. Marty had wanted to meet him at the *Goldene Traube* at midnight.

The streets were deserted. Sam didn't know if the street cars ran that late, or if he could find a cab. Conscious of how slippery the soles of his low quarter GI shoes were, he walked carefully to the *Goldene Traube*.

He got there in time to see Marty's Green Beetle out in front. The engine was running. Sam hurried to the car and knocked at the window, which was all steamed up from inside. "Hey, Marty!"

Marty opened the passenger door. "About time. I was about to give up on you. I thought you forgot." He was irritable and seemed to be in a hurry.

"Still want to go out for a beer?" Sam asked. "It's kind of late."

"I want more than a beer. There are always some broads at the Dolly Bar, even this late."

Sam wrinkled his broken nose in disgust. "What? Don't you get enough sex with Yetta?"

"That's not it," Marty said as the Volkswagen accelerated out of the parking space. "Yetta wants more than a romp in the hay."

"Meaning what?"

"She wants to get married. She's coming on too serious."

"I thought you were serious about her, nursing her when she was hurt and all that."

Marty was sucking on his tiny pipe again and speaking through clenched teeth. "I was just being sympathetic."

"Oh." Sam's estimation of his roommate just fell about three notches.

"She's just a party girl, Sam. Wants to have a good time. Get drunk. Get laid, for that matter. At least that's what I thought. Now she wants to get married."

"You could do worse, Marty. Yetta's nice."

Marty took his eyes off the road. "Sam, figure it out. We're draftees. We're only going to be in the Army a short time. You're already a short timer yourself. This is just an interlude."

Sam hadn't thought about that, not in connection with his dating Fran. The only time he thought about his time remaining in the Army was Kay's alleged pregnancy and the possibility, however remote, that he might inadvertently be the father of her kid. If he got an early release to get back to college for the September term, he'd be gone before Kay's baby was born. Not that that would get him off the hook. It was just a potential possibility and all the trouble that might go with it. There were consequences of passing out drunk. He swore never to let that happen ever again.

He had no idea if Kay had had sex with him while he was drunk. At least, with Fran he'd had a condom, which was not guaranteed contraception.

"So what happened? You had sex with Yetta and she started talking marriage?"

"No. She started talking marriage and I did NOT have sex with her. We had an argument."

"So now you want to find some broad at Dolly's and vent your frustrations? Hell." To Sam that sounded pretty juvenile.

"What about you and Fran? Did you finally get laid?"

"I don't want to talk about it."

Marty laughed. "Ah, my Buddy Boy screws up again. You don't need to get laid. You need a mother."

"What?" Sam coughed. It was true that he had essentially grown up in a single parent household. His father made a real effort at parenting, but Logan Associates took most of his time, even work at home weekends on those advertising projects. But a mother? Sam didn't think he needed a mother. He needed... but he still didn't know what he needed.

Marty laughed so hard that when the Volkswagen's tires slipped on the icy streetcar tracks he lost control of the car. It side-slipped, skidded into a curb with a crash.

Swearing, Marty got out of the car, slipped on the ice and fell. As he got up he saw the damage. "I've got a flat tire. Come on, Sam, help me change this tire."

The spare and the jack were under the hood. The aging Volkswagen's spare tire was pretty bald but when they got it on it had enough air in it for them to get to an Aral station and get it pumped up.

By then, all thoughts of the Dolly Bar had dissipated. They drove in silence back to the caserne.

All Sam wanted to do was get back to the barracks and crawl into his bunk. Once there, he couldn't sleep. He kept mulling over his situation. He shouldn't have told the hotel manager Fran was his fiancée. That had put an idea in her head. But maybe that idea was there all along.

Now he was unsure of her expectations. In fact, he had no idea what they might be, if any. He had no long-range plans. Marriage was beyond his horizon. This was, like Marty said, an interlude. Thinking about marriage put a whole new light on things, just as that photo Kay took of him had thrown him off balance.

Why couldn't things just be simple? Go out, have a good time, have some good sex, without consequences, without commitment.

The sex hadn't been that good, but it could get better. He needed more experience. He didn't consider himself a hot lover. Just as Fran had her hang-ups, he had his. The affair might lead nowhere. But, in time, it might become something wonderful. If they had that much time.

. . .

Sam got to Fran's hotel promptly the next morning. To assure the management that he was not just sneaking up to Fran's room, he asked the clerk to ring her room before he went up.

"Morning, Sam," Fran said as she opened the door. She embraced him as he came into the room and gave him a warm kiss, then backed off, troubled. "What's wrong, Sam?"

He rubbed the back of his neck. "I didn't sleep well." He didn't want to talk about that business with Marty, the flat tire, and certainly not about Yetta. That was plain gossip and none of his business. "Did you get breakfast?"

"Continental. Coffee and a couple of hard rolls in the breakfast room downstairs."

"I figured that." He had made a quick stop at the mess hall, but had no appetite.

"I'm all packed, so I can check out and we can do some sightseeing."

Sam had hoped there might be a chance for an encore performance of last night, a chance to improve on his bam-bam-thank-you-ma'm unsatisfactory performance. "I'm sorry about last night."

She kissed him again, tenderly, with sympathy and affection. "Not to worry, Sam. There will be other times."

He was uncertain, preoccupied with the discussion the night before about being a short timer. "I hope so."

"Should I check out and leave my bag at the desk, pick it up later?"

"Better to check it at the *bahnhof*. Save a trip back here."

They walked to the *Hauptbahnhof*, checked her bag, noted the time her train would leave in the afternoon and, with Sam's tourist map in hand, set out on a whirlwind sightseeing tour of Munich.

She didn't seem to be the same person Sam had made love to the night before, but he knew she hadn't changed. She was the same slim, long legged girl with a small chin, sensitive features, and, he knew, perky breasts. He could tell by the warm, relaxed look in her eyes that her feelings for him had changed. In Zermatt they had been a pair on a date, staying in separate rooms. Now, arm in arm as they saw the sights of Munich, watched the famous clock with its parade of animated figures, they were a couple.

At one point Fran asked, "Did you see Marty last night?"

"Yes. You know how he drives. Skidded into a curb. We had a flat tire last night. He wanted to go to a bar, but I wasn't interested."

"Sounds like Marty."

Sam changed the subject. "How do you feel this morning?"

Fran studied his face. "I was wondering if you'd ask. Do I look different? Does it show?"

"Does what show?"

"Last night?"

Sam was clueless. "Of course not."

"But I feel so different," she insisted. "I feel like everyone on the street will turn and point at me."

"Why? Because you aren't a virgin?"

She cocked her head and gave him a sideways glance. "I wasn't that, Sam."

"They won't notice. That's just between us." He took her in his arms and affirmed it with a kiss. Now people were noticing. Only lovers kissed in public.

"Can you come up to Heidelberg next weekend?"

Sam realized it wouldn't be fair to ask Fran to make another long train trip down to Munich for just one night. He wanted a repeat performance in bed with her, but he was also a bit wary. Marty had, well, freaked out when Yetta got possessive, wanted him to marry her. Maybe she was drunk and hadn't thought clearly, asked him on an impulse. Would Fran do the same thing? He doubted it, but he didn't want to rush things.

Sam needed time to think about their relationship before he saw her again. "There's a farewell party next weekend for Sally Ann. I promised to come." It was pretty lame, a mere party when he should be with his alleged *verlobte*. He'd better make amends quickly. "You could join me, but you couldn't arrive until after ten o'clock. How about the week after? I can take Saturday morning off and be in Heidelberg in the early afternoon. That would give us more time to be together."

She thought about that. "There's a hotel on the Königstuhl by Heidelberg Castle, the *Zum Schloss Hotel*. I hear it has a great view of the Neckar valley."

The *Zum Schloss Hotel* sounded expensive, but it would be for only one night. If he stayed in Munich the next weekend, he wouldn't have to spend much. "That sounds very romantic. It'll be like a honeymoon."

It was a dangerous choice of words, but at that moment Sam was smitten. He loved being with Fran. Traveling around Munich, looking at the sights, having meals together. They were not just a couple. They were, well, pals. They had bonded. Sex did that. In Biblical language the woman "cleaved" unto the man, and they became one flesh. That physical connection bound them together, however briefly. Real bonding with a woman was a new relationship for Sam, something he had never had with Betty or anyone else. Was this the love Kay had said didn't exist? Maybe so. It was dizzying, powerful stuff.

Chapter Fourteen

The Seventh Weekend—Farewell Party

Sam was never able to clearly remember the week that followed. Fran had thought everyone would look at her and see the change. He felt thrust into a new state of being like a cowboy who straddles the Brahma bull to have the gate flung open and be propelled into the arena. He wasn't standing back and ruminating about the purposeless of life, or whatever. This was different.

His bewilderment was made worse when he got a letter from his father asking when he was getting out of the Army. His father suggested he finish his degree and take the G.I. Bill for a Master's in public relations. That's where the real money was, and he could take the courses in Chicago while working for the family firm, Logan Associates. Sam wasn't sure he wanted that, but he had no ideas of anything better. His father already had plans for stationery that said "Logan and Son, Associates."

To apply for an early release in time for the September term he'd need a letter from his university confirming that he could return to his studies. The future that had seemed so far off was closing in on him.

By Friday, still without his equilibrium, he was tired and ready for the going-away party. Yetta was the host but had not dis-invited Marty in spite of their argument.

Marty parked the Green Beetle around the corner from the *Goldene Traube* under a glowing gas street lamp that had somehow survived the bombings and post-war electrification. It was an old neighborhood of cold water flats with shuttered windows and probably a privy down in the courtyard.

In the pale light Sam glanced at his watch. "We're a little late."

"Yetta doesn't mind," Marty said as he locked the car. "She knows how punctual I am."

They walked up the narrow street toward the corner. Sam had to watch his step, for people walking their dogs didn't pick up after their pets did their business on the narrow sidewalk. Someone above and behind them banged open a shutter and there was a splash of something unpleasant thrown out into the street.

On the steps of the hotel billet Sam paused. "I thought about asking Fran to come, too, but it's not my party. It's not fair to ask her to take a five-hour train trip for a party."

"But she'll see you, Buddy Boy."

"My turn to see her on her own turf," Sam said. "I'm taking the train to Heidelberg next weekend."

"You going to stay at her place?"

"We'll stay at the *Hotel zum Schloss* up by the castle."

Marty clicked his mouth enviously. "Sounds like a plan. Good going, Sam."

Inside the musty warmth of the *Goldene Traube* lobby there were two officers in uniform at the reception desk. One was a tall captain, the other, a heavy-set man, was a warrant officer Sam recognized. They spoke in undertones, abruptly broke into the kind of laugh men save for dirty stories.

Sam whispered, "I know the warrant officer. He's from regimental headquarters. Since he got word that his wife is coming overseas he's done nothing but complain."

Marty shook his head. "Most of these guys feel best when they leave their wives at home." Marty greeted the receptionist. They were good friends by now.

Sam hung back and tried to overhear the conversation of the two officers, but they spoke in low tones. Sam wondered who they were visiting at the *Goldene Traube*.

There were footsteps on the stairs and the officers stopped talking. In a moment, a slight figure appeared. Her skin had a healthy, tanned color, but her expression was drawn, nearly haggard. She was dressed to go out in a smart, pearl-grey three-quarter-length coat with a matching scarf.

The captain said, "Hello, Kay. I want you to meet a friend of mine, WOJG Barnes."

"Just call me Slim," the warrant officer said. "Too bad you couldn't find a couple more girls for the party." Clearly for him the party had already started, for his voice was thick with liquor, an impression backed up when he drew a bottle from the copious pocket of his military overcoat. "I'd hate to finish this alone. It's single malt from Scotland, just came in a new shipment at the class VI liquor store."

Kay raised her eyebrows at the mention of single malt whiskey. "Very nice." She looked past the officers, noticed Sam, and hesitated.

It was a hesitation only Sam would notice. She had not expected to see him. He smiled and nodded, not sure if she wanted to acknowledge their acquaintance. At least he was in civvies, his German trench coat and black fedora hat which was gradually accumulating a collection of souvenir pins on the band. No need to salute those officers.

"Hello, Sam," she said with an air of finality that didn't invite further conversation. Whatever had passed between them in Obersdorf was not for public knowledge.

Sam had not shown her the print of the photo he had sneaked of her and the general at Obersdorf. She would not appreciate that he had taken it and it could cause trouble. So far as he was concerned, the photo was classified confidential if not secret.

"Hi." He wanted to ask her how she was feeling, but that would give away his knowledge of her condition.

The two officers turned suspiciously and looked at him as if trying to determine what rank was hidden by the German coat and civilian clothes. Sam was glad they weren't interested in conversation with him and Marty. If they had been women, that would have been different. Warrant officer Barnes slipped the bottle back into his pocket and announced, "Party time." He opened the door for Kay.

As she went out, Sam saw that her posture had changed. Before she was erect and self-confident. Now she slumped slightly as if tired or defeated. She had been almost combative when they argued in Obersdorf about the meaning of love. He knew now that she might be pregnant, possibly from him, or maybe the general, and he decided he must visit her again and find out how she was, what her plans were if she really were pregnant as the gossips said.

Yetta was plump as ever in a knit suit when she welcomed Sam and Marty at her door. "Late as usual, Marty."

"You know I'm never late."

As she took their coats she said, "You should get rid of that silly pipe. It looks like a baby's pacifier."

Marty hesitated long enough for the action to seem to be his own volition, then put the tiny pipe in his jacket pocket. It was a plaid sport coat, out of fashion and loud, but corporals who had only a tiny locker in the barracks for their civilian clothes couldn't be expected to be fashion plates.

Sam commented, "We just saw Kay in the lobby. I thought she might be coming to this party, too."

Yetta shook her head. "Kay is out of our class."

"What? Because she's been going out with a general?"

Yetta whispered, "The general dumped her when he got the word that she was pregnant."

"Bastard." Of course, Sam could not know if he was the father himself. Sam didn't know about morning sickness, or how soon after sex it might begin. He wanted to assume that if Kay was pregnant it was the general's, but could he be sure? He had never thought about the consequences if he got a girl pregnant. He didn't think he'd run for the hills if she identified him in a paternity case. He'd do the right thing. Marry her. Then what? Move to New Zealand to live among the sheep? "Some captain introduced her to Barnes, a warrant officer. I know he's married and a drunk."

"If she takes up with him it's her decision," Yetta muttered.

That troubled Sam. He suddenly saw Kay as being passed around among the officers like used property. Thinking about it later, he saw her as like those courtesans in the days before the French revolution. Some would marry. Others would gradually move down in the ranks of desirable lovers until they hit the streets. He hoped that wouldn't be the case with Kay. She deserved better.

If she really was pregnant, abortions were illegal and dangerous. He surely didn't want to ever put any woman in that position. If he did, he'd do the right thing. For Sam it was a matter of honor and decency.

Sally Ann, the guest of honor, sat by a radio that was playing a song by Edith Piaf. You didn't have to know French to understand the tragic tone of "My grenadier." Sally Annsaid, "Hello, Sam. How's my old friend?"

Sam took her hand, thought momentarily to bow and kiss it as a French gentleman might to a dowager countess. "Still your friend. Not nearly so old."

"Had a drink yet?"

"I've hardly got into the room."

Sally Ann got up. "We can't have anything like that, Sam. You sit right down here on the bed and I'll pour you one. What do you like? Yetta's bought some bottles for the occasion."

Sam was leery about drinking. The embarrassing disaster in Obersdorf was a disconcerting memory. "Just a small glass of wine, maybe."

Sally Ann got him a glass. "We have a new bottle of Mosel." She poured, but Sam was not in a hurry to drink.

"Cheers," Sally Ann said. Hers was a larger glass.

Sam was no wine connoisseur, but had seen people gently shake a glass to see if the wine had legs, then inhale its aroma, before taking a sip and swishing it around in his mouth. He didn't know wine at all, but pretended that it would pass judgment. He felt uncomfortable, was cautious that anything he said in the *Goldene Traube* would be passed around and exaggerated. He sat down self-consciously on the edge of the bed.

Sally Ann joined him, brushed her bleached hair back. "Still skiing?"

"A little."

"I hear you were in Zermatt, how was it there?"

That was a leading question. How was what? "I missed a train connection. Got there too late in the day." He didn't mention Fran, but she probably knew about that, since he'd ridden as far as Davos with Marty and Yetta.

"And you were in Obersdorf, too. I bet you're a pretty good skier."

"I fall down a lot." He was suddenly fearful that Kay had passed around the picture of him naked in her bed. But no, Kay wouldn't do that. He couldn't imagine the most proper Kay passing around dirty pictures like a bunch of twelve-year-old school boys. She wasn't like Yetta, who might. "This is your party. Let's talk about you."

Sally Ann tugged at the sleeves of her sweater. Her wrists seemed thinner than before. "You know I was planning on moving to Spain."

"I didn't think you'd go."

"Why not?" She drank her wine quickly, for the kick, not the taste. "I'm full of surprises."

"Not to me," Sam said. She could never have any surprises for him. The story of her life was written on her face, and it was not a happy one.

"I forget. You're an old friend, aren't you Sam?"

Sam smiled grimly. He had gone out with her only once. If that made him an old friend, she was pretty desperate. He looked over at Yetta and Marty. Marty was sitting stiffly on the couch with his back straight. Marty seemed to be staring into space, his face closed. Yetta was curled up beside him, her arm around him. She must not have given up on their relationship in spite of their argument.

Sam asked, "How's your back, Yetta?"

She looked across at him as if relieved to break the tension between her and Marty. "Better. It hurts once in awhile if I bend over to pick up something."

"I'm glad you're feeling better."

"I'm afraid I'm a non-skier for now, in Sally Ann's class—no athletics."

Yetta watched as Marty fumbled in his pocket and pulled out that silly telescopic cigarette holder. She asked, "Want a cigarette for that, Marty, or you just going to suck on it?"

Marty clenched it in his teeth, threw his head back, and did an imitation of Franklin Roosevelt, complete with a high voice, "You have nothing to fear but fear itself." He was the only one who laughed.

Sam suggested, "How about a drinking song for Sally Ann? It's her party."

Sally Ann demurred. "No song, Sam. Just a drink. Need a refill?" She took his glass from him, emptied it herself. "Mustn't sit with an empty glass, not around me." She walked unsteadily to the bureau's selection of open bottles, refilled his glass and handed it to him..

As he took it, Sam asked, "When do you leave for Spain?"

"Tomorrow night at eight. Night train. Change in Basel."

"Just where will you be?"

"There's a naval base in Rota. I bet you didn't know that."

He didn't. Germany had American troops stationed everywhere. Munich, Frankfurt, Heidelberg, Berlin and Bremerhafen where his troopship had landed were just a few. He realized that with all the U.S. military bases around the world there were lots of places a civilian employee like Sally Ann could work. It was a world unto itself, like a vast military empire, a layer of government activity most people were unaware of. He raised his glass, "To Spain!"

"To Spain," Sally Ann repeated. "To new faces and new friends."

Sam took up the toast. "To old friends and beautiful memories." Wary of what she had poured into his glass, he took only a sip. It was cognac.

Sally Ann put her arm around him. "I have no memories, Sam." She was drinking from a bottle of something or other.

"How about friends, Sally?" Sam kissed her on the cheek. "Will you remember your friends?"

Sally Ann kissed him on the mouth. She would have held the kiss longer, but Sam's lips were closed. "I'll remember you, Sam. You're a nice boy."

"And you're too old for me." It was a cruel thing to say and he regretted it immediately.

She laughed, her voice raw from too much smoking. "Sounds like an old refrain." She started to sing, trying to mimic the plaintive song on the radio, and crumpled on the bed. Her bottle fell to the floor. It was empty.

Sam gently lay her down on the bed and asked Yetta, "Do you have any coffee?"

Yetta didn't have an electric coffee maker, but did have a single burner hot plate which she plugged in.

"Don't let her drink any more," Sam pleaded.

Yetta filled and put on an old-style percolator.

Marty hadn't been paying attention. He seemed to be concentrating on getting drunk, putting down anything in the larder, wine, cognac, or whatever. Noting Sally Ann's condition, Marty said, "She's a crazy gal."

Sam thoughtfully studied the coffee pot as if waiting for the first perc. "She's not crazy. She's just unhappy."

"Unhappy?" Marty smirked. Slurring his words he said, "Unhappy me no unhappiness. Shakespeare."

Sam felt Sally Ann's defeat. Whatever she was seeking, she hadn't found it in Munich and now she was off to Rota, Spain, but we carry our troubles with us. We don't leave them behind. He had been wounded by the breakup with Betty. Letting the Army take him and send him to Europe didn't take that away. Sam looked seriously at Yetta. "She's running away, isn't she?"

Yetta agreed. "Running away never solves anything. I had a nice major in Heidelberg." She sipped her wine, grimaced, and poured the rest down the sink. "I should never have come to Munich."

"Did he want to marry you?"

"No. He was like all the rest. He was already married, wife in the States. She didn't want to be more than ten miles from her mother. He didn't tell me at first."

"So you came to Munich."

"Clean slate," Yetta said. "I guess, like they say, I ran away."

Had Sam run away? Not exactly. He'd waited until the fighting in Korea had actually stopped, so it was safe to be drafted, and let them take him. He hadn't been doing that well in college anyway, a step above being on probation. If he flunked out he wouldn't have to worry about going to work for his dad. Sometimes just doing nothing is a decision. You let others decide for you. At least knowing some German got him sent to Europe and not Korea. That was something.

He'd allowed himself to drift in whatever direction fate blew him. He'd used to not think about the future. He'd live in the now, take life a day at a time. Then he met Fran and Kay. Everything changed. There were consequences to the choices you made. Even not choosing was a choice.

He watched the coffee pot. It was beginning to rumble and steam on the second-hand, rusty hotplate. The coffee would be ready soon.

Sam went to the window and looked out. The Munich roofs were dirty and haphazard. Old chimney pots sprouted rickety TV antennas like weeds. A large section of new brick showed where the next building had been rebuilt. Like most of West Germany, little remained to show the results of carpet bombing.

Sam wondered if Sally Ann would find what she wanted in Spain.

Sam looked out the window, wondered what lives were in all those apartments. How many of those Germans had lost husbands and sons in the war? How many were relatives of those civilians burned to death in fire storm raids like in Hamburg and Nuremberg? How did they feel now that they were occupied by a foreign Army? True, there was the so-called iron curtain. The line the GI's were given was that they were protecting Germany, the old enemy, from the Soviets, the old ally.

So now he was among the occupiers, and Yetta, Sally Ann, Kay, and the rest were support personnel in what he saw as a political game of chicken. Marty did the morning report, the numbers of men in each rank and the status of each, on duty, on leave, sick—all numbers on the list. But he was a person and these were all human lives being played out.

Suddenly Marty stood up, looked green, and made for the door. The communal bathroom was down the hall. He didn't make it, but doubled over and retched. When he recovered and washed his face at the sink he said, "I'll get the janitor to clean it up."

"You will not. The janitor is off duty. You'll clean it up yourself." Yetta as stern, no nonsense drill sergeant. "There's a bucket and cleaning stuff in the closet down the hall. Now go!"

Sheep faced, Marty came back with a bucket, brush, and rags. He tried to scrub the vomit along with the remains of his supper off the carpet.

Sally Ann basically passed out on the bed and Sam stood with Yetta by the window which she had opened, exchanging the cold air of Munich's winter night for the smell of Marty's mishap.

Yetta asked, "Sam, do you know the difference between a French girl, a German girl, and an American girl after they have sex?"

"Go on."

"The French girl says, 'Encore, cherie.' The German girl says, 'When shall we marry?'"

"And the American girl?"

"She says, 'What will you think of me after all this?'"

At some other time it might have been funny. Sam didn't laugh. What had he thought about Betty? He was ashamed to recall. "And what does Marty think of you?"

"Not much," she said. "He's a nice enough guy, but he's immature."

That was the risk. The girls were too old for them; the guys were too immature. It wasn't a good match.

Yetta and Sam stood over Marty while he, humiliated, cleaned up his mess as best he could. The party was over.

Sally Ann was passed out. "I think we'd better call it a night," Sam said, apologetically, and to Marty, "You can't drive. Want to call a taxi?"

"You drive," Marty said, and handed Sam his keys.

Sam had seldom driven a stick shift. His father had a Buick with Hydromatic. He had hardly driven anything else, had never owned a car.

They made their way down the stairs and out into the damp chill of the Munich night. Sam got in the driver's seat and looked dumbly at the stick floor shift, the clutch, brake, and gas pedals.

Marty demonstrated the shift positions, neutral, first, second, third, fourth, reverse. It took several tries to start the Green Beetle and get it into first gear without killing the engine. Eventually he managed to get the car moving. The little four cylinder engine roared.

"Second, second!" Marty cried. "Look, when I say 'clutch' push down the clutch pedal and I'll shift."

Once in second gear, they were moving. In second gear they could make it back to the caserne, even though it was slow.

"Too bad about you and Yetta," Sam ventured, once they were moving along. Traffic was light. As long as they didn't encounter a red light he wouldn't have to stop, which would kill the engine and he'd have to start the routine all over again. He was beginning to respect Marty's driving skills.

"She's too old for me, Sam. I know women are expected to live five years longer than men, and girls are more mature than boys, so it's a miracle when a couple actually gets together and it works."

Sam didn't know how old Fran was, maybe four or five years older than him.

Marty was more lucid than he appeared. He took the tiny pipe out of his pocket and held its stem in his teeth. "Those gals are just over here to travel, have a good time, a vacation, maybe get laid by guys like us. Not get married. Yetta overstepped the mark."

In spite of that remark to the angry hotel manager about being engaged, Sam hadn't talked with Fran about marriage. He hadn't even thought of it. He was living in the now. He didn't look beyond the horizon which was delineated by his date of discharge from the Army. Then what? Well, finish the degree, like his dad wanted. For a guy with no plans, it wasn't a bad option.

But what about Fran?

Chapter Fifteen

The Eighth Weekend—Heidelberg

Since Fran was in Heidelberg and needed only to make a local call, Sam let her phone in the reservation for a double room at the *Hotel zum Schloss* on the hill above Heidelberg. She met him the next Saturday at the *bahnhof* about noon.

Fran looked stunning. No ski togs this trip. She wore a smart topcoat and a matching, warm beret she could pull down to the tops of her ears. Arm in arm, they walked the quaint main street, aptly named *Hauptstrasse*. They avoided dregs of snow and stepped around dog turds on the narrow sidewalk until they came to the little funicular railway that took them up to the famous castle. As the name implied, the *Hotel zum Schloss* was close by, a modern building that overlooked Heidelberg and the Neckar river valley below.

The desk clerk was an attractive, blonde young woman who might be a new graduate of hotel management. She was not suspicious of the affectionate young couple. Sam checked in, showed his military I.D. and filled in the police registration form with his date of birth, home address, length of expected stay. Fran had to do the same. Luckily for his PFC budget, it was only for one night. That it wasn't *Herr und Frau* Logan didn't seem to bother the clerk.

It was an immaculate room with a private bath and windows facing a terrific view. Down below, the buildings of old town Heidelberg were crammed together, the roof tops in the distance obscured by the smoke from numerous chimneys. Many buildings did not have central heating.

Sam tried to embrace Fran as soon as they got into the room, but she put him off, keeping him in suspense. "This time I'll be the tour guide. First you'll see Heidelberg Castle and its famous wine barrel. It's so big there's a dance floor on top of it. Then I'll show you the Zum Zeppel student bar and the Red Ox where many of the GIs hang out."

Sam went along, lost in thought about the discussion at Sally Ann's farewell party and how that might apply to him and Fran. He was also thinking about sex. Maybe this time he would have more staying power and not go off prematurely.

After the obligatory castle tour they took the little funicular down into the town. Fran took him to the *Goldene Hecht*, a nice little restaurant near the old bridge. The restaurant's sign was of a gilded pike. "This is my favorite restaurant, Sam. It's my treat." He was not accustomed to having a date buy him a meal. They had a dinner of wild boar chops served by the attentive, formally dressed waiter who liked to show off his skills as if serving them was a special treat for him.

Sam talked about Sally Ann who was by now on her way to her new job at the American naval base in Rota, Spain. Sam hoped that maybe Sally Ann would meet some nice naval commander or even a doctor who got her off the booze and gave her a life. She deserved it.

He didn't mention Kay or the weekend in Obersdorf and the unfortunate photo Kay took of him in her bed. He certainly wasn't going to repeat the gossip that Kay was pregnant, probably by her ex-general and, he hoped, not by him. He was too discrete for that. If Fran thought he had knocked Kay up she'd have dropped him in a New York minute.

Finally they stopped at her billet where he waited in the lobby while she picked up her overnight bag. The rooms upstairs were off limits to male visitors. They returned to the *Hotel zum Schloss.* Unlike the manager in Munich, the blonde desk clerk was unconcerned about this couple who were most likely not married. This was, after all, Heidelberg, USAREUR headquarters, and she had no doubt seen all manner of assignations. As long as guests were not rowdy, broke up the furniture, or needed the police, it was OK.

Once in the room Fran had hardly slipped off her coat when Sam took her in his arms and kissed her.

"Don't be in too much of a hurry, Sam."

He took off his German trench coat and hung up the black hat with its growing collection of souvenir pins. "Sorry."

"You don't want to get too excited, honey." She hadn't called him that before.

He remembered the last time and didn't want a repeat performance. That wasn't going to be easy. At least this time he was prepared, had actually bought half a dozen condoms, as if anyone would need that many!

Before they went any further, Sam locked the door and Fran closed the room-darkening blinds.

No one could see them from the outside, so high on the hill above the city, but the dark hid their shyness.

Sam wasn't shy. He wanted to see Fran naked, but maybe she felt her figure was not as voluptuous as she thought he might expect. It was one of those barriers to complete understanding that could spoil the empathy of the moment.

They undressed each other. Sam fumbled with her bra straps, until she impatiently unhooked them for him.

She found the zipper on his trousers without difficulty and they were soon in the bed embracing, naked, in the dark.

Sam lost himself in her arms. All thoughts of Betty, Kay, Yetta, Sally Ann, or anyone else were swept away in the moment. This was the Now they had talked about. Like the romantic song lyric went, there was no tomorrow, there was just tonight.

How erotic those hit numbers were with their double entendres. "I've got you under my skin," was just another way of saying your penis is inside me.

But first he had to find his supply of condoms in the dark, and somehow take the wrapper off one and put it on. It was not an act he had much practice at.

Fran waited patiently and guided him into her.

This time it was not a repeat of bam-bam-thank you ma'am. It was more bam-bam-bam, not a heck of a lot better, but she was patient and he could try again. He did.

Sam realized that sex did not come naturally or with perfection on the first try. It took experience, which he did not have, and knowledge of one's partner, which was also a mystery to him. He was not making love to a post or to a manikin sex toy. Fran was a person and he did not know her tastes, her desires, or her needs.

Fran seemed to have lost all the inhibitions she'd shown in Zermatt. She had overcome those, and knew what she wanted, and here he was at her disposal. It was her turn to make the moves, and she did.

Sam, after two rounds, was pretty well spent. He suddenly felt sleepy, while Fran was wide awake and ready. She was not going to be put off.

She had satisfied him, but she had not had enough. Not yet. She wanted more, and she wanted to be in charge.

Sam, in a stupor of after glow, observed as she removed the second condom from his now flaccid penis, and gently washed him with a cloth from the bathroom. Then she kissed his penis, and before he realized what she was doing, was sucking on it, reviving him. No one had ever done that to him or for him before.

It worked, and soon she was on top of him, making little cries of joy and pleasure.

Sam lay there, docile, in a state of wonderment. He did not climax a third time, but realized she had. When she was finished she lay on top of him, kissing him, and announced, "That's more like it, Sam."

Sam saw it as a promise of things to come. There would be other times, growing knowledge of each other's needs and desires, tastes, what turned her on, all it would take to make a perfect match. They were far from that, but it was a start. One could have a lot of fun trying.

He realized one could have a lot of misunderstandings and breakdowns of communication, disappointments, and even arguments. Relationships took time to be meaningful. Before he could work it out, he was asleep, leaving Fran beside him, awake in her own thoughts and whatever plans she might have.

When he stirred the next morning, still in a comfort zone of post coital contentment, she was in the shower. Still damp and naked from the shower, she woke him up with a kiss and slipped under the feather quilt for an encore. It was more than he expected. Fran who had previously been shy, even frigid, had awakened beyond his own wildest bachelor dreams. He was afraid he would no be able to keep up with her.

Sam was still dazed and was almost like a sleep walker through the continental breakfast. While she showed him the sights of old Heidelberg, particularly the Zum Zeppel student bar which was hung with stolen signs that translated as "Do not spit on the sidewalk" and "Danger, biting dog" he was still trying to reboot his brain after all that intense sex. Everything was a rosy blur.

When the time came for him to get the express back to Munich, they embraced on the platform.

His breath caught in his throat as he choked, "I love you."

Fran looked him in the eye and said, "I love you, too, Sam. You're my guy."

"How about next weekend?"

People were boarding the dark green carriages. The sign on the side of his said, *München Hauptbahnhof.* Doors were slamming. Somewhere at the front of the train a brief, warning whistle blew.

Fran apologized. "There's a major reception for a visiting commercial attaché next weekend. I have to be there."

"After that?"

"I'll call you, honey."

They kissed again and he was off. Watching her through the window of the second class car as the train backed out of the station, he was still so dazzled by his experience with her he could hardly think straight. So this was love.

Kay was mistaken.

Chapter Sixteen

Dear Sam

Sam had taken a full roll of pictures on that weekend in Heidelberg. As was his routine, he developed the film in the service club darkroom on Monday night and made prints the next evening. He did not have any of Fran naked. She'd taken one of him in his German trench coat and black hat while standing next to an *Anschlasaule*, a pillar for posting announcements. She'd caught his somewhat bewildered expression.

Except for confirmation that he'd finally had "his ashes hauled," the vernacular Marty used for getting laid, he didn't share any other details. What was private was private.

Yetta had news from the *Goldene Traube*. Kay had left Munich. The word was she was flying back to New Zealand.

The weekend passed and Sam was looking forward to the next one. Would Fran come to him, or would they rendezvous for a romantic trip somewhere? He tried to phone her using the Army's long distance service, but the woman who answered the phone said Fran was not available.

Well, maybe she had an errand. Sam didn't know exactly what Fran did. He knew the USAREUR office had something to do with procurement or economics or something like that. His own knowledge of how the Army worked was pretty much confined to the supply room and the Quartermaster Corps.

When it came down to it, he didn't really know that much about Fran at all, except for her small town background and something never much explained about a bad scene in New York. He knew her only in the Biblical sense.

Then he got her letter.

"My dearest Sam,

"I can't see you next weekend. At the reception I told you about I met the visiting State Department Commercial Attaché. She works at the embassy in Lisbon and offered me a job there. It's a step up from what I've been doing for the Army in Heidelberg. I can't miss this opportunity.

"I know Lisbon is too far away for you to visit on one of your three-day passes. We won't see each other again, but I want you to know how wonderful it has been to be with you. I do love you, Sam. You will always be my guy.

"Don't feel too badly, Sam, my dearest. We will always have Heidelberg.

"Love forever,

"Fran."

Sam tried to call her, but never got through to her at the Heidelberg office. He wrote, but got no answer and didn't know even if his letter was delivered. He sent a letter to Fran Wagner at the U.S. embassy in Lisbon, Portugal. No answer.

At first he cried. He was depressed and heartbroken. Looking back, he suspected she wanted more from him that he had to offer, not only in terms of a future they might have had together. It wasn't just that he hadn't finished school or started a career. He had awakened her repressed sexuality, and she probably wanted someone with more experience and virility.

Relationships demanded more than sex. It was wonderful while it lasted, but then was not the time.

In spite of Marty's bravado, his affectation of the tiny pipe and the silly cigarette holder, Marty had a sympathetic core. He said it was alright for a guy to cry.

Sam saved the "Dear John" letter from Fran by slipping it behind the framed portrait she had given him for Christmas along with the knit pair of gloves.

Depressed and wounded, Sam didn't want to go back to the *Goldene Traube* to face Yetta and the other crowd of gossips there. Marty didn't either.

As a couple of pals they continued their Grand Tour of Europe measured out in three-day and weekend passes. He was promoted to corporal which gave him a bit more cash for travel. He and Marty made trips to Berlin, Paris, London, Amsterdam, Copenhagen, and, locally, to Baden Baden to see the old Roman baths. Sam's collection of souvenir pins grew on the band of his black fedora.

Marty's hard driving the Green Beetle was too much for the little four-cylinder engine. It sucked a valve, requiring either a questionable repair or a complete replacement with a rebuilt engine. The replacement, which could take less than an hour and cost about a hundred dollars, was too much for a guy who never saved anything. With not many months left on his tour of duty, Marty did the cheap repair and sold the car to a gullible new arrival in the detachment.

Sam's application for early release from the Army came in time for him to return to college for his final year starting in September. His grades improved.

While he was back at the University of Illinois he got a letter that was originally sent to his old address at Detachment A in Munich, forwarded to his home address in Chicago, then bundled up by his father in a fresh envelope to be sent to the college. There was no return address and the postmark was smudged, but the New Zealand stamp showed a funny-looking bird called a Kiwi. The envelope included a photograph and a brief note. *"Sam: Here's a picture of me and my baby daughter Madeleine. Just to set your mind at ease, she's not yours. Love—Kay."*

The picture took a load of potential guilt off his mind. Taking that photograph of him naked in her bed was a prank, after all, or maybe the note saying it was not his baby was a lie just to soothe his conscience. Sam was always susceptible to doubts and confusion. He wondered whether signing with the word "love" was just a convention, or if their brief encounter in Obersdorf meant something to her, after all. He remembered all that argument that love didn't exist. Had she changed her mind?

He kept Kay's letter and photo in an old foot locker along with the portrait of Fran and his souvenir maps of foreign cities and remnants of his old uniforms. He even had three medals from the Army—Good Conduct, Army of Occupation, and Service Medal, all mementos of a life. There was even a little box of postcards from various cities and including the Matterhorn in Zermatt, all sentimental reminders of a time past.

After graduation, in spite of his early resistance, Sam returned to Chicago to work with his father. Logan Associates became Logan and Son, Associates. He took evening classes for a Master's in Communication and Public Relations, good complements to the advertising business.

He never forgot Fran. No matter who he met, who he dated, something in his heart always belonged to her. He thought he'd gotten over their romance, but whenever he saw the movie "Casablanca," the love story with Humphrey Bogart and Ingrid Bergman, and Rick said, "We'll always have Paris," Sam cried again. As Fran had said, they'd always have Heidelberg.

Epilogue

Nearly sixty years later, Sam Logan was watching television in his retirement apartment in Portland, Oregon. To be near his grandchildren after his wife died he had moved there. Though he had put on about thirty pounds since his trim 165 of his Army days in Europe, Sam was in pretty good health for a man in his late seventies. Though he had never served in battle, and had never liked military service, he still kept his dog tags and had a sentimental attachment to the Army. He put in hours as a volunteer at the nearby VA hospital.

The phone rang, interrupting the game he was watching. "Hello?"

A woman's voice asked, "Is this Sam Logan?"

"Yes. Who's this?" He was suspicious, afraid it was some telemarketer asking for money. He never gave anything to strange callers.

"Is this the Sam Logan whose military ID number ends with 1101?"

Sam knew that the military had long ago abandoned the old ID numbers. His had begun with U.S. for Army of the United States, meaning draftee. He still had his original dog tags. Now the military used regular social security numbers. An old military ID number could not turn into a case of identity theft. "Yes."

"Was your laundry mark L1101?"

"Yes, it was."

"Did you know a girl named Fran Wagner?"

"Yes." How could he forget? "What's this about?"

"Fran Wagner is my mother, now Fran Smalley. She has a souvenir handkerchief with the laundry mark L1101. When I asked her the story, she told me about you."

So she had kept the handkerchief, just as he had saved her photo and her farewell letter. Sam was stunned by a flood of old memories. He'd forgotten about the handkerchief. "My God. How did you find me?"

"The internet, of course."

He remembered his Christmas gift for her. "Does she still have a little German teddy bear dressed in lederhosen?"

"Oh, that. She gave it to me when I was little. It was my favorite. It lost the hat and it's pretty threadbare, but I have it. Would you like to talk to her? She's right here."

He didn't recognize the sound of her voice. After all, it had been so long ago. "I wondered what became of you," he ventured. "You got that job in Lisbon. Then what?"

"I married a fine man who worked in the office of the commercial attaché. We were posted to several places, but when I had my two girls he left the Foreign Service and we settled down in Houston. What about you?"

"Nothing very exciting," Sam admitted. "Went into my father's advertising business. Raised two sons. My wife died three years ago. Cancer."

"I'm sorry."

"Life happens when you're making other plans," Sam admitted. He was still mourning. One doesn't forget.

Fran must have been on speaker phone, for her daughter asked, "Do you Skype?"

"Yes, sometimes. Talk to the grandchildren."

"Let's set up a Skype call," Fran's daughter said, taking charge.

They did. Sam booted up his already obsolete PC and the speaker was soon chirping with the Skype video call. He picked up and soon in a little box on the monitor was his face, his white hair, still the old bumpy nose which he'd never had fixed even though his wife had suggested plastic surgery. He realized he needed a haircut.

When he saw her face he was reminded of the shock when he attended his high school fiftieth reunion. All those old people! He'd remembered them as they had been, not what he saw at the reunion. What he saw when Fran's image came on his computer screen was the face of an old woman he didn't recognize. Well, maybe he did. As we grow older, the years are written on our features. Somewhere in that face was the remnant of an old memory.

She was the first to speak. "You got old, Sam."

"Yes. Beats the alternative."

There was an awkward silence. They both realized that over the years, all those life events had made them strangers. What they had in common had happened a very long time ago. Any romantic fantasies they had held onto about Germany,

Heidelberg, and young love were just memories. That was then.

At length, Sam ventured, "You still remember Heidelberg?"

She admitted, "Some." She didn't elaborate. Her daughter was listening.

He apologized, "I was young then. I'm afraid I let you down."

"What's past is past, Sam."

Their conversation deteriorated to clichés and talk about the weather. Finally, sensing they had nothing more to say to each other, she said, "Take care of yourself, Sam. Maybe send me a Christmas card some time."

"I'll do that."

After she hung up he realized he hadn't asked for her address.

The End

About Harley L. Sachs

 Though born in Chicago and raised in Indiana, Harley L. Sachs considers himself an international, having lived in Germany, Sweden, Scotland, and Denmark. He earned a degree in English at Indiana University, then served in the U.S. Army in Heidelberg Germany. After getting his Master's degree at I.U. he returned to Europe and worked under cover for several years. He met and married Ulla in Stockholm, Sweden and they spent a year's honeymoon in a Scottish castle. Returning to the USA, Sachs taught English briefly at Southern Illinois University then moved to Michigan Technological University in the Upper Peninsula where he and his wife raised three daughters. He took early retirement and now lives in Portland, Oregon.

If you liked this story you may enjoy a romantic mystery, *Ben Zakkai's Coffin*. Here's a sample:

The Union Bank was having a grand opening and my boss wanted some unusual shots beforehand, so I set up my Hasselblad on a tripod in the lobby. It's heavy as a brick but has the advantage of being a single lens reflex with interchangeable lenses and switchable backs. The fisheye lens distorts the image, but the effect can be dramatic. The Union Bank has this huge, abstract bronze sculpture in the middle that must have cost the shareholders their dividend. Ugly thing. I set up in front of it. I was getting ready to shoot a long, slow exposure when through the viewfinder I saw the revolving door starting to turn. From it emerged a young woman, looking tiny at first in that massive breadth of field, then looming suddenly bigger as she walked right up to the camera. I looked up.

That was it.

I remember that I thought, if I were to take her portrait I'd put everything in shadow except those hypnotic eyes. She wore tiny gold earrings but none of the facial hardware that I find so objectionable.

I imagined this sultry woman in a fashion photo. She could pass as a model, the prescribed size seven. Physically she was beyond my own dreams of manly glory and conquest. She had a figure that didn't need the enhancement of push up bras or clothes designed for seduction.

Her outfit was a combination of all business and female sexuality. She carried a black, leather shoulder bag that could serve as purse or briefcase big enough for a laptop. She wore a crimson power suit like some women wear in the board room, as if the right clothes can break through the glass ceiling. There was enough cleavage to make you want to burrow down there like a mole trying to escape from the worries of the world.

I must have looked pretty foolish, startled, my eyes wide open and my mouth agape as she quietly took hold of the Hasselblad, folded the tripod legs, and hefted it with a little grunt of appreciation at its weight.

"What's this?" was all I could muster.

She put one finger to her lips, pointed to my bulky equipment bag on the floor, and moved her head in a way that said "follow me." She didn't have to say anything else. I picked up the bag and followed.

I protested, "I've got permission from the bank manager to do this shoot."

"Take them tomorrow." Her low, husky whisper suggested I didn't need to be told the reason.

I wasn't about to wrestle the camera away from her. If it fell and broke that lens I'd be out of business. Insurance might cover the cost, but not the replacement. I followed her out of the bank, the blades of the revolving door making a soft hiss as I moved out of my reality into... what? If I had an idea I was afraid to think it.

The new Hilton hotel is next door to the Union Bank. She walked past the uniformed doorman, into the lobby, and up to the registration desk. I could feel people watching us, or watching her with me tagging along at her heels like a pet dog. She whispered something to the clerk, was handed one of those electronic keys, and headed for the elevator.

I'd have followed her even if she wasn't carrying my precious camera.

Inside, she punched the button for the tenth floor but didn't say anything. I didn't either. This was not a scene I could have rehearsed, like what will I say to pick somebody up in a singles bar? She stood close to me, her red dress brushing against my blazer. I could smell her scent, couldn't figure out if it was perfume or her natural, erotic essence. I thought, pheromones, the come and get me essence perfume makers would die for. Natural or synthetic, it made me hard in the crotch and weak in the knees.

She noticed my ID badge pinned to my breast pocket, "Herman Bachrach, Banking Insider." Claire, God's receptionist and do everything gal, does those on her computer. "Banking Insider" is ambiguous, could mean I'm a member of the board of directors of an international banking cartel or a trainee teller. As if she couldn't read, I said, "Herman Bachrach" as a way of introducing myself.

"Diana." No last name. I remembered vaguely that Diana was a Greek goddess, the huntress or something. If that was her karma, I was prey.

I followed her down the hushed hallway of the Hilton's tenth floor to the room, a suite as it turned out, with adjoining bedroom. She shut and dead bolted the door, carefully lay the camera and tripod on the couch, and took me by the sleeve into the bedroom. She unbuttoned my jacket and slipped it off my shoulders.

Dry mouthed, I finally got the courage to say something. "What is this?" I asked. "Does someone at the office think it's my birthday and you're the birthday girl?" I could imagine Lewis/Louise, the Banking Group's bisexual art director, pulling a stunt like that, but he'd be as likely to send a boy.

Those eyes were fixed on mine as if she was mentally stripping off my clothes. "Is it your birthday?"

"No. My birthday is September 6, Labor Day." My mother used to joke about that, going into labor on that holiday, but this didn't seem the right time to tell that story.

Now she had my black tie, slipping it off with a single, smooth movement before she started on the shirt buttons. "Happy birthday anyway," she whispered, occupied with getting my clothes off.

. . . .

Ben Zakkai's Coffin is available as an ebook, in paperback from Lulu.com, and as an audio book in MP3 format.

Harley L. Sachs

Other books by Harley L. Sachs

THE MYSTERY CLUB SERIES

THE MYSTERY CLUB SOLVES A MURDER
First and most popular of the Mystery Club series. Mary Higgins finds the body of Dora Reed on the roof of the Plaza retirement building, notifies the police, then tells the Mystery Club. They assume several suspects: the manager of the Plaza, Dora's son Donald, or a Plaza employee. Dora's husband, Ed Sutherland, is in Hawaii on board the yacht Miss Chief with an all girl crew. Carrying on their own investigation, the Mystery Club finally suspects Sutherland, though he seems to have a perfect alibi. If they can prove it to their satisfaction, will a court ever convict him—if he can be found somewhere in the Pacific?

THE MYSTERY CLUB AND THE DEAD DOCTOR
Second in the Mystery Club series. The Mystery Club consists of five elderly women who live at the Rose Plaza and discuss mysteries written by women. The Mystery Club ladies have no idea of the consequences when Viola Cartwright, their blind member, asks them to go over her Medicare bills. That leads to suspicion about the identity of her personal assistant, Dorothy Anderson, who turns out to be using a stolen identity. Viola's doctor runs a phony clinic owned by a member of the Russian Mafia. Soon the investigation of Medicare bills leads to murder and tragedy, stopped only by the courage of Mary Higgins.

THE MYSTERY CLUB AND THE HIDDEN WITNESS
Third in the Mystery Club series. The ladies of the Mystery Club discover one of the residents is a crook under WITSEC, the witness protection program. He apparently keeps dipping into the employee gift fund. The Mystery Club bands together to track down the missing money, but what they discover is danger.

THE MYSTERY CLUB AND THE SERIAL WIDOW

Fourth in the Mystery Club series. Caroline Kostinsky, new resident at the Rose Plaza, is a widow four times over and she's looking for a fifth husband in retired General Hardcastle, but when drunk she says she killed all of her husbands. Except for her confession, there's no evidence. Now what?

DELIVER ME FROM EVIL

Responding to a posted invitation for new members for the Mystery Club, Judge Ira Kahane and Ursula Besette show up. Ursula, at a turning point in her life as a new Rose Plaza resident, is interested in Wicca and Kabala. Roberta Nelson believes one should not suffer a witch to live. Judge Kahane tries to lead Ursula on the right path, but there is conflict and tragedy coming.

WHITE SLAVE

Sequel to *The Mystery Club Solves a Murder.* The appearance of Ed Sutherland's gold bracelet in a Portland pawn shop revives retired detective Casey's interest in the cold case. He doesn't know that Sutherland has been picked up and is a slave on a Korean fishing boat. Sutherland, penniless, .without clothes or identification, is stranded in New Zealand. Can he find his way back to Portland and be somehow redeemed or face a death sentence for first degree murder?

THE IRWIN GLASS SERIES

BETRAYAL

Prequel to *Retribution.* Irwin Glass, BA in Russian, MA in International Relations, has a promising career in the Foreign Service in Moscow until he is snared in a classic "honey pot" seduction. He's young and naïve, honest, always wants to do the right thing, but at every turn he is betrayed. The incident in Moscow destroys his career. He is accused of being a paid Soviet agent and is pursued by the consequences of his encounter with the KGB twenty years later. Some enemies never let go

RETRIBUTION

Sequel to *Betrayal*. Newly married to Ivy Hartshorn, Irwin Glass gets a dunning letter from the IRS for taxes on interest at the Washington, DC account he didn't think he had. It's a joint account with his missing birth daughter and the balance is huge. Assuming it's money Katya's KGB father of record, Vladimir Putinsky (now Putin) deposited for her living expenses, Irwin moves it to force her to contact him. But Ivy warns him that he is laundering money and the people it belongs to will come after him. Irwin's complicated life is catching up with him, but this time he will find retribution.

BURNT OUT

Irwin Glass is approached by FBI Agent Wilkins who asks for Irwin's lists of foreign students. Not satisfied he wants more and is looking for potential terrorists among the Moslem students. Gradually Irwin is sucked into the role of FBI informant on the Michigan Institute of Technology's Muslim Students' Association and the results are tragic.

OTHER MYSTERIES

MURDER BY MAIL

German exchange student Klaus Hitz is more interested in making money than in asking questions about his work assignment. He doesn't know that the industrialist father of his punk girlfriend is using him in a terrorist conspiracy to kill everyone in the United States with a mass mailing of a scratch and sniff virus. The plot begins to unravel when a Polish nurse brings blood samples from Libya and alerts a CIA agent. While the CIA and FBI track down the terrorists, Klaus Hitz gradually figures it out. How can he avoid being murdered or imprisoned for being naive?

MURDER IN THE KEWEENAW

CIA agent recovering from Post traumatic Stress after failed missions in Finland and a divorce is fishing in Lake Superior when he snags a corpse. He thinks he has seen the girl before and his attempt to identify her leads him to a ring of deadly pornographers. It almost costs him his own life.

CONSPIRACY!

Technical writer Tom Godot can't believe his luck when CONSPIRACY!, the book he has co-written with the elusive Harold Stevenson, is a hit. The book details a plot to hijack communication satellites. As Tom crosses the country on his book tour, he is disturbed by people interested in early drafts and dogged by an NSA agent. Communicating by fax with his editor and by encrypted e-mail with the mysterious Stevenson, Tom reaches out in his loneliness to his California girlfriend Sylvia Hanson who turns out to be a pivotal figure. There is another conspiracy, and Tom is part of it

THE GOLD CHROMOSOME

When Adam Rottman's childless Aunt Sadie Gold died, the eight cousins learned her estate was in an irrevocable trust, the proceeds going to Adam's sister Sarah while she lives. After Sarah's death, the money would go to the last surviving cousin. It's a fatal tontine Adam's lawyer brother Harold set up. Would the cousins kill each other for one million dollars? Sarah's car is found in the river, but not Sarah. That begins a series of mysterious deaths. Coincidence? Or Murder? Who will be next? Adam and his psychologist wife Deborah must stop the chain before he, too, is eliminated.

BEN ZAKKAI'S COFFIN

Born of a Jewish father and a Catholic mother, Herman Bachrach insists he has no religion, but he is drawn by circumstance into a holocaust vendetta over gold stolen by a Swiss bank from Jewish depositors. Seduced by a woman who calls herself Diana, no last name, Herman is suspected by detective Sheehan to be her murderer. Someone else wants him dead. His Jewish boss provides him with a lawyer, but sends him to Switzerland to finish the job "Diana" started. It's an assignment he can't refuse. The result is an epiphany of identity that changes Herman's life forever.

THE LOLLIPOP MURDER

A warning for wannabe novelists! What happens when a stable of neurotic novelists who live in their pseudonyms and are bound by iron clad contracts are invited aboard their miserly Florida publisher's yacht for the Miami Book Fair only to find that they have no hope of ever earning a dime of royalties for their books? All this as Hurricane Gerta threatens to sink the yacht at the dock. It's grounds for murder

SCI-FI AND FANTASY

NEVER TRUST A TALKING HORSE

The narrator of this dystopian novel escapes preventive detention into a world he discovers has gone mad. Hungry, he is told he can eat for free at Lachumba's supper club, only to discover that he might be the main dish. He rescues Iris I. Iris from the ovens and in a series of episodes explores the insane world in search of a livelihood. He gradually realizes why he was incarcerated in the first place, but by then it is too late. His and Iris's roles have been reversed. Arrested, they are given a sadistic sentence which is their final challenge.

THE SEARCH FOR JESSE BRAM

Jesse Bram, the young hero of this metaphysical science fiction adventure, is unaware of his Jewish roots. An Eldre of mixed breed, he is marooned on the post apocalyptic shunned planet URth where technology and books have been destroyed. The URthlings variously view Jesse as a bringer of cargo for the half-breed prefect Hrod, as the reborn Savior by crypto-Christians, and as a link to the past by a remnant of Jews. The Galactic Federation suspects him of treason and he is pursued by an enigmatic Trinian policeman. If Jesse survives, will he be convicted? If acquitted, what next?

SHORT STORIES

THREADS OF THE COVENANT: THE JEWS OF RED JACKET

A collection of twenty-one short stories about Jewish life in small town America centering about two main characters, David Katz, the only Jewish boy in Red Jacket, and Richard Goldman, the only Jewish professor at Copper country Community College. Each story depicts another aspect of what it means to be a Jew in a small town as each character comes to realize his own identity.

MISPLACED PERSONS

Though set in different locales what these stories have in common is a central character who is out of his element, in the wrong place, coming to grips with cultural, generational, or physical displacement. In PROBLEM FOR THE TEACHER an expatriate fumbles for a living; in LIMBO an ex-GI is adrift in Copenhagen; in TRIUMPH OF THE WILL a nervous wreck seeks recuperation; in MISCALCULATION a would be tax evader succumbs to his own fears; in THE LIE a drunk gets himself into difficulties, and in THE GIRLS OF FREDERIKSHAVN an old man is trapped by girls looking for action.

YOOPER TALES AND OTHER FUNNY STUFF

Extracted from the massive volume of Sachs's published Essays and Columns: 1992-2011, this collection of stories related to Michigan's Upper Peninsula, known as the UP, home of Yoopers, reveals the truth about snow fleas, ice worms, the humungous fungus (world's largest living thing) and the rigors of winters in the remote north woods. You can also learn how to catch and cook the Mosquito Giganticus and why visitors won't come. Sachs has several awards for his humor.

AHOY! QUARTERDECK!

Originally published as IRMA QUARTERDECK REPORTS but re-released with new illustrations and, in the paperback edition, with sea shanties, this funny book is a series of boating anecdotes about Irma and her bumbling husband Ralph ("I can't believe I lost the anchor") Quarterdeck in their many boating adventures and mishaps. One reviewer says the book is as informative as Chapman's famous manual, but more fun. Readers will find plenty of laughs in this book and at the same time learn a great deal of boating fundamentals.

ANNA-LENA'S TROLL AND OHER STORIES

Each of the three Sachs daughters has a story in this children's book. "Anna-Lena's Troll" explores the nature of trolls, which represent the dark side of human behavior as Anna-Lena's nasty letter to Santa is rewarded by the gift of a nasty troll. "The Return of Baby Suzy" is the true story of Cynthia's worn out doll and its resurrection. "The Stars for Christmas" is the remarkable surprise Belinda got along with her new eye glasses. Other family stories are Christmas related.

NON-FICTION

THE MISADVENTURES OF CPL. SACHS

Adrift through college at Indiana University, author Sachs was drafted at the end of the Korean War. Physically unfit for combat, he was sent to Queer Company for basic training, then by a fluke was shipped out to Germany instead of Korea. Thus began his own version of the traditional Grand Tour.

FREELANCE NONFICTION ARTICLES

This third edition of a monograph on freelance writing first published by the Society for Technical Communication is newly updated. This little manual provides tips for interviewing, article structure, article preparation and submission, photography, and business practice.

CHILLY-CHILLY-BANG—HOW WE FREELANCED THROUGH EUROPE'S COLDEST WINTER IN A VW WITH A KID

Companion piece to *Freelance Nonfiction Articles*. The former is a how to book. This is a "how we did it" memoir. The author knew nothing about Volkswagens when they set off, but as they worked from VW dealer to dealer getting the old Combi fixed, he learned! It's as much a book for VW enthusiasts as it is for writers.

Both FREELANCE NONFICTION ARTICLES and *Chilly-Chilly-BANG! How we Freelanced Through Europe's Coldest Winter in a VW with a Kid* are combined in a double volume, *The Writing Life*.

THE 1957 SACHS ARCTIC EXPEDITION

After military service in Germany the author took the GI Bill to Sweden. With no income in the summer, and not even sure there was a road to the far north, he set off hitchhiking to North Cape, the northernmost point in Europe in search of the midnight sun. Illustrated.

FROM TENT TO CASTLE: MEMOIR OF A YEAR LONG HONEYMOON

Setting off from Stockholm, Sweden on rebuilt one speed bicycles, Harley and Ulla embarked on an open-ended honeymoon with no fixed destination and equipped with a tent, a thin double sleeping bag, a tiny gasoline stove, and $3000. After arriving in Britain, Ulla discovered she was pregnant. Tired of unrelenting rain, they advertised for a cheap place to spend the winter. They were offered the gatehouse to Borthwick Castle outside Edinburgh, Scotland for $25 a month by British author Theo Lang.

"IS"

As Bill Clinton said, "It all depends on what the meaning of "is" is."

A problem we all have is distinguishing between what is real and what is not. This is in fact an age-old question. This volume switches between classical instances of the problem to the author and his psychiatrist and his wife. What is real? That all depends on the meaning of "real."

QUEER COMPANY

Not a gay novel, this is a fictionalized memoir of an experimental basic training unit at the end of the Korean War. All the draftees were physically unfit for combat but the Army didn't want to discharge them. Instead they got modified training in a company unfortunately designated Q. In the Army phonetic alphabet Q is Queen, but Q Company was called queer. A copy is in the U.S. Army historical archives.

www.ingramcontent.com/pod-product-compliance
Lightning Source LLC
Chambersburg PA
CBHW021500240626
47154CB00002B/447